Fate Throws the Dice

Dice Twice
A Silver Creek Press
Tête-Bêche Book
Volume III
featuring:
Fate Throws the Dice (from 1908)
As the Dice Fell (from 1912)

The stories in this book are works of fiction. All names, characters, places and scenes described herein are the results of the author's imagination and genius. Any resemblance to actual persons, living or dead, is purely coincidental; and that includes actual persons depicted.

These stories were published at a time when political correctness had not yet caused serious cultural and moral decay. Certain ideas, terms and social conventions found herein are no longer considered acceptable (some for rational reasons, others not). A mentally healthy reader (the kind for whom this book was lovingly compiled) will understand that, and not give the matter further thought.

The text in this book is version 1.0. Anyone finding erors, please send them to the e-mail below. You will be acknowledged (anonymously or by name, as you wish) in a subsequent version.

Dice Twice
ISBN: 978-1-945307-13-3

Book compilation and design by Rodney Schroeter.

Cover design generated by Amberlight, www.escapemotions.com

The Silver Creek Press
PO Box 334
Random Lake WI 53075-0334

rschroeter@silentreels.com

Albert Payson Terhune

Fate Throws the Dice

SCP ə̣ɟə̣L-Bêche
Book III

Silver
Creek
Press

2021

CHAPTER I.
The First Cast.

"I WIN!" I remarked with quiet satisfaction, leaning back in my chair and letting my eye stray to the pile of gold pieces and pink, blue, and white bank-notes heaped up before me. "Do you want your revenge?"

"I want justice on a card-sharp!" blurted out the boy, his efforts at sportsmanlike stolidity breaking up in a half-hysterical outburst.

I looked him over coolly, dispassionately, in a way that has brought many a better man to his senses. But the lad's flushed, furious face turned an angrier red under my gaze of contempt, and he cried:

"I was warned against you. I might have known. I was told in this very card-room that you were a swindler—a down-at-heel soldier of fortune; a man who lived by his wits; an American who knocked about the Balkan Peninsula because his own country was too hot to hold him. I was told all this, and yet—"

"Who told you?"

I like to remember how fine a contrast my own quiet, steady voice offered to his incoherent, almost sobbing plaint; how clearly it gave me the mastery of the whole situation. I think it was that very coolness, coming like a dash of ice-water in a hot face, which checked his babyish tirade. I was forced to repeat:

"Who told you these things about me?"

"What business is that of yours?" he snapped, womanlike. "I—"

"It concerns me this much," I retorted with the same cold calm; "if a grown man said it, he must answer to me. If it was a callow school-boy like yourself—"

"Well, what then?"

"I am afraid I should be at the trouble of caning him. So take friendly warning and—"

"You pretend to look down on me, as younger than you, now that you've won all my money you can get!" he interrupted, quite beside himself—for youth is ever the most infuriating charge that can be made against youth—"but you looked on me as man enough to cheat, and I'll make you look on me as man enough to fight!"

I laughed. I did not mean to, but his fury was irresistibly amusing. I am afraid my laugh did not serve to check his wrath.

"I'm man enough to take my own part, I tell you!" he roared. "I was half-back on our varsity team at—"

"Are you *quite* certain it wasn't the ping-pong or hide-and-seek team?" I asked gravely. I don't know why I continued to plague the poor boy. Perhaps with somewhat the same idle malice as that which leads one to stir up a bantam rooster by shaking a hat at him.

"Are you man enough to fight me?" he bellowed—"to give me satisfaction?"

"Are we to have a rough-and-tumble barroom fight and be kicked out of the hotel?" I queried politely.

"We are on Greek soil," he replied grandly. "Even though dueling is extinct in America it still flourishes here, and I have no doubt we can arrange—"

"Pshaw!" I broke in, disgusted. "You read that in a book. I hoped you were going to be at least original in your squabble."

I rose with a yawn and began to gather together my winnings. I was commencing to grow genuinely bored. Moreover, though the smaller card-room of the Hôtel d'Angleterre chanced, as usual at this time of day, to be empty except for ourselves, young Clyde's loud voice might readily draw loiterers from the outer foyer.

And a public scene centering about a misunderstanding at cards was something I could not afford, if I were to continue my stay in Athens. So it was that I sought to end the affair as quietly as possible.

But the boy had other ideas—or, more likely, was too far gone in rage and chagrin to have any ideas at all.

"If you refuse to fight me," he roared, "I'll brand you as a coward from one end of Athens to the other! I'll—"

"You read *that* in a book, too," I scoffed. "Now, let me tell you something. No sane American fights duels—they're babyish and old-fashioned. And even if they weren't, I'm no child-killer. Think it all over quietly and you'll decide it's wiser to take your medicine gracefully and keep your mouth shut. That's all. Now—"

Before I could turn to go he had snatched up a handful of the scattered cards upon the table and hurled them in my face. I think he had not meant to do so banal and foolish a thing; for the violence of his own act seemed partly to sober him, even while he stood pluckily braced for whatever retaliation I might make.

But I made none. I stood stock-still, looking at him, while such of the cards as had lodged on my waistcoat or shoulder fluttered one by one to the ground. I looked at him, I say, and I felt that the banter and cynical amusement were gone from my expression, leaving something less easy for him to face.

Even as I gazed I saw the fury ebb out of his eyes, leaving there a look akin to sheepish uneasiness. For we Americans are not prone to melodramatics, and when we do indulge in them the action usually leaves us with a sense of having made fools of ourselves.

I waited until I saw that reaction, as well as my own greater coolness and magnetic power, had momentarily mastered him. Then I said quietly:

"Sit down."

Apparently to his own surprise, he obeyed.

"Now listen to me," I went on. "You spoke just now of branding me as a coward all over Athens. I am fairly well known here. Go out into the square and tell the first man you meet that you have struck Bruce Graeme across the face.

"He will call you either a liar or a lunatic. The fact that you are still alive will be proof enough for him that you are one or the other.

"This cut over my right cheek was from a Turkish saber. A bashibazouk cavalryman gave it to me in a skirmish in Macedonia. He never boasted of it—for he collided with my own sword about fifteen seconds later.

"The bullet-wound that sometimes makes my shoulder a little stiff came from a Druse sharpshooter in a brush in the Vale of Tempe in '96. He was a full three hundred yards away from me, up among the rocks—but my carbine was lucky enough to find him.

"There are other scratches strewed here and there around my anatomy, and most of them have a similar history. And yet *you*, a beardless schoolboy, talk of branding me as a coward."

It was a boastful speech, I grant, and overlong, but it had its effect.

"So much for my cowardice, and for the blow you struck," I resumed. "You accused me also of cheating you at cards. I will not waste breath by protesting my innocence—it is of no import to me whether you believe me or not. But when you think of me again as a cardsharp just stop to reflect whether a man like myself, who has made a study of *écarté*, for fifteen years, would need to cheat in order to win from a boy who has perhaps played the game a dozen times in all his life."

He fidgeted and made as though to speak. But I gave him no time.

"I was introduced to you in the bar three days ago," I continued. "I did not seek your society. Kindergarten associates do not appeal to me. You asked, that evening, to join in a game a few of us were playing. I won some money from you. So did all the others.

"But as I won more than they, you hunted me out to-day and wanted a chance to win back what you had lost. I consented, and I have cleaned you out. There is the story in brief.

"Think over every step of it, alone; and when you're through remembering your own share of it, you may possibly feel inclined to revise your mental list of the world's great men and give yourself a somewhat lower place in it than you've hitherto occupied.

"As for the money I've won from you, here it is"—shoving across the table the entire stakes. "Better turn them over to papa and let him dole you out a few francs a week."

I turned on my heel and strolled out, leaving him sitting there, eyes bulging, mouth open, and the gold and notes lying untouched before him.

I crossed the marble foyer to the main entrance of the hotel, where I lighted a cigarette and stood looking out upon the broad plaza that stretches between the Angleterre and the royal palace. Autumn dusk was falling and had already blotted out the far shores of Hymettus. Even the Acropolis, with its crown of white and gray temples, loomed up dim and misty in the gathering night.

The square was ablaze, and likewise the palace beyond. Ever-increasing groups of loiterers began to fill the whole plaza, while police and Albanian guards bustled here and there. For a moment I was puzzled at such unwonted activity. Then I remembered:

His Imperial Majesty the Kaiser of Germany was due to arrive from the Piræus at about seven this evening, on a visit of state to his somewhat less imperial brother-in-law, King George of Greece. The procession from the station to the palace was to be an Occasion, with the largest sort of capital "O," as are most public appearances of the German Emperor.

I stood there idly, my mind drifting back from the reception preparations to my own miserable affairs. For, now that the petty affair was over, I looked back on my scene with young Clyde with far less composure than I had shown or felt at the time.

My chief regret, I confess, was for the money loss involved. In fact, except for a few pieces of silver, the incident had left me penniless.

Thoughtlessly I had slammed upon the card-table not only my winnings, but—as we had been playing for table-stakes—my own available capital as well. The two sums aggregated in all perhaps nine thousand francs, of which nearly one-third had been my own money—all I possessed.

Now, it was not wholly a new thing for me to find myself stone-broke in a foreign land. From boyhood I had played a losing game against fortune. Cast out of my own country, branded, through no fault of mine, with another's disgrace, I had been Fate's battered plaything for more years than I cared to remember.

A *gaucho* in Mexico, a revolutionist in Brazil, a filibusterer in Cuba, a professional "patriot" in Macedonia and Bulgaria, a captain of irregulars in the Turko-Greek War, a blockade-runner in Peloponnesian ports, I had been jack of all trades, desperate player at every game—winner in none.

I recalled young Clyde's angry charges—soldier of fortune, swindler, and outcast from fatherland. The first and last counts I must admit.

As to that of swindler, I myself was in doubt. I had never marked or "slipped" a card, it is true; nor practised any of the countless arts of trickery with which central Europe in general and Greece in particular abound. But, as in Clyde's case, I had not scrupled to oppose my superior skill at cards against the boastful ignorance of rich young fools.

Nor had I hesitated to embark on various schemes which, if not actually dishonest, had at least brought me into close association with some of the rarest crooks and scoundrels of the whole Grecian Archipelago.

Coming back to Athens with scarce five hundred francs to my name after an unsuccessful smuggling-trip in the southern Levant, I had put up, three days earlier, at the Hôtel d'Angleterre to await a new chance for activity.

There were a dozen lesser hostelries in the Greek capital where I might have lived more cheaply—fifty houses where I could have found a shelter by reminding their owners of past bonds between us that they would not dare ignore.

But it has ever been part of my policy, as well as of a certain inborn fastidiousness of which I could never, at my very worst, wholly rid myself, to choose the best available lodgings, wearing-apparel, and food. Such a course pays in the end, besides being far pleasanter throughout.

My first meeting with Clyde had not, perhaps, been quite so accidental as I had led him to suppose. But at all events I had won from him fairly, and with the knowledge that he could well afford his losses.

For he had been pointed out to me as the son of an American multimillionaire who, with his family, was cruising in the Mediterranean and intended to make a long stay in Athens. I knew the elder Clyde by name—and by more—and what I knew did not lead me to harbor any especially merciful thoughts toward his son.

My first game with the lad had netted me a handsome sum, wherewith I had at once taken pains to pay a month's advance board at the Angleterre, and to make a deposit at the exclusive little English tailor-shop in the Corso. The remainder I had staked in my second game, and my unprecedentedly quixotic attempts to make the lad ashamed of himself and to prevent him from starting uncomfortable rumors about me had cost it all.

I stood well-dressed, well-lodged, and without five francs in the world. Nor did any immediate chance of new and profitable employment await me. Cheerful prospect for a man of thirty-five!

A cough at my side roused me from my unpleasant thoughts. I looked up to see young Clyde. Still red of face, he was, nevertheless, a far different person from the furious collegian who had thrown the cards at me in impotent rage, and I could see that the redness of his visage rose from quite another cause.

"Mr. Graeme," he began with a stiffness doubtless intended for dignity, "it occurs to me that I—that—in fact, I've made something of a fool of myself. I have been thinking over what you said, and I wish to apologize.

"Between men, you know, an—an—oh, hang it all!" he broke down, emotion knocking to pieces the last remains of his floundering dignity, "I'm *sorry*, old man! I behaved like a measly, unlicked school-boy, and I'm so ashamed I wish I had a third foot so I could kick myself with it. What a beastly little cad I was! Say, won't you try to forget it?"

"Why, certainly," I assented, trying hard not to laugh. "I understand. We'll say no more about—"

"Yes, but we *will!*" he contradicted vehemently. "I've got to get a whole cargo of remorse out of my system, and now's the time to do it. I behaved like a baby, and—"

"So you said," I interrupted soothingly. "Let it go at that."

"I can't!" he grumbled. "I wish I could. But I'd never be able to look myself in the face again unless I squared myself with you now. On the level, Mr. Graeme, I don't know how I ever happened to act so. I liked you a lot from the minute I met you. Then yesterday when that fellow—it was Kampf, of the German legation—told me you were a—a—"

"Swindler," I supplemented, as he paused in embarrassment.

"I told him I didn't believe a word of it," protested the lad—"and I didn't. Only, when I lost every hand we played to-day I got mad at my own bad playing, and I was too stuck on myself to confess I'd played like a blind apple-woman. And I'd read about card-sharpers at European hotels—and I lost my head and made a fool of myself and—"

"And acted like a white man afterward by admitting it," I added to help him out, speaking very gravely, as though to an equal age.

"No, I'm *not* a white man," he insisted, loath to leave his self-dug "Valley of Humiliation." "I'm a brat that ought to be in freshman year still. To think of my challenging *you* to a duel, when I don't know one end of a sword or a pistol from another, and when you've been fighting all over the world since before I was born!

"If you'd accepted and cut me all to pieces, or if you'd taken me over your knee and spanked me in public when I threw those silly cards at you—if you'd done anything on earth to me, I couldn't have felt as rotten as when I remember how you didn't even think it worth while to resent an insult from a mangy little piker like me. You just stood there and looked at me as if I was a crying baby—you with battle-wounds—"

"Drop it, lad!" I cut in, his mixture of self-contempt and boyishness again proving almost too much for my gravity. "All young men make fools of themselves now and then. It's one of the penalties that are sent to punish the glorious crime of being young. Shake hands and—"

"I had a dandy speech all framed up," mourned Clyde. "I was going to tell you I was sorry I'd ever for a minute doubted you were a gentleman and a white man, and to say I hadn't doubted it anyhow, and to ask if you wouldn't be friends with me, and that it'd be an honor to me if—"

"Consider it all said, then," I answered. "You were much more effective in what you really did say."

"Won't you dine with us this evening?" he went on eagerly. "With my father, my sister, and myself? We dine at eight, in our suite. Number eight, it is, on the entresol floor. I want my father to know you. He would like so much—"

"Not to-night, Clyde," I broke in. "Thank you, all the same. I've an engagement."

His eager face fell—while I considered regretfully the effect my debut into the Clyde family's social life might well have had on my finances. But I did not care to break bread with old Barzillah Clyde, nor did I think he would be likely to welcome me very heartily on his scatterbrained son's unbacked indorsement. So I escaped from the dilemma as quickly as I might without hurting the lad's feelings.

"I'm sorry," he muttered. "Perhaps to-morrow evening, then?"

"I'm late for my appointment," I interrupted, pretending not to hear the last words and making play at consulting my watch. "Good-by."

"Good-by, then. You're sure you've forgiven my—Oh, wait!" he broke off suddenly. "I forgot the main thing of all."

Thrusting his hands into his pockets, he jerked forth a great handful of large-denomination bills and gold.

"Yours!" he said, nervously thrusting it at me—"your stakes and your winnings."

I drew back, but he waxed doubly eager.

"You *must!*" he insisted. "It's your own money, fairly won. If you refuse I shall know you're still thinking of me as a kid, and that we aren't really friends, as I'd hoped."

I saw his reasoning and saved him from another outburst of apology by accepting the sum, mentally resolving to lure him into another game of *écarté* at the first opportunity and lose back to him his share of the money.

"Thanks, Mr. Graeme," he sighed gratefully. "And you'll let me be your friend, won't you? It'll mean such a lot to me. And—and won't you tell me some day the rest of the story about the time the Turk in Macedonia slashed your face and you cut him down?"

He was such a *boy*—such a natural, ingenuous youngster—that there was no resisting him. I knew that there is no other adoration in all the world quite so deep and all-powerful as the hero-worship of a lad of twenty for an older, more experienced man.

But at the time I had no faintest notion of how well that same boyish friendship was some time to serve me, and how mighty a part its effects were destined to play in my future.

Fate, unknown to me, had made her first cast in the greatest of the many life-and-death games she had enjoyed at my expense.

CHAPTER II.
The Woman in the Case.

As I walked aimlessly down the steps of the Hôtel d'Angleterre toward the now overflowing plaza, a figure in the hurrying throng caught my eye. A very gorgeous figure, indeed it was, clad in the dress uniform of a German hussar captain.

I followed after, and catching the hussar roughly by the shoulder spun him round. The man's big, blond face contracted in displeased surprise, and his hand involuntarily sought the hilt of the saber that clanked at his left side. As he recognized me his frown lost some of its insolence, but deepened its displeasure.

"Good evening, Herr Graeme," he said distantly."You have eccentric ways of attracting people's attention. In my country we do not accost casual acquaintances by seizing their shoulders and—"

"Step in here!" I interrupted, never releasing my grip and piloting him roughly through the crowd toward a half-filled *cabaret*.

"I am not accustomed—" he began angrily, as he writhed in vain to shake himself free. Then, changing his tone to one of nervous importance:

"I am on duty, to-night, and in haste. His imperial majesty—"

"His imperial majesty," I finished grimly, thrusting him into a seat at a table and sitting opposite him, "will be minus one of his Athenian legation attachés by this time to-morrow, Herr Kampf, unless you sit here until I am through talking to you."

"You threaten me?" he blustered, half rising and again reaching for his saber.

"I certainly do," I replied gently, without moving a muscle; "and you know enough of my record to be aware that I seldom threaten for the mere pleasure of exercising my lungs.

"Herr Kampf," I added, leaning far across the table and looking him full in the face, "it has come to my ears that you have referred to me as a swindler, and by other lying terms.

"I do not publicly chastise you for this, simply because I do not care to lend enough importance to your vaporings. But I have this to say: If ever again I hear of your mentioning my name, in any connection whatsoever—and I *shall* hear of it if you do—I shall cane you publicly, in the corso or on the plaza there."

He sputtered wildly, but I paid no heed and went on—cold, deadly, unemotional—my eyes not once releasing his:

"You are a coward at heart, Kampf. Yet if I thrash you in public, you will have no recourse but to challenge me. And then—be it saber, pistol, or dueling-sword—well, you know reasonably well my reputation with all three. Also, that I am a man not given to idle threats. If a man's mouth must be stopped—it must be *stopped*."

I had finished. There was no need to say more. The sudden fear of death had leaped unbidden into his round blue eyes. I saw I had stripped the man of the military bluster and shallow bravery that ordinarily cloaked him. He was as securely muzzled, so far as I was concerned, as though he already stood in front of my sword or dueling-pistol.

Without another word, I rose and left him sitting there, staring dully straight ahead.

As I elbowed my way through the press, pursuing my aimless course, a great revulsion of spirit swept over me. Of what use was this wretched existence of low adventure, gambling, and political intrigue? What profited the life of an American—a college man—a gentleman by birth—if at thirty-five he must knock about the world, self-exiled. a cheap soldier of fortune, keeping his fellow man at arm's length by bullying, and holding off insults with his sword's point?

There were times when such thoughts had me by the throat; and then life seemed very empty, and I could see the future stretching out before me dreary and barren as a rainy sea.

To-night these miserable fancies held riot in my brain. The incident with Kampf reminded me more clearly than ever that fear was no fit substitute for respect. Perhaps it was the honest hero-worship in Clyde's flushed face that had stirred my long-sleeping sense of shame. Perhaps—

The thickening of the crowd brought me and my sour meditations to a halt. I was close to the curb. Up the avenue from the station a file of gaudily attired cavalry were riding, the *gendarmes* and Albanians clearing a way for them through the throng. The spectators whirled about in eddies of excitement, and more than once I nearly lost my footing.

A hand touched my shoulder lightly. Beside me stood a large, heavy man, dressed as an Albanian shepherd, the upper folds of his cloak twisted about his head and face as if to shut out the autumnal chill. Figure and gesture were familiar, and savored to me vaguely of the underworld.

"Greeting, brother," I said in the modern Greek vernacular.

"And to you," came the reply in a rough, rumbling voice.

"Padapoulos!" I whispered, "and with eight thousand drachmas on your head! Right in the center of Athens—"

"And where safer?" rumbled the big voice beneath the cloak. "Is there any spot so safe as a crowd—and by night? Hymettus grows lonely and my boys are poor company. I wished a glimpse of this German Emperor who comes tonight. What a prize if—"

I laughed softly over this outcropping of the man's ruling passion.

"A golden prize, indeed!" I agreed, in the same whisper, "and one that would set the mountains of Greece swarming with a hundred thousand soldiers. My poor Padapoulos, they'd smoke you out, you and your band of worthy cutthroats, inside a week."

"I suppose so!" he agreed with a sigh that showed he had already given the prospect some thought.

"No, no!" I went on in the strain of banter. "Content yourself with rich foreigners and government paymasters. A kaiser is higher game than even the famous Gorgias Padapoulos could net in his mountain trap. Fly lower and safer, old chief!"

"I am no fool!" he grunted, not greatly relishing my laughter. "I gave the matter a thought, but only a thought. I merely wish to look at him."

"And you have traveled twenty miles from the other side of Hymettus just to—?"

"For that and another reason. My scouts here sent me word of an American man of millions who is here in Athens—coming on his own yacht, living like a king, and scattering gold like so much dirt. I came to consult with certain dragomans—I could not trust my own men in so great a matter—to see if he could not be interested in a pleasure-trip to the hills and—"

"Who is he?"

"His name is Clyde," replied Padapoulos, pronouncing the foreign cognomen barbarously. "Ah!" noting my look, "you know him? You are of his country, too. If you could lure him into the hills—giving me warning in time—well, my friend, you would see that old Gorgias Padapoulos is grateful. You could return to your own savage country a rich man. The ransom should be fully—"

A new commotion in the crowd checked him.

The cavalry and Albanians had succeeded in clearing the center of the avenue. But now, debouching from a side street, a small cavalcade broke through the thick-massed spectators, with scant heed of the pedestrians' life or limb, and proceeded to cross the cleared space toward the opposite highway.

There were but six riders. The foremost was a giant in height and shoulder-span, and sat his huge horse as though the two were one body. He was a bearded man, plainly dressed, yet carrying an air of conscious power and unconscious distinction that would have marked him anywhere. The five who rode behind him were evidently servants.

That any one should dare thus to break in upon the carefully arranged route laid out for royalty seemed to strike the police motionless with amazement. The broad avenue was almost crossed by the little cortège before an officious guard-officer recovered himself sufficiently to gallop up to the foremost horseman and reach for his bridle.

The giant made no move, but two of his followers speeded between their master and the policeman's profaning touch. At the same time an Albanian, who had run up on the other side, caught a glimpse of the leader's face and halted uncertainly, all the pompousness gone out of him. A murmur ran through the crowd.

The six horsemen continued their progress unopposed, the throng pushing back to left and right to make way for them. And so they passed out of view toward the Hôtel d'Angleterre.

"Who is he?" I asked Padapoulos, in wonder at the odd sight.

"One Greek celebrity that even the wise Bruce Graeme does not know, eh?" chuckled the old bandit in an access of national pride. "That is Prince Vlasto. Small wonder you do not recognize him! I do not think he leaves his Hymettus castle for Athens once in three years. He regards town-dwellers as scum."

Now I knew, and I wished I had looked closer at the gigantic rider. For to me, as to all who have lived long in Greece, the name of Konstantin Vlasto was as interestingly familiar as would be that of the sole survivor of the dinosaur or pterodactyl tribes. Vlasto, like them, was unique in his line, and represented as much as they a now extinct species.

He was, in fact, probably the last living scion of the medieval Greek nobility—the nobility who, claiming with justice a straight genealogy back to the Attic sovereigns, had ever retained the old pride of birth and position, and had looked down on the heterogeneous mass of

Levantines, Orientals, Balkans, and Turks who make up the blended population of modern Greece as on mere animals of a lower order.

For ages these nobles, growing yearly fewer and prouder, had led the lives of fourteenth-century feudal lords in the hill-castles of the interior. They were adored by their vassals, over whom they exercised power of life and death—a power as unquestioned as it was self-appointed.

Considering themselves above the law, looking down on the present Greek sovereignty as a nest of foreign upstarts, these lords of the old régime formed a phase of modern existence as remarkable as it was rare. It is related how one of them, during the middle years of the nineteenth century, challenged—by sheep-skinned emissary—the ruler of a European country to mortal combat, because the latter had refused the Greek his daughter's hand in marriage.

Konstantin Vlasto was perhaps the last of this strange race left alive; yet, from all reports, he had abated not one jot the ancient prerogatives and dignity of his order.

"Perhaps," rumbled on Padapoulos, "he is in Athens to get a glimpse at his fellow sovereign, Kaiser Wilhelm. Hohenzollern blood must be almost old enough to warrant even a Vlasto's interest. Perhaps—"

"*Zito!*" yelled the crowd as a second cavalry troop clattered past and a band at their rear broke into *"Die Wacht am Rhein."*

"The imperial carriage is coming!" muttered Padapoulos.

The throng in front of me eddied again. Then a man laughed coarsely, and the laugh was taken up by others.

"Don't be scared, *ma belle!*" called one fellow in execrable French. "I'll lift you upon my shoulder and you shall see everything. But one kiss, first, as payment!"

Again the crowd roared with laughter, and I rose on my toes and looked over intervening heads to see the cause.

Some eight feet away was a girl—slender, small, fragile. How, with that look of refinement and breeding, she came to be alone in such a place, I could not understand. But as a stout Levantine attempted to encircle her waist with a not overclean sleeve, and as the Greek bystanders laughed delightedly at her scared efforts to elude him, I caught one good look at her face.

Pretty it was—decidedly pretty, and very young, but stamped with such an aspect of panic fear that it turned me sick. The sight of fear in animals, children. and women is one to which I can never wholly accustom myself, and which always gives me a queer constriction about the heart. On this instance it drove me instinctively toward the frightened little woman.

Now, understand me, I had no heroic ideas of chivalry. I am not a squire of dames, nor am I troubled with any high-flown ideals concerning the other sex. As for this girl, she was doubtless some milliner or actress who had been drawn by curiosity to see the spectacle of the parade from close quarters, and whose rashness was being repaid by insult.

But she was frightened. And that, at the time, was quite enough for me.

I found myself beside the Levantine just as he had succeeded in cornering her and had caught her around the waist. His dirty, unshaven face, with its aura of garlic fumes, was pressing forward in an effort to kiss her. With one uplifted hand she was seeking to push him away, and in her averted eyes that look of dread had deepened well-nigh to madness.

My mind was made up instantly.

No, I was not like the hero of a dime novel. I did not fell the burly ruffian with a blow of my fist and clasp the rescued heroine to my bosom with appropriate sentiments. I considered that a girl who would wander abroad alone in the streets of Athens after dark scarcely merited such heroics, even were I the sort of man to indulge in them.

Instead, I simply caught the Levantine by the nape of the neck and, giving him a shake that loosened his grip on her waist, propelled him with a none too gentle shove among his laughing mates.

I know men fairly well. The type of central European who annoys women is not the sort to resent chastisement. So I was in no way surprised when he did not turn back to call me to account. But a surprise, nevertheless, awaited me.

The girl was shuddering, her face in her hands—they were little hands, I noted, well-shaped and well-gloved. Reaction had, for the instant, robbed her of speech and of independent motion.

"I am sorry for your fright," I said in Greek, "but he will not trouble you again. May I suggest that you are likely to be still further insulted if you stay here? You see—"

I stopped. She was looking up at me without the faintest glimmer of understanding.

"I am not Greek," she faltered in Parisian French, "and I cannot understand you. You speak French?"

"Yes, *mademoiselle*. I was advising—"

But she cut me short.

"Thank you—oh, thank you *very* much!" she cried. "I was—"

"You were in a somewhat daring mood, if I may say so, *mademoiselle,* to venture out alone. The streets of Athens are even less safe at night for unescorted women than those of your own Paris."

"Alone?" she repeated. "I was not alone. My—"

"What? That greasy Levantine surely wasn't—?"

"I never saw him before," she interrupted with another involuntary little shudder. "I—my father and our dragoman were with me. We were waiting to see the Kaiser pass. And there—there was some sort of struggle in the crowd when the cavalry rode by, and—somehow I was separated from—from—"

"A thousand pardons, *mademoiselle,*" I apologized, in a very different voice. "I did not understand. May I have the honor of taking you to your hotel, or trying to help you find *monsieur* your father?"

"Yes, if you will be so kind," she answered, recovering herself a little and accepting my proffered arm. "It was my own fault. I was so anxious to see the Kaiser, and—"

"And there he is, *mademoiselle,* directly behind you," I interposed, glad to distract her thoughts from the memory of her late fright and to give her jarred nerves a chance to quiet down.

We were almost on the outer edge of the crowd, close to the guard-lines. As we turned, the imperial landau was abreast of us. For one fleeting moment we saw its four occupants—the two gaudy aides with their backs to the horses, and facing them two mustached men.

"There is the Kaiser," said I, speaking loudly to be heard through the storm of cheering—"the one to the left. The other is King George."

The German Emperor's helmet blazed back the thousand lights of the street. The shoulders were squared in military fashion under a heavy army-cloak. A second later the carriage had passed on.

"Did you get a good look at him, *mademoiselle?*" I asked, as I turned and began to pilot the girl carefully out of the crowd.

"A very good look, thanks to you," she answered gratefully. "He is quite handsome, isn't he?"

"I should not have expected to hear a Frenchwoman say so," I retorted lightly. "Most of your countryfolk—"

"My countryfolk? Why, I am not French. I—"

My eyes fixed themselves on her searchingly.

"I *thought* your accent was too precise for a born Parisian," I said. "I seem fated to make blunders this evening. Accept my compliments on your pronunciation. It's perfect."

"You Frenchmen all say that to foreigners, I believe," she countered, slightly embarrassed. "It is very kind, but—"

"But I'm not a Frenchman!" I protested. "I am an American."

"An American!" She halted, and broke into a laugh—a beautiful, silvery little laugh that no one but an American girl could possibly have compassed. "Why, so am I!"

I do not know why her laugh proved so infectious. But for a full half-minute we two grown people stood in the deserted byway to which I had led her and laughed at each other like children.

It was foolish, of course, but the heartiest laughter always is, I think. And as we recovered our decorum, I instinctively felt that the mutual laugh had somehow established a subtle bond of sympathy and incipient intimacy between us that a week of casual acquaintance could not have formed.

"How absurd!" she exclaimed as we started on our way again. "We two Americans were jabbering so solemnly to each other in a foreign tongue, when—but you do not look like an American," she broke off.

"Probably not. I have not been in my own country for many years. But, speaking of absurdities, I think we both must be bewitched to-night. Does it occur to you that I am supposed to be taking you to your father or to your hotel, and that I don't know where to look for either?"

This brought her in a flash to earth and to a rather belated sense of the proprieties.

"How careless of me!" she murmured. "We are stopping at the Angleterre. It would be better to go there at once, if I may trouble you, rather than to try to find papa in that mass of people back on the avenue. He will probably have hurried on to the hotel, anyway, to look for me."

We moved on more rapidly, a certain constraint falling between us. By the shop-window illuminations I stole occasional side glances down at her. Yes, she was pretty—prettier by far than I had thought, now that the color had returned to her face and the light to her eyes. Petite, slender, infinitely graceful; scarce taller than a child, yet with a gracious womanliness in look and manner; a flower face, slightly up-tilted nose, small mouth, and a pair of dark eyes that seemed two sizes too big for the rest of her countenance—such, in brief, was my description of the girl I had so strangely met.

Little by little the constraint wore off, and by the time we reached the Angleterre we were chatting with the gay freedom of old acquaintances. I saw that her late fright still underlay her thoughts, and admired the pluck that led her to mask it so brightly.

"You will come to our suite, of course?" she said as we entered the wide lobby of the hotel. "My parents must thank you in person for what you have done. I want you to meet them and—"

"Hello, little girl!" shouted a voice behind us. "The pater's wild about you. He's been sending to the police and the American minister's and—How'd you get lost? Who is—?"

It was young Clyde, and he caught up with us as he spoke, recognizing me for the first time. The girl turned to me in introduction.

"This is my brother, Mr.—Why!"—she checked herself with another embarrassed laugh—"I don't even know your name!"

CHAPTER III.
TEMPTATION.

YOUNG Clyde stared from one to the other of us in frank dismay. Plainly my acquaintance with his sister seemed less odd to him than did her ignorance of my name.

"I was lucky enough to meet Miss Clyde just as she got separated from the others," said I, "and she allowed me to bring her home. The streets are rather crowded."

"Thanks," replied the lad; "awfully good of you to take the trouble!" Clyde was at the age when a boy cannot understand how it can be other than a "trouble" for another man to do a service for his sister. "And now I'll go and stop the pater before he has the national guard and the fleet called into the hunt for you. There he is now, over by the desk. I'll—"

"Here he comes," broke in his sister, "and," she added quizzically, "before he gets here, Jimmy, won't you please introduce this man whom I've been talking with for a solid half-hour? You seem to know each other, and it is becoming almost—"

"Oh, I beg pardon!" cried the boy. "Certainly, Elinor—this is my sister, Elinor—Mr. Bruce Graeme. Oh, it ought to be the other way round, oughtn't it? But it's all the same. Well, Mr. Graeme's the whitest chap I know. See that scar on his face? He got that in a battle with—"

Before I could stop the young idiot his father had borne down upon us, puffing, red, excited.

"Elinor!" he panted, "where *have* you been? We've—"

Quietly, yet with none of the snubbing superiority which so many girls nowadays seem to feel it necessary to assume in order to keep their parents in proper subjection, Miss Clyde checked the outflow of paternal agitation by introducing me. Then she went on with a brief yet embarrassingly glowing account of our recent adventure.

"And Mr. Graeme never said a word about it!" crowed Jimmy as she finished. "Just told me he'd met her, and said not a thing about licking that Levantine cur or—"

"Mr. Graeme!" boomed the older man with all the tremulous pomposity of the true stage father, "you have put us under very, very heavy obligations, which none of us can ever forget. Accept my thanks, my heartiest—"

Perhaps gathering from my manner how distasteful were his eulogiums, he paused, and then went on in a different tone:

"Graeme? That is an unusual name for an American. From what part do you come?"

"From Boston," I answered. It was nearly as true as it was false, for I had spent at Harvard the four years just previous to my exile.

"Boston?" he ruminated nervously. "No relation, I suppose, to

Bruce Graeme, the former New York banker? Or—"

It was the first time I had heard my father spoken of in fifteen years; but long control of nerve and muscle left my face unmoved.

"My own name is Bruce Graeme," said I indifferently. "The banker of whom you speak was a connection of mine—by marriage. And the Graemes, of New York, are a branch of our family."

The old man's face cleared marvelously, and his manner underwent a complete change. Hitherto, I knew, he had looked on me as a possible doubtful stranger to whom he owed perfunctory thanks for the service rendered his daughter, but who might not prove a wholly desirable acquaintance. Now, the knowledge of my antecedents made him view me in a totally new and infinitely friendlier light.

That I could not meet him half-way was my own fault. The reason need be no mystery—I do not believe in mysteries. Yet as the subject is a bitter one to me, I will touch on it as shortly as may be.

My father was a New Yorker of old and high family. He was a bank president. The misrepresentations of a friend of his boyhood, then powerful in the financial world, led him to put his own fortune and large sums of the bank's money into a venture that his friend advocated and vouched for.

The deal failed utterly, and my father was ruined both in fortune and reputation. His "friend," as it turned out in the investigation, had been on the other side of the deal and had reaped rich profits thereby. My father's heart broke through the double shame and grief; he died, and I, his only son, went out into the world branded by his disgrace.

That is all the sordid little tale—all except that the "friend" was Barzillah Clyde.

"And now," prattled on the old gentleman, glancing at his watch, "we dine in twenty minutes. Just time enough for us all to dress. You dine with us tonight, of course, Mr. Graeme. No, I'll hear no denial, no refusal. We don't mean to lose sight of you, young man, I can tell you. In twenty minutes, remember. Suite eight."

And I accepted. Why, I don't know. It was one of those blind impulses that come over a man sometimes, strangling his better judgment, his logic—even his inclination.

Yes, I accepted, and I went. I have no very vivid memories of the evening. There was a sweet-faced little old lady—Mrs. Clyde—who made me welcome with a gentle graciousness that did my heart good. Then there was a golden hour after dinner when I sat beside Miss Clyde on the low window-seat as we all looked out at the illuminations and fireworks in the plaza.

These, with Jimmy's eager, boyish friendliness and old Clyde's elephantine efforts at good-fellowship, are about all I recall of the affair. Yet, I went away with my brain in a tumult.

What was there in a simple, informal dinner to confuse a grown man's mind? Just this: for the first time in years I found myself in surroundings where I was neither on the defensive nor on the lookout for spoils. In other words, I was tasting again the life to which I had been born. And it was as strong wine to an unaccustomed brain.

Of the fortnight that followed there is little to tell. Daily, almost hourly, I was with the Clydes. The old man, to my amused chagrin, grew to take a prodigious fancy to me.

Mrs. Clyde also took me into her ample, maternal heart with a kind motherliness that sometimes brought a lump to my throat. Jimmy, in his hero-worship, stuck to my heels like a pet dog, accepting as the Voice of Wisdom my most commonplace utterances.

As for Miss Clyde, it was my fortune to be her constant companion in ride, drive, and walk—in rambles over the Acropolis, in trips to Eleusis—in all manner of excursions among the environs of the wonderful Old-World city.

I did not try to analyze my emotion. I was content, for the time, to drift with this pleasant, unwonted tide. Of one thing alone was I certain: Barzillah Clyde had ruined my father—and I hated him.

It was sometimes not easy to dignify by the name of hatred the feeling inspired by that pursy, pompous old mass of self-importance. Yet, whatever it might be called, my feeling against him was strong, and I knew that sooner or later he must pay for what he had done.

Fate had thrown him in my way, through no effort of mine. Like most men who have lived the hand-to-mouth life and have laughed in Death's face, I am a fatalist. And I knew that our meeting was not a matter of idle chance.

Why then, knowing this, did I remain on terms of intimacy with his family? A man who, after long sojourn in darkness, finds himself unexpectedly in all the glory of spring sunlight, will understand. To him who does not, I cannot explain. Nor do I justify myself—but it is easy to drift.

For my association with Clyde himself, I need no defense. Had he not professed friendship for my father and then betrayed him? Was I not paying him in his own coin? And more and more, as time went on, I recalled old Gorgias Padapoulos's hint.

To lure Clyde to the mountains, to let Padapoulos strip him to the very skin of his windy self-esteem, and to wring him dry of fortune as the price of life and freedom—that could be easily accomplished. Scarce a year passes that some such thing, on large or small scale, is not done in the Archipelago.

Then, for my rightful share, a comfortable fortune and new life in America. In America again, free, well-to-do, happy! The thought set my blood athrob with all an exile's yearning.

But at such times a vision of Elinor Clyde's big, dark, honest eyes had an uncomfortable way of rising before my mind, and my clear thought would grow troubled.

The most eventful happening, just then, in Athens, next to the Kaiser's visit, was the sojourn at the Angleterre of Prince Konstantin Vlasto. Indeed, to most born Athenians his presence outranked in importance that of the German Emperor himself.

To me, the oddest thing about it all was the fact that Vlasto—who looked on untitled foreigners as mere peasants—should consent to become acquainted with Barzillah Clyde, for become acquainted he did, less than a fortnight after my own introduction to the family. And what was more odd, he treated them all with a civility—even a dignified deference—wholly unlike his customary hauteur.

It was a chance remark of Vlasto's own that at last explained it to me, and ridiculous enough the explanation was. An Athenian paper, in its account of distinguished strangers in the city, made mention of Clyde as "one of the financial kings of America."

Vlasto, in his massive, primitive ignorance and indifference concerning everything outside his own domain, read the paragraph in the literal sense, jumped to the conclusion that Clyde was a representative of American royalty, and at once sought his acquaintance.

Laugh, if you will, at the simple absurdity of it. But how was a man whose life had been passed in the Attic mountains and whose reading and outside education was more than limited—how was such a man to know better?

At all events, Vlasto did not. And many and perilous complications were to arise from his ignorance.

A splendid fellow he was, physically. Fully six feet six inches tall, built on the massive lines of a Farnese "Hercules," classic of feature, magnetic and compelling of mien, he was the sort of man to catch and hold any woman's fancy. And as I realized this one day when he stood talking with Elinor Clyde, I became aware of a wholly illogical thrill of anger.

It must be remembered, too, that the title of "prince" has an uncommonly sweet sound to democratic ears; and the sight of Athenians uncovering in respect as Vlasto passed along the streets could not have failed to impress the average American girl.

Cordial as he was to the Clydes, Vlasto accorded to me much the same treatment he would have bestowed on Jimmy's bull-terrier. When we chanced to be fellow guests in suite eight, he behaved toward me with cold, haughty civility.

At other times he ignored my existence. I did not object to this—long experience has taught me that every land has its own customs which a foreigner will be wise not to resent. Yet others, less wise, noticed it too.

One afternoon, for instance, as Miss Clyde and I were returning late from a walk to the Temple of Jupiter, she spoke to me about the matter.

"You came out from the breakfast-room just ahead of us this morning," she said. "You passed Prince Vlasto in the foyer, and you did not look at him or speak to him. Why not?"

"Chiefly," I answered, "because he did not either look at or speak to me. One must draw the line somewhere, and I draw it," with a smile at my tame witticism, "at not speaking to people who refuse to recognize me."

"But why doesn't he 'recognize' you?" she persisted.

"Why should he?" I countered. "He looks on me as a foreign commoner, a sort of hanger-on of your family's. The old Greek princes regard such people as the barons of the Middle Ages regarded serfs or tradesfolk."

"What utter nonsense!" she cried indignantly. "We are living in the twentieth century, and—"

"*We* are," I assented, "but *he* isn't. Time stopped, for him and his, five hundred years ago. There is something pathetic and yet almost grand about such an attitude."

"It's very silly," she contradicted, "and I suppose his politeness to us is due to that silly paragraph about financial kings. I wanted to explain to him, but papa begged me not to. It gives poor papa such genuine pleasure to be taken for a king that I haven't the heart—"

"That may have accounted for Vlasto's original attitude toward you all," I replied; "but I think there's a decidedly stronger reason now."

I paused, but she didn't answer; and in the gathering dusk I thought her cheek grew a deeper rose.

"Don't *you?*" I asked bluntly, I don't know why.

"How can I tell?" she returned almost impatiently. "We've spent enough time talking about him. I'm only sorry you are so meek and humble about being snubbed."

"I'm afraid it isn't anything quite so worthy as humility," I said. "It's more like indifference."

"You are the most indifferent man I ever met!" she cried, now in real impatience. "Nothing seems to move or excite you. You've the air of having been through everything before. Is there nothing you really care about? Nothing, no one, that has the power of lifting you out of yourself and making you feel as though—?"

"Yes," I cut in quietly, "there is. And you know it."

"*I* know it?"

"If not you, then no one does or ever shall," I blundered on. And I give you my promise I spoke the crazy words without either will or premeditation—they tumbled out like money from a broken-stringed purse. She could not have been half so surprised as I.

Yet, now that I had spoken, I must say more. I could no more have checked myself than can the man who has inadvertently swam too close to Niagara's falls.

But the checking came from another quarter. Jimmy, at the top of the hotel stairway, had spied me as we drew near, and was bearing down on us in joyous, horribly unwelcome greeting.

"Listen," I said to her hastily, lowering my voice as he approached. "You are going to the opera this evening, so I can't get a word with you alone. If—if you feel any curiosity as to my lack of indifference for some one, may I call to-morrow at ten and tell you more about it? Will you care to hear?"

"Say, old man!" bawled Jimmy. "What do you think? There is a man named Paddy—Pad—Poul—Something-or-other, who's no end of a brigand, and hangs out over on the other side of Mount Hymettus, and the police have found out that he was here in this very city not a month ago. Came here, bold as brass, and got away without one of them recognizing him. What do you think of that for official punkiness? Not one of them got onto his being here. I wish we could have had a squint at him."

Elinor had slipped past us up the stairs. Cutting Jimmy short in a decidedly unenthusiastic fashion, I went to my own room, my head awhirl.

Well, I was committed now, if ever a man was! I stared at myself in the glass as at a stranger. The impulse of a moment had undone the self-control of years. Where now was my beautiful plan for luring Barzillah Clyde into the mountains beyond Hymettus and giving him over to his just deserts? My plan to avenge my father and at one stroke to become a rich man?

I had plotted it all so carefully, too. And here I was, without a moment's conscious warning, head over heels in love with the old blackguard's own daughter. So much for revenge and wealth and all I had dreamed of!

I—a man of the world, noted for coolness and caution even among men to whom those qualities were the breath of life—I had tumbled in love like the veriest schoolboy with five feet of fluffy loveliness, with glorious dark eyes and a face like a half-opened blush-rose! Fallen in love without an atom of warning, and at the cost of wealth and vengeance.

I shook my fist at my asinine self in the mirror. But, to my surprise, that same self grinned back at me, behind the clenched fist, in a halo of idiotic beatitude; and I groaned and blissfully gave myself up for lost.

"To-morrow at ten!" I found myself humming, with outrageous

lack of tune but plenitude of fervor, as I dressed for dinner.

Nor did morning bring me sanity. I dressed with a solicitous care worthy of Beau Brummel. My hand, that had never shaken on pistol-butt or sword-hilt, trembled awkwardly as I adjusted my tie.

As for breakfast—who could have descended to the gross function of eating earthly food at such a time? The hours dragged mercilessly. It was still some twenty minutes short of ten when, unable to bear the waiting any longer, I left my room and made my way to suite eight.

As I reached the outer door Barzillah Clyde, coming up from the foyer, hailed me.

"You're just the man I want to see!" he exclaimed as he reached my side. "I want to talk to you about something. Come in, won't you?"

He opened the door and made way for me to precede him. Inwardly cursing the old reprobate for his hearty welcome, I went in ahead of him and entered the little drawing-room of the suite. There, Mrs. Clyde, who was reading some letters, looked up at me with her bright, motherly smile.

"You'll find only the old folks at home," she said. "Jimmy's over at the Embassy Club, and Elinor has gone riding with Prince Vlasto."

My face as I halted, dumb with dismay, told her something, but she misread my expression and went on:

"I know it isn't customary for girls to go riding unchaperoned with foreigners. But I never can make my children understand that every quarter of the globe isn't just like safe old America.

"The prince wanted especially to show her some new excavations just this side of Eleusis, and she seemed so anxious to go that I hadn't the heart to refuse. So I sent one of the footmen along, as groom, to play propriety. Are you feeling badly?" she asked with real concern. "You look pale and ill!"

I made shift to stammer some commonplace denial, but in my head rang the words: "She seemed so anxious to go!" Knowing well what this morning was to have meant to me, Elinor had not so much as waited to hear me out and refuse me. Vlasto had raised a beckoning finger, and she had obediently run to do his bidding.

Well, so be it! Could I blame her for preferring a prince to a beggarly adventurer? And yet her eyes had seemed so honest!

But what was to be expected of the daughter of Barzillah Clyde?

In my bitter fury I mentally thanked Fate for this latest rebuff, for, cruel as it was, it had awakened me from my golden insanity and brought me back to my old shrewd, calculating self.

Then, with a thrill, I caught the import of the words old Clyde was speaking.

"Yes," he was saying, "the children have been at me for days to take them on a short camping-trip among the hills before winter sets in. The dragoman says he often provides outfits and guides for such parties, and it seems it's quite the thing to do when you visit Greece.

"But all this talk about brigands has rather scared me. Now, I understand you know this country like a book. Tell me, honestly, is it safe? I told them this morning I'd leave it to you, and go by your decision. How about it?"

It seemed almost too good to be true. With difficulty I forced my voice into a decent indifference as I replied:

"Safe as a church. There is not a brigand any more dangerous than a common pickpocket within a hundred miles of Athens. To prove what I say, I'll join the excursion if you'll let me. It would be a shame for you to leave Greece without at least seeing a sunrise from the slopes of Hymettus."

My unwonted enthusiasm infected Clyde; and so busy did he keep me answering questions about the journey that I had to plead a pressing engagement in order to get away.

A glance at the clock as I passed out of the suite told me that it was still five minutes to ten. Fifteen little minutes! And a whole world changed for me.

An hour later I was cantering decorously away from the city. Once out of sight, I clapped spurs to my beast and hurried at full gallop toward where Hymettus rose, snow-capped, above the foothills—and where, incidentally, one Gorgias Padapoulos, brigand, held camp.

CHAPTER IV.
I Trade Love for Revenge.

I RODE steadily, first through the fairly good roads leading westward from the city; then over the winding lanes, and finally into the craggy hill-paths that skirt the north slopes of old Hymettus. Pressing my horse as hard as I dared, considering the length of the journey before me, I pushed onward doggedly, raging, until the sun reached the meridian and passed it.

The hill shadows were sloping long and black away from the sun, and there was a mountain sting in the late afternoon air when, finally, I struck off the regular path into a rocky trail bearing southward and up.

Here there was no question of hurry. A slow, cautious footpace up the treacherous incline was the best I could hope to make. After a time, I abandoned even this, as beyond my town-bred horse's ability. I dismounted and worked my way up through the boulders, leading my mount behind me.

A hill pony would have covered the ground swiftly and safely. But, to a horse unfamiliar from birth with the path, the climb held countless perils. I had far too much at stake just then to risk a broken leg, or a knock in the head.

Then, as the valleys beneath me grew dusky, and the peaks above and behind were the only points whereon the sun still streamed, the thing I had for half an hour been looking for happened.

I was rounding a great rock. From its shelter stepped a man, clad in sheepskins and carelessly fingering a long, old-fashioned rifle. That he was an outpost of Padapoulos's, and that he had doubtless observed my progress from the moment I had turned off the beaten path, I did not doubt.

"M'sieu has lost his way?" he asked in broken French, his dull eyes roving in evident appraisal over my well-groomed figure, and resting with a look of real affection on my watch-chain.

"Yes," I replied, also in French. "Perhaps you will set me right?"

He grunted pleased acquiescence; ran his arm through my horse's bridle, and, keeping abreast of me, turned off from the trail and started in a true line across the north slope of the mountainside.

We were both happy: he, that a traveler of means had offered no resistance, but had stupidly consented to be led straight into the trap; I, that I had not been forced into asking to be conducted to Padapoulos. Had I done so, it was ten to one the scout would have suspected a trick, or an ambush, and would have refused.

He might even have carried his disapproval to the point of lodging a bullet or knife-blade somewhere in my anatomy in order to remove any danger of my returning. One must use forethought in dealing with the Greek brigand class. It was with this in view, for instance, that I had for the occasion donned much more jewelry than I am wont to wear. I knew it would serve as a bait, and also that it would be as safe as in a deposit vault, once it was understood that I was under Padapoulos's protection.

We continued our way without speech. My guide glanced sidelong at me now and then, at first, to make sure I was too thick-headed to realize that he was leading me away from the main road instead of toward it. Finding that I seemed to harbor no suspicion, he doubtless placed me in the brainless tourist category, and henceforth showed no more doubt of me than of my stumbling, tired horse.

It was perhaps a mile or so farther that, coming to a sharp turn in the shoulder of the hill, we skirted a deep gorge. It was black at the bottom. Through the stillness, I could hear the far-off swirl of running water through its bed. What caught my eye was not the gorge itself, but what lay beyond. The farther sides rose almost precipitously in tier after tier of brown rock; culminating about a mile away in a peak, and forming a steep, rugged hill by itself, whose summit was capped by a mighty sprawling gray stone building.

I knew a little about architecture, yet that of the edifice across the gorge was almost foreign to me. The house must have antedated the Crusades, and had evidently been built for resistance rather than for beauty. A feudal castle, practically impregnable from its position and strength; and, to judge from smoke-wreaths that drifted over the slope, with a large or small village nestling against the southern base of its cliffs.

I broke silence to ask my hastening guide: "What place is that?"

"The castle of Prince Konstantin Vlasto," he returned, a tone of genuine unwilling respect permeating his surly voice.

He vouchsafed no more information, but quickened his pace until an angle of the mountain cut the castle from our view.

I wished I might have had longer to gaze on the strange spectacle. My busy imagination could picture the castle in bygone centuries, its battlements swarming with armed retainers; the war banner of the Vlastos streaming from the highest turret; the cliffs alive with the charging men-at-arms of some hostile prince, or with troops of peasant tenantry coming to pay their yearly homage and tribute.

Truly the ancient glory had departed! Yet there, as strong to-day as then, stood the frowning castle. At its foot, and in the neighboring mountains, dwelt vassals as loyal to their overlord as their ancestors had been to his. And—not there, but in Athens, making stately love to the girl I had lost—was Prince Konstantin Vlasto himself; a man born five centuries too late.

The moon had long since risen when we came to a halt, my sheep-skinned guide and I. How he could have thought that even a tourist could be so stupid as to still believe himself on the way to Athens, I do not understand. But the Greek peasant does not waste much time in thinking. It was probably enough for him that I did not resist.

He halted me on what seemed the verge of a precipice. But, as I looked down, I saw a cup-like valley, hidden wholly from casual notice, wherein twinkled two or three camp-fires. About these fires lay or sat more than a score of men. Some were playing cards; some few busy clearing away the remains of a meal; but the majority were wrapped in the apathetic sloth that so characterizes the Levantine in his very frequent moments of repose.

My guide, I say, halted me, and shouted to those below. At the first sound of his voice a half-dozen men scrambled to their feet and came running up the valley's steep sides toward us.

"What is this?" I asked in innocent surprise. "You were to guide me to the Athens road, and—"

"You will do quite as well here," he chuckled in his wretched French, as the others crowded about us. "We need you more than do the hotel-keepers there."

"As you wish!" I assented cheerfully, dropping into modern Greek and using purposely the odd accent affected by the denizens of the Levantine underworld. "I am content. Is it too late for Gorgias to see me to-night?"

Had I drawn a brace of revolvers and begun firing among the disreputable crew they could not have been more dumfounded. While they still gurgled forth incoherent profanity, I thrust a way for myself and ran down the slope to the nearest camp-fire.

A pistol-shot followed me—and flew wide. I strode up to the fire, kicked its logs into a brighter glow, and beckoned to a grimy rascal who had been squatting before its embers tying up a wounded hand in a very dirty rag. The fellow had leaped up at my approach, and had half drawn his knife. But my insolence had left him doubtful as what next to do.

"Tell Gorgias I must speak to him at once!" I ordered sharply. "Jump, man! I've no time to waste!"

The others, recovering from their amaze, were closing in, uncertain, but noisily wrathful. The pistol-shot and their jabber must have waked the echoes. I leaned forward, oblivious of their presence, and warmed my hands by the blaze. Every gesture should have its meaning. In a crisis such as I faced, minor matters count. I have seen a yawn avert a barracks fight, where a start or look of surprise would have been the signal for a dozen knives to flash.

My indifference now probably saved my life. One cannot stroll unmolested into a nest of robbers and send one's card to their chief. Such men are prone to slay first and ask questions afterward. Nor is there an adequate postal service between Athens and the headquarters of Gorgias Padapoulos. I had, in fact, chosen the least perilous way of gaining audience with the chief.

The fellow whom I addressed had not time to obey or disregard my command before the blackguards were shoved unceremoniously to either side, and Padapoulos himself pushed past them and was before me.

The old fellow was half dressed; his eyes heavy with suddenly disturbed sleep, his short gray hair and stubby white beard bristling with anger.

"What is this?" he roared. "Who shot without my orders? If one of you dogs has killed another—"

He stopped; his eyes focusing at last to the light and recognizing me. It was amusing to see how wonder replaced wrath in his gnarled old face.

"Graeme!" he cried.

"At your service, always," I returned, bowing.

"But—"

"You have often asked me to visit your retreat. I am here at last to—"

Pleasure chased the surprise from his eyes.

"So?" he cried exultantly, "you have staked life once too often, at last, have you? And the law-boys are after you? And you've come to throw in your chances with—"

"I am come only as your guest, chief," I answered formally, and held out my hand.

Out of the corner of my eye I noted the change in the men's expression. It was a crucial moment for them. Should the chief ignore my proffered hand it was a sign that I was prisoner. My jewelry and tailor-made raiment would go to some of those who were so covetously eying it. My ransom would swell the band's exchequer.

If, on the contrary, my hand were accepted, I was, henceforth, during so long a time as I might choose to stay in their domain, sacred from molestation by any member of the band. Yes, and each and every man in Gorgias's following would be responsible with his very life for my safety and well-being. So runs the immemorial oriental law of the mountains.

Before my arm was half extended, Gorgias had gripped my hand with a pressure that numbed me to the elbow. It may have been my fancy, but I thought I detected an almost inaudible growl of disappointment. To try still further the temper and loyalty of the rascals I drew out my handkerchief; managing as I did so to let fall to the ground behind me a goodly roll of bank-notes.

At once several men darted forward. One of them, picking up the money, returned it to me intact, with a bow that held perhaps more of regret than politeness. Meantime old Gorgias was booming forth greetings, orders, and questions.

"Well, guest or recruit, you're welcome!" he bellowed. "I've seen you fight and I've seen you plot. And you'd be useful to us both ways.

But how did you find your way? Mitri!" he yelled to a lad, "Wine and food! Not here. In my hut. Now, who fired that shot?"

"I beg you will let it pass," I intervened, as the men glanced uneasily at one another. "The fault was mine. I am here on business of import. Business that may mean much to you. Can we talk apart?"

Padapoulos led the way across the sward, out of range of the camp-fires, to a hovel whose door stood open. Passing in ahead of me, he lighted a couple of guttering candles and waved me ceremoniously to a seat on a couch, whose covering of tumbled skins attested to the chief's recent sudden awakening.

"Wait!" he said, as I began to speak. "Food first. Then tobacco. Then speech. That is our guest law."

The boy Mitri came in as he spoke, bearing a wicker flask of wine and a smoking dish of goat flesh. The wine—as is common in Greece—reeked of turpentine. The meat was tough and ill-cooked. Yet an all-day ride had given my appetite an edge that would have consumed much worse fare. Still, I laughed inwardly as I thought of dyspeptic old Barzillah Clyde's misery when he should find himself forced to subsist for weeks on such food. The thought added zest to my rude feast.

My host sat opposite me, on a rickety stool, saying no word, nor looking in my direction. When platter and flagon were empty, Mitri set before each of us a narghile with a live coal atop of its tobacco, and beside it a cup of cognac. Then he withdrew.

"Now," said Gorgias complacently, "we can talk."

"You spoke to me, in Athens, two weeks ago to-night," I began, "of an American multimillionaire, Barzillah Clyde."

His complacency was gone in a flash, and he was on his feet in keen excitement, almost upsetting the tall narghile.

"What!" he shouted, "you can get him for me? If you're joking—"

"I am not given to jokes," I interrupted, growing cooler as the bandit's excitement increased.

"You mean you can really wheedle the old miser into—"

"I do not like your way of stating the case," I objected. "What I say is: I think I can interest Mr. Clyde into taking a trip through the hills in this part of the country. If I do so, and he should happen to fall in with a detachment of your men—"

"Oh, I understand," he grunted contentedly. "Put it any way you like. Only there is no need of offense at my way of talk. It is as good as yours, and—"

"Your sheepskins are as good as my fifteen-guinea riding-suit," I retorted. "They keep out wind and weather as well. Yet I am foolish enough to prefer tailor-made clothes, and—"

"Tailor-made talk!" he supplemented with a big laugh.

"Quite so. A mere preference of mine. Respect it, please."

"As you like," he agreed, in nowise ruffled; though he would doubtless have flogged one of his own men for less. "Now, go on and twist your tailor-made talk into telling me what we are to do."

As briefly as I could, I outlined the plan I had formulated during the day's ride.

During the following week or later, the Clydes and I would start on our camping-trip. I would suggest to them the most attractive route, and, if need be, would tip their dragoman to indorse my suggestion. This route would lie in the same general direction I had taken during the first part of my ride toward Padapoulos's headquarters.

We would start early in the morning and pitch camp, the first night out, on a flat little plateau I had noted just before I had reached the rock where Gorgias's scout had met me. The place would prove a good half-way spot on our proposed ascent of Hymettus.

I had observed among the rocks, a furlong or so above the plateau, a blasted tree that was visible for miles in each direction. On the night of our arrival there I would tie a red handkerchief to its trunk. A scout of Gorgias's was to be on the lookout for such a signal. At daybreak on the morning it should appear, the scout was to carry the news at once to his master.

Gorgias and one or two picked men could then readily precede the party to our next night's halt, at the summit. On that second evening I would engage to lure Clyde into a stroll with me to some point out of earshot from the tents. There Padapoulos could quietly capture him. There would be no outcry, no disturbing or frightening of Elinor or Mrs. Clyde.

The affair was ideally simple. My part of it could readily be carried out without attracting suspicion. Then, when the first hue and cry should die down, I would find opportunity to visit Clyde in Padapoulos's camp and let him know to whom he was indebted for his present plight, and why. This item was my personal affair.

Padapoulos could demand what ransom he chose. My only stipulation was that one-third of the sum should come to me. I knew the old robber well enough to be sure he would hold to any promise he might make me. I also knew that Barzillah Clyde, through sheer shame and through fear of stirring up the half-forgotten story of my father's death, was not likely to make public later my own share in the matter.

America—freedom—wealth!

The three words, to my surprise, gave me less intense pleasure tonight than when I had so often whispered them to myself earlier in my acquaintance with Elinor Clyde. Vaguely, I wondered why.

Padapoulos heard my plan through to the end, rubbing his big, bony hands together in silent joy, and nodding occasional approval of some point in the project. When I had ceased speaking, he smote me a resounding whack on the shoulder.

"Magnificent!" he cried, "and so simple it is almost childish. You shall have your third. You will deserve it. But, boy, how did you know those points you spoke of? The plateau, the blasted tree—the—"

"I am trained to note the ground I pass over," said I indifferently. "Every soldier should be."

"Then you had never come that way before?"

"No farther than the outer path. I knew the general direction of your camp. All I had to do was to travel in that direction until I came upon an outpost."

"And having once traveled it?"

"I could find my way to this spot from Athens on a dark night," I replied, seeing that a little boasting would not come in amiss. "You should teach your men to blindfold their captives."

"What need, with nine out of ten? It is a rare man who has that hunter faculty of studying each rock and tree and hill as he passes it. I wish you were one of us."

"I see you are a neighbor of Vlasto's," said I. "His castle cannot lie more than five miles distant from here, across the gorge."

"Yes," he grinned, "I have great neighbors. But there is scant acquaintance between Vlasto Rock and my valley. He does not molest me, and I do not prey upon his vassals. It is 'live and let live' between us. If he takes the trouble to remember we are here, it does not greatly annoy him, or he would have destroyed us before now. I am wise enough to give his lands a wide berth. I've no wish to see a hundred of his mountaineers swoop down on me some fine day, I can tell you."

I remembered my guide's haste in passing the castle's range of view, and now better understood his motive.

"Graeme," said Padapoulos, presently returning to our first theme, "you are a puzzle to me. I have never before been able to interest you in bringing 'guests' to me. Why do you do it now?"

"Perhaps for the money."

"And perhaps not," he caught me up. "There is another reason. Well, it doesn't concern me, so I get Clyde here. But why not his wife and children, too? There would be larger—"

"It is out of the question," I interrupted, with a finality that left no room for reply. "You can squeeze him dry, for all I care. But I take no step in the affair until I have your oath that neither you nor any of your men shall harm a hair of the others' heads. Is it so understood?"

"It is understood," he agreed sulkily.

The sun had not yet risen when I left Padapoulos's camp and retraced my steps over the mountain-shoulder toward Athens. I refused the old brigand's hospitable offer of a guide, confident of my inborn gift to retrace unerringly any path I had once trod.

Nor was I mistaken. Past the gorge with its opposite castle-crowned hill, over the rock-path, down the slope of Hymettus, and so to the highway, I led my horse in safety. Then, rapidly, I rode on to the city.

Dusk had fallen as I entered the Hôtel d'Angleterre and hastened to efface by a bath, a shave, and a change into evening-dress the marks of my two days' journey.

As I entered my room and switched on the electric-light, my eye fell on a slip of white paper that had been pushed beneath the door.

I stooped to pick up the white object, and found, as my fingers touched it, that it was a visiting-card. Crossing to the light, I read:

PRINCE KONSTANTIN VLASTO.

I stared at it in mild wonder.

"It seems I have been having a distinguished guest," I mused. What on earth can Vlasto want of me, and why did he demean himself by paying a visit to a mere mortal? His need must have been great indeed.

The more I thought of it, the more puzzled I grew. The man had ever ignored me with a lofty air. In my absence he had deigned to pay me a personal call.

"In my absence"—the phrase gave me an idea. Was it not probable he knew I was away and had left the card, in full perception that I, according to Greek etiquette, must return the call of my superior in rank at the earliest possible opportunity? In which case—

"I sha'n't return it," I decided aloud.

CHAPTER V.
Prince and Plebeian.

"WHEN do we start?" I asked Barzillah Clyde, as, three days later, he and his dragoman Demetrius and I finished planning the itinerary for our camping trip.

"As quickly as Demetrius can get the equipment together," he answered. "I hope it will be soon. I haven't done any camping or horseback-riding to speak of since war days. The prospect of another taste of tent life begins to appeal to me."

I knew well Clyde's connection with "war days." As a boy I remember hearing that the foundations of his later wealth were built then by shrewd and tireless attention to business, in the glorious calling of sutler's assistant.

I bit my lip to refrain from a timely reminder on the subject. I could not afford to risk losing an atom of the almost infatuated friendliness wherewith he nowadays showered me.

I well understood that had I appeared before him in the light of a poor adventurer he would never have favored me with a second thought. But he looked on me as a well-to-do fellow countryman whose exploits and unassumed character of man of the world appealed strongly to the old New Yorker, whose whole life had been shut in by walls of money.

"We can start by—let me see, this is Tuesday—we can start by Friday if your excellency pleases," computed Demetrius, as he departed to make ready for the trip.

"Unlucky day for beginning a venture!" I suggested lightly.

"Nonsense!" retorted Clyde in indulgent reproof. "Faith in superstition argues a distrust in Divine justice and—"

"As Rochefoucauld says," I supplemented with intentional absent-mindedness.

He frowned; then, otherwise unruffled, went on with the ponderous jocosity that always unreasonably jarred upon me:

"Never believe in signs and omens, my boy. You'll never get far if you do. Why, if you'll believe me, it was on Friday—the thirteenth of the month, too—fifteen years ago—that I put through the most fortunate deal of my career."

My back was to the light, and I was glad. Hardened in self-control as I was, the sudden recalling of my father's ruin made me wince. Yet I answered with the same indifference:

"Perhaps it was not so fortunate for every one."

"Mr. Graeme," he replied, "in finance there must always be losers. As to our little excursion, I have not the slightest unpleasant feeling about starting on Friday. In fact, I am rather glad. For when we return safe and happy, I can perhaps make you believe how foolish a foible superstition is. Your going with us will add greatly to our enjoyment. I wish we might have seen more of you during the past day or two. You have quite shunned us."

"I have been rather troubled over some business matters," I lied glibly.

How could I explain my real reason for avoiding the Clydes, or the bitterness that had been mine at knowing myself to be so near and so immeasurably far away from the woman for whom in a mad moment I had once been on the point of casting away revenge, wealth, and future? Well, that dream was past. Henceforth, as for so many years past, I was to be solitary devotee to the great god Self.

"Business matters?" echoed Clyde. "That is where you make a mistake. Let business alone when you are on a holiday. Now, I always—"

"You can afford it," I said curtly. "I can't."

"Surely a man as young as you, who can afford to spend years in wandering at leisure about Europe, is fortunately enough situated to—"

"To turn my back on business?" I supplemented, ignoring for the hundredth time in our acquaintance his suave attempts to gage my financial status. "Not quite yet. But in a short time I hope to be permanently independent of all business worries."

"My dear boy!" he cried enthusiastically, pump-handling me with one of his puffy white talons, "I congratulate you with all my heart. You are still under forty. You cannot mean to let your capital lie idle. Some day you and I must have a little talk. I like you, and I think I may be able to interest you in one or two operations which would enable your wealth to be of benefit to your fellow man, and at the same time vastly increase it. Now, for instance. I—"

"Now, for instance," I interposed, "I have just such a scheme under consideration. If you will let me I should like to talk it over with you. Not just now, for the arrangements are not quite complete. But perhaps before the end of the week."

"I should be delighted! You can count on any cooperation of mine that—"

"I *am* venturing to count on your cooperation," I replied, rising from my seat on the rear terrace of the hotel and tossing my cigar-stump over the low white parapet. "In the meantime, I fear I shall be too busy to see as much of any of you as I should like to until our start on Friday."

"But this evening," he urged, "you will dine with us, won't you? Quite informally. And afterward—"

"I am sorry," I answered, "but I have an engagement. I will be ready for our start Friday. During the trip I think we may see more of each other, and get to know each other better than ever before."

He seemed piqued at my refusal to dine with him. Yet I was resolved not to be his guest; not to break bread at the expense of the man, now that I had planned his undoing. There is limit to even a scoundrel's unscrupulousness. And, unlike many great men, I cannot accept favors from a person whose enemy I am. Since my visit to Gorgias I had not as much as taken a cigar from Clyde's hand.

For the same quixotic reason I had risked serious quarrel with him by insisting on paying my own share of the forthcoming excursion and refusing pointblank to go on any other basis.

Clyde, huffed, strutted into the hotel, leaving me alone on the terrace. I was about to follow indoors a minute later, and had reached the threshold, when the entrance way was blocked by a huge figure.

I recognized Prince Konstantin Vlasto and drew civilly aside to allow him to pass out. But I saw at second glance that it was I whom he was seeking.

Yet I ignored his arrogant gesture to stop, and as he came out onto the terrace I made as though I would go in. I was not minded to be beckoned as a waiter, even by the man who regarded me as lower than one, and who had apparently been able to impress with a sense of his superiority the woman I had loved. I would force him to speak. I did. It was a petty victory, but I felt a sort of miserable enjoyment in it.

"Monsieur Graeme," he said in French, as I stalked past, "one moment, please."

"Prince Vlasto," I retorted, purposely in Greek, "at your service."

A second minor victory. When he spoke again it was in Greek.

"You did not return my call," he began stiffly.

"I did not," I assented.

"Why not?"

"I did not choose to."

"Perhaps, being an American, you are ignorant that etiquette demands—"

"Only if further acquaintance is desired. I did not desire it."

Even his monumental calm seemed ruffled by this rude retort. I suppose it was the first time in the man's life that any one had dared be uncivil to him, and it came as a surprise.

"Gentlemen do not speak in that fashion," he said coldly, as though correcting an unduly awkward servant.

"How do you know?" I answered, and there was no flippancy in my query. "You are only a Greek."

His face darkened momentarily, yet cleared in an instant. There was no pose in the man's calm. I could see he regarded me as so far beneath himself that my worst insult could scarce hope to pierce his conscious superiority. The knowledge nettled me. And it hurt my pride—personal and national. I longed senselessly to wound this mountainous dignitary who regarded me as the dust beneath his feet.

"I do not wish to send for my fellows to horsewhip you," he said hesitatingly, "but—"

"If you have any future need of their services it might be inadvisable," I agreed pleasantly. "But was it to discuss your servants that you called on me the other day?"

"No," he answered, after a pause, and I noted with joy that a shade of bewilderment had crept into his quiet mien. "I wanted to tell you my wishes concerning yourself."

"Your wishes?" I cried with a really very creditable laugh. "Since when has it been the custom for a Greek mountaineer to express 'wishes' to a *gentleman*—a man from a civilized country? My friend, you grow impudent. I am willing to make all allowances for your rustic ignorance and boorish manners, but—"

"Be silent!" he ordered. The stern command in his voice well-nigh broke down the line of bluff I had suddenly decided on. "What can a tradesman like you—a commoner from a nation of tradesmen—what can such a person know of the respect due—"

"Due a Greek countryman who comes for a holiday to Athens to sell his crops and to show forth his best clothes—of season before last?" I finished. "You are quite right. Now, you'll listen to me a moment."

I lighted a cigarette with intentional slowness, for I say my very effrontery interested him despite himself. I had decided on my course of action. His strength lay in his belief in his own greatness and my low rank. On this ground alone could I hope to meet him equally. If only I, too, could assume a superiority as colossal as his own I might in time find a chink in his hereditary armor of pride.

"You speak of me as coming from a nation of tradesmen," said I. "It is true. America is a nation that sways the trade of the world—yes, and the Old World's fortunes, too. While your miserable little kingdom has been quietly rotting away from old age and disease, we have fought our way against mighty foes to the top of the nations. When Greece was a cheap little Turkish province in 1821 it was my country more than any and all others that fed your starving countrymen and bullied the Sultan into giving you a freedom you don't merit. *You* are ignorant of all this, perhaps, because you and your personal ancestors had been spending your time in a drafty old rock-pen up among the barren hills, surrounding yourself with half-starved peasantry and playing that you are still great men instead of old-fashioned, powerless fools. Why, you are nothing but a harmless scarecrow wrapped in the tatters of a bygone feudalism."

Laugh if you will at my mode of addressing him, and put me down as a half-witted braggart. When one encounters a man like Vlasto, one cannot deal with him by ordinary means. His slow-moving, primitive brain was wholly swamped by my rapid, nonsensical verbiage, catching only the fact that I for some unknown reason apparently regarded him as an inferior, and that I was a man of more or less exalted station in my own land.

Hence, Vlasto spoke to me next less as to a dog and more as though I were a human being whom he disliked. It was a refreshing change.

"We need not detain each other in a companionship that is distasteful to both," he said with cold dignity. "My business is quickly spoken. I wish you to cease your visits to the apartments of His Excellency Clyde."

"You wish it?" I gasped, utterly amazed.

"I wish it," he repeated in the same quiet command. "I do not wish you to continue your visits there. Your presence annoys me."

"And what business is it of yours?" I shouted furiously, finding my voice and losing my temper in the same breath.

"I do not choose," he went on, his massive air of authority almost impressing me, "I do not choose that you shall associate with the woman whom I am to marry."

"What?"

I gaped dumfounded at him.

"Therefore," he concluded, "you will discontinue your visits. That is all."

He moved in stately stride toward the doorway; but I was there before him. Huge and powerful though he was, I would, if necessary, have contested his passage.

"Wait!" I cried. I think my tone held as much authority as had his. "Do I understand that you are to marry Miss Clyde?"

"I cannot stoop to discuss—"

"Oh, yes, you can. You may stoop a whole lot further before I'm done. You'll answer my question. Are you betrothed to Miss Clyde? I have a right to ask."

"What right?" he sneered in cool contempt at my wrath.

"The right of an American—of a fellow countryman of hers. The right any white man would have to prevent a gently-reared American girl from being so dazzled by a silly title as to shut herself up for life in that gray old tomb of yours on Hymettus with no better companion than a savage, half-civilized mountain ruffian like you. That is my right. And you'll find me very, very much on hand to defend it. So I ask you again if you are betrothed to—"

"I refuse to waste words on you. You have had my order."

He walked toward the door in his splendid strength and contempt as though I had not been standing on the threshold. I held my place, as he came on, and felt the moment of crisis was upon us.

CHAPTER VI.
A Strange Proposal.

PROBABLY Vlasto realized what was in my mind. Yet, as he advanced to within one pace of where I stood, blocking the doorway, no expression of any sort crossed his handsome, bearded face. A step nearer—

Even as I braced my muscles, the lust of battle died in me, and Vlasto retreated a step. Coming through one of the long windows leading from her suite, Elinor Clyde stepped out on the terrace, not ten feet distant from us.

I was glad, even in the instant of reaction, that Vlasto and I had been speaking in modern Greek and not French. For, even had Elinor overheard us, she could not have understood a word. She advanced to where we stood, and Vlasto turned eagerly to greet her. As he did so, my mind was made up to a highly unconventional move. I also started toward her; but before I could speak she had turned from replying to the prince's ardent welcome and spoke to me hastily, under her breath, in English.

"You were quarreling," said she. "I could not understand what was said, but your voices were angry. What is it?"

But I was too far gone in my new resolve to be checked. Raising my voice, and speaking in French, so that Vlasto might understand, I said with formal perfunctory politeness:

"*Mademoiselle*, I owe you a humble apology. Prince Vlasto has just told me of your betrothal to him and has explained—"

"My—my betrothal?" she cried incredulously.

"And has explained to me," I continued, unmoved, "that my presence in your apartments is distasteful. Had you given me a hint that I was unwelcome there, believe me I should long since have ceased my visits. I ask your forgiveness for my lack of perception and I beg to offer my felicitations on your engagement."

I paused. I doubt if any stilted speech ever before or since had quite such an effect on its hearers. Elinor looked from one to the other of us, her face flushing, her big eyes bright with embarrassment and indignation. Vlasto, for the first time in my experience with him, changed color and was thrown off his wonderful balance of self-control.

"*Mademoiselle*," he began excitedly. But she interrupted him.

"One moment," she said. Turning to me, she went on with an effort: "Mr. Graeme, you are laboring under a strange misapprehension. I am not engaged to Prince Vlasto, and I have never expressed a wish that you should not come to see us. I—"

"Then," I returned placidly, "it seems that our worthy friend, the prince, has lied. A not uncommon trait among the Greeks."

The insult did not move him. Indeed, I doubt if he so much as heard it. And I somehow felt small and plebeian at his neglect. He was standing before her in appeal. For all my dislike, I could not help seeing the pathos of so proud a soul stooping to plead.

"*Mademoiselle*," said he, "I have been put in the wrong. I have not said that I am betrothed to you, but—"

"But that you were to marry her," I interrupted.

"I am forced," he resumed, ignoring me, "to speak otherwise and sooner than I had hoped. But I have talked with his excellency, your father, *mademoiselle*, and I have his consent, conditional upon yours. I have the unmerited honor, *mademoiselle*, to request your hand in marriage."

Now, if there is an embarrassing situation on earth, I was in it. To be the third person at a proposal was the one tight place into which I had never before blundered. Devoutly I wished myself anywhere else.

I moved aside and would have stolen quietly away, had not Elinor laid her hand on my sleeve.

Vlasto saw the gesture and flashed me a look I was not likely to forget. Yet, almost at once he was again seemingly oblivious of my presence. If his inamorata wished a witness to his proposal, she should have one. This was no doubt his thought. Still ignoring me, he went on, his great organ-voice vibrant with intensity:

"*Mademoiselle,* I am Prince Konstantin Vlasto, of family as old and as illustrious as your own can possibly be. I beg the honor of your hand. I have never before loved a woman, nor have I before met one whom I believed worthy, in person and rank, to become princess of my line. But, as the lowliest of servants I crave your love, my queen. My life is in your fair hands."

"There is one other matter, prince," she said, evading a reply and speaking in the same hurried yet dangerously steady voice. "Monsieur Graeme tells me you presumed to order him from our apartments. By what right?"

He shook his massive shoulders impatiently as though dismissing a matter too petty for consideration.

"I ask forgiveness," said he, "if I have overstepped the line of my rights or have caused you displeasure. But my heart is at your feet. Surely other matters can wait. Can you not give me a reply?"

By a queer intuition that is sometimes mine, I felt that his pleading manner was inspired rather by courtesy than by any doubt as to her answer. In olden days—the days wherein he still lived—a father's consent alone was necessary. The daughter's ensuing "yes" was a mere formality. He had Clyde's provisional assent to his suit. He waited confidently for Elinor's. Yet she hesitated, and, almost in wonder, he repeated:

"Will you not give me a reply? It is cruel to—"

"Yes," she said slowly. "I will answer you. I am deeply honored, prince, at your offer. I am also aware that my rank is by no means equal to your own. By asking me to be your wife, you waive many things and seek a far humbler match than your exalted station might demand. I—"

He had already taken her reply for granted. So had I. I turned away, sick, weary, inexplicably wretched. He sprang forward, seized her hand and, dropping on one knee, kissed it. Oh, why had she detained me here to witness this? To see my own doom and lifelong misery sealed? She continued:

"But, while I am aware of the compliment, I cannot accept it. I must—I am sorry—I—"

Her punctilious manner failed, and she paused. I halted at the threshold and wheeled about; a wild, utterly unreasonable joy setting my blood to run riot. Vlasto rose dazed.

"You cannot mean?—" he began.

"I am sorry," she said again, and there was infinite gentleness and regret in the three simple words.

He stared at her unbelieving.

"It is not a morganatic marriage I offer," he said at last. "Perhaps you do not quite comprehend. I—"

"I quite understand," she interrupted, less regretfully. "My answer is, no."

Stunned, wholly shaken from his grand serenity, Vlasto stared dully at her. Then he looked at me and back at her again, turned on his heel and walked heavily into the hotel. This time I made way for him unasked. I think I have never been sorrier for any one—not even for myself. A big man—big in every way—has so far to fall! And Konstantin Vlasto was the biggest man I ever knew.

I stood a moment, looking—dully as the prince himself—at Elinor Clyde. For I had all at once realized that Vlasto's rejection made no difference whatsoever in my own relations toward her. She had sent him about his business, it is true. But the fact remained hideously unchanged that she had shown her true state of feelings toward me by refusing to remain to meet me, that morning five days ago, when she knew I was coming—and *why* I was coming—to see her.

Had she been merely heartless in breaking the appointment and leaving me to go away with all my wealth of love unspoken? Or, had she chosen that drastic method of sparing my feelings and showing me that I must not speak? I could not decide. Yet in either case the result was the same. The tale of my love must not be told. And in my bitterness I assured myself I was glad it was so. For now, with no troublesome qualms, I could play my chosen part and force Fate's dice to score a victory for me at last.

Her voice cut in on my morbid thoughts, dispelling them as her lightest word has somehow ever had a strange way of doing.

"Are you satisfied?" she asked, a little break in the unwontedly angry tones.

"Satisfied?" I echoed stupidly. "I don't quite follow you."

"Are you satisfied that you have made me ridiculous—that you have made me ridiculous and forced me to publicly humiliate and chagrin a man who honestly loved me? It must be a rare triumph for you!"

I stared at her, as awkward and abashed as any bumpkin. I could not understand the outburst in the very least. You see, in my wanderings, while I had attained a very fair knowledge of my fellow man I had had absurdly few dealings with women. When Jimmy Clyde had blazed out at me in the card-room I had been perfect master of the situation. Yet when this mere child, his sister, adopted similar tactics I was utterly at a loss and knew not what to say nor how to say it.

I think the best woman has somewhere in her make-up a tiny tinge of mercilessness. For my silence and confusion seemed only to augment Elinor's wrath.

"It must indeed be amusing to you," she went on cruelly, "to witness such a scene. No doubt it will make an excellent smoking-room story."

"Stop!" I cried, indignation coming to my help, "you have no right to say that, and you know it isn't true. What I was unlucky enough to see and hear just now will go no further, as you very well know. I didn't want to wait or—"

"Then why did you?" she snapped.

"Why did I what?"

"Why did you wait? It would have been much better of you to go away when he began to—"

"I was going away," I declared, "but—"

"But why didn't you, then?"

"Because you stopped me. You put your hand—"

"I stopped you?" she repeated, with the same dazed incredulity she might have employed had I accused her of kissing me, "*I?* Surely you are—"

"I'm not mistaken," I asserted doggedly. "You don't suppose it was any pleasure to me, do you, to stand here feeling like a fool while another man proposed to you, or to—?"

"Then, why did you do it?" she insisted.

"I've told you. Because you held me."

"Really!" she exclaimed in sublime sarcasm, "I held you by force from escaping! Truly, I am strong. You must be fully six feet tall, while I—"

"While I'm not strong enough to break away from the touch of your hand," I blurted out.

The very sincerity of my words must have overcome their banality. Her bright eyes softened ever so little, even while she reproved me:

"That is doubtless meant for a pretty speech," she scoffed. "It will hardly serve this time. You were—"

"Listen," I interposed, emboldened by her look into something like composure. "Do you mean to say you didn't put your hand on my arm and stop me as I was going away? Didn't you?"

"Of course I didn't," she flashed.

"Are you sure?"

"Why, how could you think such a—"

"Honor bright, now?"

"Well, perhaps, just without thinking I might possibly—I—oh, how *dare* you catechize me like this? Is it fair? Is it manly to—?"

"But," I protested, once more reduced to abject weakness by the sudden filling of her eyes, "I didn't mean to hurt you! I'm so sorry—"

The impending tears gave place to a laugh as musical as an April brook's, and once more I was at utter loss.

"Oh, you great overgrown child!" she stormed mockingly. "You have a saber cut on your face and you have been through dear knows how many adventures. Yet you don't know the first thing about women."

"I'm afraid I don't," I admitted mournfully. "You see, I haven't had much to do with them. But even if I had had," I went on, with gathering courage, "I'm blessed if I believe I could understand all that's happened since Prince Vlasto left the terrace here, ten minutes ago."

"After that battle in Macedonia," she said with apparent irrelevance, "were your nerves at all shaken by what you'd been through?"

"I suppose so. Most men's are at such times. Why?"

"What did you do?"

"To the best of my recollection I'm afraid I swore."

"Exactly," she cried in triumph. "Well, a woman can't do that. So she does—as—as I just did."

"Takes it out on the unlucky man who happens to be nearest and—?"

"And tries to make some one else just as miserable as she is," concluded Elinor. "If the 'some one' understands women, he knows it is only her shaky nerves that are being unkind and unjust to him and not her real self. So he doesn't argue with her or deny anything, but just lets the storm blow over. For he knows how sorry she'll be and how nicely she'll try to treat him afterward to make up for—"

"I am supposed to be thirty-five," I murmured in meek awe, "and you are probably somewhere under twenty. But I confess you are, at the very least, ten thousand years older and wiser than I can ever hope to be. I traveled two hundred miles once to learn an Italian fencing trick. What you've just taught me is worth a trip around the world. Now that I've mastered the first lesson, will you let me pass on to the second by asking why you made me stay and listen to Vlasto's proposal when—?"

"Good morning, Graeme!" hailed Jimmy from the doorway. "So we're starting Friday, are we? Say, Nell, who do you s'pose I met in the foyer, just now? Vlasto. He left his good-byes for you and for the others. He's—"

"His good-byes? Is—"

"Says he's just got news that takes him back home in a rush. His servants are hustling like a bunch of longshoremen to get his luggage under way. But he isn't waiting for 'em. Just ordered his horse and galloped off. Too bad, isn't it? He was a good chap—or would have been if somebody hadn't frozen him up, about ten centuries ago. If he could melt out once he'd be all right."

I glanced covertly at Elinor to see how she took the news. But her face was averted. Jimmy prattled on:

"I knew you'd all be sorry to lose him. So I tried to persuade him to stay by asking him to join our picnic to Hymettus. But it was no go. He seemed interested about it and asked a lot of questions, but he wouldn't wait. I asked him if he wasn't coming to say good-by to you in person, Nell. But he said, 'There is no need, because I am going to see her again very soon indeed.' What d'you s'pose he meant by that? Is he coming back in a day or two, or—?"

"No," I volunteered, "I don't think Prince Vlasto will come back soon to Athens. I think you must have misunderstood him when you thought he said he was going to meet Miss Clyde again very soon. Your understanding of French, Jimmy, is even worse than your ability to speak it, if such a thing is possible. So you probably—"

"Maybe I did," he assented in perfect good humor. "Ever since the time I asked a waiter in Paris for a cab and he brought me a live pig I've had my own doubts about it."

We all three entered the hotel, and strolled forward to the office to see if the foreign mail had arrived. On the way, we encountered Nikola, Vlasto's fat majordomo, staggering down the main stairway under the weight of two heavy traveling bags. Nikola was a silent, surly fellow, devoted to his master and aping the latter by ignoring the existence of every one else. Even to old Mr. Clyde he had never deigned a salute in passing.

Hence, both Jimmy and Elinor were amazed when, catching sight of us now, the majordomo dropped both his valises, removed his red cap in reverent courtesy and surreptitiously made the sign of the cross on his breast. Then he gathered up his burden and hurried on.

"What a strange sort of bow!" commented Elinor as he went. "I never saw anything just like it. Did you, Mr. Graeme?"

"No," I replied curtly.

Therein I lied. For Nikola's salute was the sort used by Greek peasants when unexpectedly meeting a funeral procession or on entering the presence of those about to die.

For which of us three had it been intended?

CHAPTER VII.
A Camp Surprise.

FRIDAY night. At a little after sunrise we had left Athens. With our dragoman, a half-dozen servants, and four tents, the Clydes and myself had formed quite an imposing little cavalcade as we cantered out of the city on our sure-footed little ponies.

Mrs. Clyde was a timorous horsewoman, and had, as the morning progressed, dropped to the rear. Elinor rode beside her. Jimmy, too full of animal life and youth to keep the sober pace, had spent most of the day taking short gallops ahead or exploring by-roads. The arrangement had thrown Mr. Clyde and myself much together, and I had been duly bored by his prosy, pompous platitudes. My one consolation was that by the same time two days hence he and I would be in a position where I could do all the talking and he be the listener. I could safely guarantee my remarks would be of interest.

So the day wore on. A long stop for lunch, on the first rise of Hymettus's foot-hills; then an easy afternoon's ride, and at sunset we found ourselves toiling up to the little plateau, where we were to spend the night.

The servants, taking less time for luncheon than we, had gone on ahead, and on our arrival we found the camp already pitched and everything in readiness. From the central tent flew an American flag. From one of the others the blue and white standard of Greece.

Above and beyond the camp rose a crag whose summit was crowned by a blasted tree. This drew my eye at once. From that tree the signal to Gorgias was to float at dawn to-morrow.

The novelty and charm of the scene delighted the Clydes. The bracing air of autumn was growing chill, and the newly lighted camp-fire in the center of the little ring of tents was grateful. We dined with tremendous appetites and afterward sat about the roaring fire for a time. Mr. Clyde raked out of the past for our benefit a choice assortment of dreary lies which he served up as Civil War camp-fire reminiscences.

But the long ride, the cold mountain air, and the flicker of the flames proved an even more powerful sedative than did the old financier's yarns. Little by little the conversation slackened. At last, with a prodigious yawn, Jimmy stumbled to his feet.

"I don't know about you people," said he, "but *I'm* trained down to the minute for a spirited bout of pillow pounding. Me for the hay. Coming, Graeme?"

"Not quite yet," I answered as the others rose to retire. "I'm not sleepy. A camp-bed calls for a good case of drowsiness before it can be termed exactly comfortable. I'll sit here and smoke another cigar before I turn in. Good night."

Mrs. Clyde and Elinor moved off toward their sleeping tent and the two men toward theirs. Demetrius and the servants, too, in the kitchen tent beyond, were making ready for bed. Soon I should have the waking world to myself, so far as our party was concerned. This was what I wanted. I had work to do.

My cigar burned down and I lighted a second; then, throwing another stick or two on the waning blaze, resumed my seat on a pack-saddle and waited. Late as it was growing, I resolved to remain where I was for another hour, until every one should be too sound asleep to permit any note of my departure.

Then for a clamber up the crag, barely a furlong distant, to tie about the single low branch of the blasted tree my red silk handker-chief. Padapoulos's scout would, I knew, see it by the very first glimmer of dawn.

I need not be absent from camp more than a half hour, and could, on returning, roll myself in my blankets and sleep in the sweet knowledge that my plan was at last under way. We kept no guard in that safe spot. No one was likely to see me go or come; or seeing, to suspect anything.

It grew very quiet, there on the slopes of the world-old mountain. Except for the occasional stamp or snort of a restless horse, tied in a line under the trees behind the tents, nothing broke the silence of the autumn night. Above shone the great white stars in a black sky, and far out on every side stretched the sleeping wilderness. I had the world and darkness to myself.

I shivered a little, in the growing chill, and wrapped my great coat closer about me. Then I fell to wondering how Elinor and her mother would take the worthy Barzillah's disappearance. I was sorry for them; sorrier than I dared let myself think.

There is no pleasure in causing women unhappiness. I resolved that they should hear as quickly as possible from Padapoulos, and that old Clyde himself should be coerced into writing them that he was comfortable and well cared for in the brigand's keeping.

The whole affair—terms, negotiations, payment and all—ought not to occupy more than a few weeks at most. Then—America, wealth, freedom!

Once more I wondered why a vision of Elinor Clyde's big, dark eyes came between me and the elation the words ought to have aroused in my brain.

To banish the thought I began to speculate on the furor the news of Clyde's kidnaping would cause in New York.

Some one moved softly behind me.

I sprang to my feet and whirled about, hand on my revolver.

Then with a laugh I snatched off my cap and stepped forward toward the slender white figure that glided into the radius of firelight.

It was Elinor Clyde; and she wore a flimsy silk negligee of some sort that made her look smaller and fairer and younger than ever.

Her heavy masses of hair were caught up carelessly and piled atop of her dainty little head. Her great dark eyes were wide, and her flower-face flushed from recent sleep. With a finger on her lips she checked my exclamation of surprise at her advent.

"I don't want to disturb the others," Elinor began in a guardedly low voice; "I woke up, and—the stars and the silence and the wilderness seemed to call me. I came out here to sit by the fire a few minutes. I—I didn't know you were still here. It's very late, isn't it?"

"Not too late to catch a bad cold by wandering around out of doors in that fluffy tea-gown, or whatever it is," I answered, slipping off my greatcoat and wrapping it about her as I would have about a child. Yet the uninvited thrill that caught me as my arms were momentarily around her was a very different emotion, and I mentally cursed myself for my folly.

"You mustn't give me your coat," she protested quickly; "you'll take cold. And, besides—"

"And, besides," I added, "you must obey if I let you stay out here. So keep the coat close around you and sit down on that saddle. It's fairly comfortable. Now, sit still, and be good while I put more wood on the fire. I suppose you know it's very bad form for you to be sitting out here this time of night. If—"

"But I didn't know you were here," she protested; "I told you that. And I don't like to be treated as if I were a baby. I'm nineteen years old—nearly twenty—I'd have you know, and—"

"You didn't know I was here? That's odd! I was sitting where you are now—quite visible from your tent."

"I—I saw *some one* was here, of course; but—"

"But you thought it was one of the muleteers?"

"Yes. And so I—"

"And so you came out for a pleasant chat with him? In what language was that momentous conversation to have been? They can't speak French or English, and you don't understand Greek. It would have been a delightful little talk. I'm sorry to have spoiled it."

"You're horrid!" she assured me. "If you think you're going to pin me down to a statement that I saw you sitting here looking so lonely and melancholy that I made up my mind to come out and sit with you a while, you're very, *very* much mistaken."

"Of course I am," I agreed solemnly, as, having replenished the fire, I threw myself on the grass beside her seat. "Any one could see that. But now that you *are* here, won't you let me tell you how glad I am it happens to be myself and not a muleteer?"

I had tried to keep up my light tone to cover the embarrassment I felt. For, since that day on the terrace when she rejected Konstantin Vlasto, I had purposely avoided all tête-à-têtes with Elinor Clyde. Such things could lead to nothing save an augmenting of the heartache that by now had become a part of my being. Yet, since we were alone together through no act of mine, I felt a certain miserable joy in her presence.

Elinor had returned no answer to my flippant query, but sat, elbows on knees, her pretty hands clasped under her chin, staring into the flickering embers. I lay at her feet, studying the picture presented by her dainty, fire-lit face and figure against the dark mountain background. At last she spoke.

"It is so still—so solemn!" she murmured in a hushed voice. "I feel as though I were in a cathedral."

"You are," I answered, falling in with her whim, "in the vastest and oldest. I've watched late by many camp-fires in the wilderness. I know the feeling it gives you, and I have never quite gotten over the same sensation."

"It must be easy to be very good when one is often so close to Nature's night secrets," she mused.

"I have not found it so," I answered curtly. Her simple words awoke memories of what I had been so recently planning beside that very fire.

Perhaps my tone jarred upon her, for she lifted her head and looked at me.

"There is much written in your face," she said reflectively, "if I can read it aright—sorrow, pain, weariness, disappointment. But nothing worse. Why do you speak as though there were?"

"Could it interest you to know of such things?" I asked, with less indifference than I had intended. "They don't come into *your* life."

"If I were not interested," she replied, "I should not have asked. I like to read faces. They tell me so much. Yours, for instance, speaks of trial, of broken hopes, of more than I can wholly understand. The story behind it must be very—"

"Very crude and commonplace and sordid," I supplemented, with bitter gaiety. "Nothing more. I'm sorry to have no romantic tale to regale you with. But—"

She winced as though I had sworn at her, and a revulsion caught me. The hour, the solitude, and the hypnotism of firelight had wrought upon her, turning her speech from conventional channels. Perhaps somewhat the same mood now seized me. For, even as I noted how my sneering interruption had pained her, a crazy impulse came to me, and I said:

"I did not mean to be rude. If you are interested in the story, you shall have it in a nutshell. Lieutenant Kampf, of the German legation, stated it quite clearly and briefly to your brother last month when he referred to me as a 'swindler,' a 'down-at-heel adventurer whose own country was too hot to hold him,' and 'a man who lives by his wits.' There you have the character of Bruce Graeme, Failure. And having it, can't you fill in the minor details of the story to suit yourself?"

I paused. The girl was leaning forward, looking down into my eyes. Her own were alight with a look I had never before seen in them.

"Why do you say such things?" she panted. "How *dare* you? You know there is not a word of truth in them."

"There is so much truth that—"

"What did Jimmie say when Lieutenant Kampf told him that?"

"I believe he politely told Kampf he lied."

"That's my answer, too—with the politeness left out."

"Thank you," I answered simply. I could say no more at the

moment. The glorious, blind loyalty of her divine, unreasoning sex is a wonderful thing. This was my first taste of it.

"I wish you would tell me more about yourself," she said, after a time. "Won't you?"

"Yes, if you like," I retorted, forcing myself to be honest and speaking with intentional brutality. "When I was twenty my father was ruined in fortune and name, and he died. I inherited his stained name and nothing else. I was too much of a coward to stay at home and win new reputation for myself, so I sneaked across to Europe. Instead of seeking some decent employment as a naturally honest man would, I became a sort of upper-class tramp and vagabond.

"When fighting was to be done that would win me a few dollars by fair means or foul, I did it. At other times I lived by gambling, smuggling, and any other dishonest shift that presented itself. That brings me up to the present hour, I believe.

"Except," I added, "for one thing: until I met your family I had not in fifteen years talked with a woman of my own original class, or associated with any people who were not either possible accomplices or victims in some crooked scheme."

She did not answer me at once. Then she said:

"Why did you tell me all this?"

"Why?" I echoed, taken aback. "Because you asked me."

"I asked for the truth. You have not told me the truth. A man such as you have just described is not a gentleman. You are a gentleman. So you have not told me your true story, after all. Why?"

"It is a more favorable version than half my acquaintances would have told of me," I answered, in doubt, yet vaguely stirred again by that splendid, illogical faith of hers. "In any case, it can't matter greatly to you. You say you have the gift of reading faces. Strike an average, if you like, between my face's story as you see it and my own story as I told it. That surely should be enough for a casual acquaintance's curiosity."

Again—if the firelight's flicker did not trick me—she seemed to flinch. But when she spoke her voice was formal.

"Yes," she agreed, "I forgot for the moment that we are 'casual acquaintances.' It was good of you to remind me. I was impertinent to pry into your personal affairs. Pardon me."

A dozen answers sprang to my lips, but I choked them hack and said nothing. And again for a space we were silent—she gazing into the fire, I staring at her.

"You have strange eyes," I commented at last, apropos of nothing. "They are as big and innocent as a child's, yet they seem full of all the wisdom of the ages."

"That is very pretty," she vouchsafed. "My eyes are said to be like my father's."

"Your father's!" I cried, wondering how any besotted idiot could compare those eyes of hers with Barzillah Clyde's shrewd little washed-out orbs. "Why, Mr. Clyde has—"

"I mean my own father's," she corrected.

"But Mr. Clyde is—"

"My father? Why, no. My father died when I was a baby. When mama married Mr. Clyde, Jimmie and I took his name. I thought you knew. He has been just like a father to us always, and—"

I heard no more. Darwin's principles of heredity were triumphantly vindicated. I might have known it all along.

"I'm glad," I said involuntarily, continuing my thoughts aloud.

"Of what?" she asked, puzzled.

I caught myself up in time and answered with cheerful mendacity: "Glad I didn't have to sit out here all alone."

"Why were you sitting out at all? You spoke of waiting to get sleepy enough to overcome a camp-bed's discomforts. But to a soldier, used to sleeping on hard ground, surely—"

"One grows effeminate after a term of town life," I evaded, "and, besides, I hated to lose the beauty of this night."

"It *is* beautiful," she sighed, looking past the fire, over the miles of dark mountain-peaks. "Thank you for telling me about yourself," she continued, harking back to the old theme, with no apparent relevance.

I was unreasonably nettled.

"I am always willing to serve as subject for anybody's idle hour," I scoffed, "but you'll forgive me if I say I can't see just what amusement you get from taking advantage of my maudlin campfire mood and making me tell you things better left unsaid."

"Don't talk so!" she begged. "Is it kind to—"

"You don't understand, I'm afraid," I went on roughly. "What I am puzzled over is, why you were so eager to hear what I didn't want to tell just now, and why you refused to hear what I wanted above all the world to tell last week."

"You're right," she said in genuine perplexity, "I *don't* understand. We seem to be talking at cross purposes. Won't you explain?"

"Gladly, if you really wish it," I assented stiffly; "but you can hardly have forgotten in one short week what it was I begged leave to say to you."

She did not answer at once, and her eyes, that had been looking down into mine with such troubled wonder, suddenly hid themselves under their long, soft lashes.

"You begged leave to speak," she breathed at last. "Yes, I remember. Is a woman likely to forget?"

I supposed this new phase of voice and word must be coquetry, whereof I had often read and heard. Just why I should be its victim I did not know, and I dully resented it.

"She is not likely to forget that, I suppose," I retorted, "any more than she forgets any egregious idiot's compliments. But—don't you think she might have found a gentler, more tactful way of silencing that same idiot?"

"What do you mean?" she asked, raising her eyes again to mine in what looked like honest wonder.

"Must I humiliate myself once more by explaining in full? I mean that it would have been kinder to me had you let me call that morning at ten, as I had asked, and to have heard me out—even if, after hearing, you had—"

She broke in hurriedly.

"That morning? Then, why didn't you call as you said you would?"

"Why didn't I call?" I repeated stupidly.

"Yes," she hurried on shyly, her face turned away. "You said you would be there at ten. I waited for you till noon; and then—then Jimmie told me he'd seen you riding out of town an hour earlier."

"Do you mean to say," I asked, "that you were at home at ten o'clock and waited for me—for me—"

"Certainly," she replied at once.

"I think," I said, and my moment's anger had turned to sorrow, as though it were some beloved little child I had caught in a lie, "I think you had better go back to your tent. The night air grows damp. May I take you as far as the door? No," as she rose, "don't take my coat off yet. Wait till you're at the tent."

She obeyed meekly, with not a word, and walked along at my side out of the firelight, looking smaller and more fragile than ever beneath the folds of my huge coat.

At the door I bade her a formal good night and returned to the fire. All at once the work I had to do seemed delightfully easy. My last scruple was gone. What claim on me had this girl with the face of a child and the heart of an arrant flirt? Why should I shrink at harming her stepfather?

I reviewed, with self-torturing rage, the scene I had just been through. How utterly she had bamboozled me! First, by seeming sympathy, to draw out my wretched history for her idle curiosity's gratification; then to lure me into hinting again of my love, and, by way of playing me on, to deny she had not been at home on that cursed morning! I had allowed myself to be danced about like a puppet to fit her whim!

The cold caused a twinge in my old shoulder-wound.

"That scar was never made by a bullet," I growled to myself in contempt; "it was caused by a ping-pong ball at worst. I belong somewhere in the kindergarten. I ought to thank my luck that I didn't blab to her about this plan to kidnap old Barzillah. That would probably have come next. And now, for the tree on the crag!"

I pulled out from my pocket the red silk handkerchief I was to tie about the limb, and rising, turned from the fire.

"Mr. Graeme!"

At sound of the whisper I halted in dismay, as though actually caught in my plot. Elinor Clyde was coming toward me once more from her tent. I crammed the red handkerchief back into my pocket and, in no good humor, walked to meet her.

But she did not speak until, regaining her old place by the fire, she seated herself again on the saddle.

"Mr. Graeme," she said, as I stood, puzzled, before her, "you thought I was not telling you the truth a few minutes ago. I could see that you did. It hurt me; so I couldn't speak at the time. But—but I can't sleep, and—oh, won't you please clear up the whole horrid mystery? I hate misunderstandings."

What new trick, what fresh sorcery, was I to fall foul of now? Before answering I put my coat once more around her as she sat. Then the appeal in her eyes got hold of my brain once more, and I not only knew I was a fool, but morbidly rejoiced in my folly. Yet I attempted one feeble stand for self-mastery.

"Yes," said I, "I thought you were telling me an untruth. To be accurate, I *knew* it. What then?"

"I ought to be angry at you," she murmured, more to herself than aloud. "I wonder why I am not. I wonder why I came back. I never thought I—" Checking herself, she asked more coldly:

"Will you please explain just what you mean?"

"With pleasure. I called at your suite that morning and was informed by Mrs. Clyde—who was in the drawing-room—that you were not at home. Of course, you may be able to persuade me that you were there or that your mother—"

"Is it quite necessary to be brutal?" she asked.

"I'm sorry. But the truth is seldom anything else."

"We are still some distance away from the truth, I'm afraid," she replied sadly, "and we don't seem to be getting much closer to it."

"Perhaps the best way of getting there," I suggested, "might be to tell it."

"I am not in the habit of telling anything else," she replied, "although you have charged me with falsehood several times in the last few minutes. Here is the truth—believe it or not, as you choose. I tell it for my own self-respect, not to force your credence. From ten o'clock until noon that day I was at home and waiting for you to call. You did not come, and ever since then you have seemed to avoid me. I know no reason for it, and I could not ask. I have told you the truth. Do you believe me?"

Our eyes met—hers calm, fearless, honest—mine, first politely incredulous, then wavering, then—

"Yes," I said—and I meant it—"I believe you. I don't know why, but I do."

"Is that satire, too?" she asked wearily.

"Is it?" I countered.

She looked again at me searchingly.

"No," she said, "you are in earnest. Thank you."

"We are still as far as ever from understanding it," I remarked, inwardly contemptuous of my own easy credulity.

"There is nothing hard about it to understand," she returned, as though arguing away the fears of a baby; "you asked me, the afternoon before, if I would be at home at ten the next morning, as you had—something—to tell me. I had an engagement to ride to Eleusis with Prince Vlasto at nine the next morning. I knew we could not get back in much less than two hours. So that evening at the opera I asked him to ride an hour earlier. We started at eight, and the clock was striking ten just as I reached our suite. I—"

Now I understood—as any one but a thick-headed dolt would have understood from the very first. It was so disgustingly simple that a child would have known better.

"I called at twenty minutes of ten," I blurted out, feeling only a degree less foolish than deliriously happy. "Mrs. Clyde told me you had gone riding, and I supposed—well, the upshot of it was that I stamped out of your suite at five minutes of ten, too chagrined, too blind with disappointment—"

"You poor boy!"

"But," I said suddenly, "surely your mother mentioned—"

"No, she and papa were just starting for a drive when I came in. The carriage was waiting, and they were in a hurry."

"And you sat there two mortal hours, wondering why I didn't come? What a graceless cub you must have thought me!"

"Not as bad as all that," she said, with a hysterical little laugh; "only—I didn't quite understand."

"You knew what I wanted to say that morning!" And my own voice was little less shaky than hers.

No answer.

"Didn't you?" I insisted.

"I—I don't know. I thought—that perhaps—"

"*Didn't* you know?" And now my voice was all mastery.

Again no answer.

"Didn't you?" More compellingly.

The faintest possible nod.

"You thought, then, I was a rich man, knocking around the world for amusement," I pursued, some of her own honesty stirring me to a sense of decency. "Whatever your answer would have been at that time, you know me now for a penniless, disreputable adventurer, with no future, no profession, no means of taking care of any woman.

"No, you mustn't interrupt me. There is something I have to say, whether I want to or not. Then, I was carried away by selfish love. Now I am saner—perhaps because I love you ten thousand times more, and because that mighty love is bringing out what little there is of honor and manliness in my worthless nature. So I won't ask now for a reply. I don't even ask you to bind yourself to *think* of me.

"But I go out into the world to-morrow with a real object in life for the first time in all my misspent years. I shall earn an honest livelihood and win an honorable name for myself among men. And when I have done that, I am coming back to find you and to win you—to win you against the whole world, if need be!"

I had spoken hurriedly, almost incoherently, not daring to look down at her, where she sat at my feet, lest my high purpose weaken.

Oh, I was in a mood for great deeds. The wresting of fame and fortune by honest means from a universe that is grudging of both, seemed to me the simplest of tasks. With her heart for my possible goal, there was nothing I could not—*would* not—accomplish. No knight of old went into battle for his lady-love with a stouter—and, for the instant, purer—heart than would I for mine.

And until the hour of my victory should arrive, I was resolved to flee temptation by not so much as touching her little hand. It would be hard, after such contact, to leave her—to deny myself the bare possibility of hearing her say she cared. Then—

Then my eyes were drawn downward to her. She was looking at me, and the embers' glow showed me a face such as the martyred saint might hope to see when first he opened his eyes in paradise.

And I was on my knees—foolish scruples, lofty ambitions, quixotic resolves, all blown to the four winds—and my arms were about her, pressing her slender little body to my heart, covering her flower-face with kisses, whispering words of mad endearment.

I wonder if you will laugh—the men who had lived and fought with me would have roared at the preposterous idea—when I tell you that it was the first time in all my wretched life that I had felt about my neck the warm, soft arms of a girl, the first time a woman's kiss had responded to mine! It was worth while to have retained ever that one scruple, just to know the heaven I knew then.

After a little time we spoke no more, but remained silently, movelessly happy—there in the solemn night of autumn—the big white stars smiling benignly down upon us, the sleeping night witness to our new-pledged love.

At last sanity came back to me—a little of it—and I withdrew my arms from about her, but still knelt at her feet.

"I have done the craziest, worst thing I *could* have done!" I cried in a voice that tried very hard to sound self-reproachful. "First, I have told you of my love, and then I have let you tell me of yours—and I had no earthly right to do either. Oh, you ought to despise me, Elinor!"

For a moment she did not answer. Then she sighed as if in a dream:

"Oh, it is all so wonderful—so *wonderful!*"

"Is that all the rebuke you have for a man who has stolen a heart he had no right to?" I exclaimed in mock wrath, quite involuntarily kissing her as I spoke. "What will the worthy and wealthy Mr. Clyde answer when I go to him and say: 'Sir, I am a beggarly ne'er-do-well, with no prospects. I respectfully ask your daughter's hand'?"

"Why should we care what he says?" she answered pluckily. "We have each other."

"This is the most glorious insanity ever spoken or heard!" I vowed; "but what I said to you when I was still sane, a few minutes ago, is true, none the less. I am going out again into the world to win you fairly and honorably, and to earn the right to the love I've stolen."

"When do we start?" she whispered.

"'We'? But I—"

"You have had fifteen bitter years of loneliness and toil and disappointment. Shall I, who love you, send you out alone to a still harder fight? No, no, dear heart! We'll share the future together, let it bring what it may. Your victories shall be my victories, your defeats my defeats."

"But this is madness! And your family—"

"I'm over eighteen, Mr. Bruce Graeme; and, moreover, I am not used to being contradicted or refused anything. Jimmie himself will tell you I'm spoiled and set on having my own way. Well, just now and henceforth my way is your way—wherever it leads. Of course, if you don't *want* me—"

Here I interrupted in a fashion which, I am told, is not at all unusual. And blessed Saint Idiocy took us again temporarily into his keeping.

"I shall win wealth for you, just the same," I said at length. "I feel that I shall."

And I meant it. Hope, such as I had never before known, surged triumphant through me. I knew that henceforth failure and I had no more in common. The gross underworld life had fallen from me as a foul, disused garment. Henceforward I was to be a man.

The cold and darkness of the late night crept in upon us as we sat, divinely happy, in each other's arms, before the dying fire; but we did not feel its chill. Her loosely piled hair had slipped its fastenings and fallen in a shower of tawny gold about her shoulders, enveloping her in an aura of shimmering light.

The first faint gray tinge of dawn lay in the east, beyond the hills and sea. I noted it and rose, lifting her tenderly to her feet. As I did so something slipped from my pocket and fell to the ground.

"It is a red silk handkerchief," she said, straining her eyes to see it, in the dim light, as we turned toward the tents. "Aren't you going to stop and pick it up?"

"No," I answered, delirious in my awful happiness and tempting my old enemy, Fate, by my idle words. "I have no need for it now—nor *ever!*"

CHAPTER VIII.
Fate's Next Throw.

SHE was gone, and I stood alone under the stars, trying to glean some coherent idea of what had befallen me and to analyze the gorgeous, buoyant delight that had transformed me into a boy again. Oh, it was glorious, this being in love! I wonder if any one else ever felt it just as I did?

The sky was paling. That first gray streak had flushed into a roseate mist. In fact, all the world was roseate just then.

It was high time for a man who expected to ride all the next day to go to bed. But the idea of turning into a stuffy tent with Barzillah Clyde and Jimmie for snoring neighbors seemed almost a sacrilege in my present state of mind. I wandered away among the rocks, on past the crag with its blasted tree whereupon my signal should by this time have been fluttering had not life changed so divinely for me during the past few hours. Looking back on my plans of the day before, a tinge of almost physical nausea smote me.

To think that I—the man Elinor Clyde loved—could have sank to forming an alliance with a murderous old Greek kidnaper and had looked forward to fattening on a fellow American's ransom! Faugh! It had been some other, some viler being who for years had usurped my mind and body, and who now, by a woman's kiss, had been exorcised.

"Some day," I thought happily—"some day I'll tell her all about it, and what she saved me from."

I moved onward up the hill with no thought of time or distance. Thus I came to a little summit, perhaps a mile above the camp. There, on a couch of dry moss, I threw myself down to watch the coming of dawn. From my elevation I could see, in a gap through the lower peaks toward the east, a misty, shifting ribbon of gray—the sea, some ten miles distant. I knew the general direction, and remembered that the Clyde's huge white steam-yacht lay at anchor somewhere in the lower harbor not far from that opening.

Many a short cruise had I enjoyed on the trim craft in the first fortnight or so of my acquaintance with her master, and I wondered if, in future, I would be as welcome a guest there. A struggle of some sort I confidently looked forward to when I should present myself to the estimable Barzillah as suitor for Elinor's hand. Well, I would not delay the crisis. That very morning, as soon as—

I started up in surprise. The sunlight was pouring down upon me. I glanced at my watch. Eleven o'clock!

Eleven o'clock; and we were to have been in our saddles at nine! What must they be thinking of me, down below there?

As I rose I could look straight down on the distant camp. Yes, there it was, the tents still standing, the horses in their impromptu open-air stable at the rear. And this struck me as odd, for even if the

Clydes were waiting for me, why had not the camp been struck and the tents and luggage sent on ahead to the summit as we had planned?

I broke into a run down the rough slope, for it suddenly occurred to me how odd my stupid absence must have seemed to them all, and how nervous Elinor would be.

I gained the lower ground, providentially avoiding a breakneck fall over the boulders that strewed the hillside. Then, without slackening speed, I swung off toward the now hidden camp.

Rounding the last curve of rocks I came upon it. The place was strangely still. I walked into the circle, past the dead camp-fire, my soldierly eye noting that though breakfast had been prepared it was still uneaten.

My heart beat more quickly than was its wont as I entered the central tent. The table was laid for breakfast. A jar of autumn cyclamen and narcissus stood in its center, and on a chair close by one of Elinor's dainty gauntlets and her riding-whip.

The men's sleeping-tent, too, was empty. No sign there of the outing-clothes worn by either father or son, nor, what was more peculiar, any of their portmanteaus.

"If they'd just gone for a walk, or to look for me," I muttered aloud, "the luggage would still be here. They haven't sent it on, for all fourteen of the horses are tied at the line. I counted them. If it's a practical joke—"

I went on to the tent Elinor and her mother had occupied. Its flaps hung untied. I called. There was no answer, and I pushed aside the canvas and stepped inside. The two camp-beds were stripped of their coverings, ready for removal. Here again no luggage, no clothes.

Running across to the kitchen tent and hastening into it, I nearly fell over a heterogeneous mass of cooking-utensils, bundles, and boxes. Here was plenty of luggage, but it was that of the camp in general and of the muleteers. Not one article belonging to the Clydes or myself. And now it struck me for the first time that my two suit-cases, like the rest of our personal impedimenta, had been gone from our sleeping-tent.

So all our effects were missing, together with their owners; the servants' baggage was here, and the servants themselves gone! What on earth did the riddle mean?

Corning back to the center of the camp, I lifted my voice in a long halloo. The shout reechoed from hill to hill, and as it died a slight scuffling sound from somewhere near by came to my straining ears. I listened, but it was not repeated. I called again. Again the voice-distorting echoes, followed by a repetition of that rustling noise. One of the tied horses whinnied.

There was something uncanny about all this. I have no nerves to speak of, yet this midday mystery was almost too much for them.

A third shout, and with bent head I harkened to observe the direction of the faint sound that had followed my two other cries. Sure enough, it came, and I located it. It had emanated from somewhere behind the kitchen tent. I drew my revolver and advanced cautiously around the guy-ropes beyond the tent-wall, alert for a surprise, expecting I knew not what.

At the rear I paused. No sign of life was visible among the stunted undergrowth that stretched away for a hundred yards or so beyond. I took one step forward.

A frantic thrashing and rustling came from the low bushes at my very feet, and something writhed violently down beneath their cover. Still holding my pistol in one hand, with the other I parted the bushy fringe of twigs.

There, flat on his back on the ground, tied hand and foot, and gagged, lay Demetrius, the lordly dragoman, his blue-and-gold uniform torn and soiled, his swarthy face purple with semi-suffocation.

Even after I had cut his bonds with my pocket-knife, removed the handkerchief gag, and pulled him to his feet, the trussed-up dragoman was still too weak and frightened to speak intelligibly.

With my arm supporting him he managed to hobble to the kitchen tent. There I made him swallow half the contents of my flask, and watched in itching suspense while his faculties came back to him.

This they did in a rush. For suddenly he sat bolt upright and, clutching my arm in terror, croaked:

"Where was excellency when they came?"

"When they *went,* you mean? Where are they?"

"Those muleteers run away!" he jabbered, his eyes lighting on the tumbled baggage. "They see 'em first, and they run away before they can be stop. But I stay, and I get tied up like a goat for fear I raise alarm. Those muleteers won't tell. They too scared. But I'm person of high connections, so they don't dare leave me loose, an—"

"You chattering fool!" I yelled, shaking him till I thought his backbone would have snapped. "Where is Miss Clyde? Speak, or I'll strangle you!"

"They took her away—those men of the mountains—her and the rest. But I, sir, I was tied up like—"

I heard no more. Already I was clear of the camp and running with all the speed love and fear can lend a man, along the mountain-track that stretches upward and southwestward from the plateau.

For now I understood, and I cursed myself for the idle delay. Gorgias had broken faith with me. Learning, doubtless, through other channels of the whereabouts of the party, he not only had not waited my signal, but had violated his promise concerning the two women and Jimmie. In my absence he and his men had swooped down on the camp and had borne away the whole party.

"I might have known better than to trust his word," I reproached myself angrily, hopelessly, as I rushed on. The picture of Elinor in the hands of that grimy gang of blackguards was more than I could bear to dwell on. And—so ran the eternal undercurrent of self-reproach—I, the man who adored her, was indirectly responsible for her plight. But for my foul plan for abducting her stepfather, none of this horror would have befallen her.

That Gorgias would willingly relinquish any prey his talons had once closed on, I had no idea. That I, single-handed, could prevail against him, or by force or inducement make him release his captives, seemed an absurdity.

And yet I ran on toward his distant valley, hot rage welling higher in my heart at every stride. I had no definite plan of action. I must be with Elinor—must rescue her or die for her. That was all.

Even in my blind fury my subconscious instincts, acquired through many a campaign, were at work. I knew that there was no hope of overtaking the marauders before they should reach their little cuplike glen, for they had had too long a start.

We were to have breakfasted at eight. Breakfast had been ready, but not eaten. The absence of clothing from the sleeping-tents and the presence of Elinor's whip and riding-gauntlet on the dining-tent table told me that the attack must have come just as they were assembling for the morning meal—perhaps while they were waiting for me. It was now well after eleven. Padapoulos had had a full three-hour start of me. Slowly as he would be forced to travel, I had no chance of catching him up on the journey.

So I plunged onward over the broken, rising ground, now stumbling, now recovering my balance on some cliff-edge, now sprawling headlong among the thick-strewn rocks. Bruised, bleeding, sweating, weary, faint, I reeled onward. My lungs felt as if they would burst my chest. My eyes burned like coals, and my throat was parched. I had eaten nothing in eighteen hours, and I was weakening. Still I kept on.

I could picture Elinor's morning—the happy awakening, the hasty toilet, and the hurrying forth to meet me, only to find me gone. Then the onrush of savage, unshaven, picturesquely tattered ruffians—

"The attack must have been well planned," thought I with the idle undercurrent of mentality that underlies our wildest crises. "Not a chair overturned—not one mark of struggle."

I was passing the gorge on whose opposite bank Konstantin Vlasto's age-worn gray castle reared its rough walls. An idea came to me. Were I to stop there, tell the prince of the Clydes' abduction, and entreat his aid, there was just a chance that he might for once waive his "live and let live" policy toward his outlaw neighbors and send men to the rescue. I half-stopped as the notion dawned on me.

But at once I staggered on. I recalled my last meeting with Vlasto, the death-sign his majordomo, Nikolo, had made, and the look the prince himself had cast on me. The chances were, if I should turn aside to seek speech with him, Vlasto would have me killed out of hand before I could pant out my message. No, I would reserve Vlasto as a final resort should all else fail.

And I lurched onward, falling oftener and oftener, my head swimming, my limbs like lead.

A shout from an outpost, a leveled musket, an exclamation of recognition—and dully I knew I was at the ridge above Padapoulos's camp. Other shouts followed, and my blood-engorged eyes vaguely made out forms coming to meet me. I started down the steep slope, stumbled, and rolled headlong to the foot, where for a minute I lay, too tired and buffeted to move.

Men were crowding about me. Above the dinning of the blood in my ears I could hear ejaculations of surprise, of query, of wondering surmise. Some one lifted my head. Another put a skin bottle to my lips and, without being aware of the act of swallowing, I felt a glow and a shadow of returning life pulse through my worn-out body.

Then, as on my former visit, the crowd were shoved aside and I heard a deep, booming voice call my name. At sound of it my faintness gave way to a keen onrush of memory and purpose. The mists cleared and I was sane.

I reeled to my feet and, still swaying from weariness, confronted Gorgias Padapoulos.

"Where is she?" I demanded, my voice sounding hoarse and indistinct. "What have you done with them, you Levantine swine?"

I strove to pierce the circle with my tired eyes and catch, if might be, some glimpse of the captives.

"Where are they?" I cried again.

"He is mad—stark mad!" I heard the old chief mutter. "Take him to my hut and—"

But I broke feebly away from the outstretched hands.

"I am not crazy!" I protested. "You lying dog, you gave me your word not to lay hands on Clyde until I should—"

"Clyde?" bellowed Gorgias. "I know nothing of him!"

"You lie! He is here, or you have hidden—"

"Hush!" he commented in rough gentleness. "Your head has given way and you talk like a drunkard. Clyde is not here. I have not seen him. Even now my scouts are waiting for your tree-signal. We expected—"

But I was not listening. I had seen his face, and past it into his mind. And I knew that he was speaking the truth.

CHAPTER IX.
I Fall into Bad Hands.

FOR what seemed like an eternity I glared foolishly into the old thief's puzzled face. Then I asked, in futile hazard:

"Perhaps a detachment of your men—"

"My men are all here," he replied, "except the two who are on the lookout for your signal. Go and rest."

"My mind is not turned!" I said, with the dull quiet of dawning despair. "I almost wish it were. Barzillah Clyde and his whole family have been kidnaped this morning. They camped last night on the plateau just above the—"

Padapoulos let me get no further. With a bound he was upon me, seizing my throat in his powerful grip.

"*Kidnaped!*" he shrieked. "And they camped last night on the plateau? If you are not mad—!"

With a momentary rally of strength I cast off his grip.

"I am not mad!" I snarled as furious as he, "but if you lay hand on me again—"

His gusty rage had taken a new turn.

"I ask pardon," he exclaimed. "I see it now: you raised the signal, and my curs of lookouts were off duty somewhere. By Saint Gorgias, when I set eyes on them again they will wish they had died in the cradle! They—"

"I raised no signal," I answered, careless of consequences, anxious only to be away and once more on my search.

"Raised none? But—"

"It is as I say. Now let me go. I have much to do—"

"You've sold me!" he cried, "*sold* me, you foreign cheat! Another offered you higher pay, and you gave Clyde over into his hands and come to me with a silly lie to turn away my suspicion. And you think you can cheat Gorgias Padapoulos!"

He had caught me by the shoulder, and other angry hands were upon me. I struggled fiercely. But even had I not been spent and weak, what chance could I have had against a dozen or more? Within a minute I was overpowered, and lay panting and glowering up at the ring of dark, scowling faces above me.

Gorgias was shouting orders right and left.

"Paul! Ritojonyi! Philipo! Merzos!" he called, summoning up four of his men. "Quarter the district among you till you pick up their trail. Then report, and we'll be after them. They can't be many, and they have far to go, for there's not another company of us within fifty miles, and those who have taken our prize must be Macedonians or Bulgars. The women cannot travel fast, so we may overhaul the party in time.

"Now," to the others, as the four hunters bounded off up the slope, "carry this vermin," with a jerk of the thumb at me, "to the south end of the camp, by the spring, and put him in the sheep-pen. See that he's securely tied. We've no time now to attend to his case. After we get back we'll see how a traitor likes slow death. See that he's fed, and one of you watch him all the time."

I made no protest, partly because it would just then have been useless, partly because that last struggle of mine had sapped my scant remaining strength and left me helplessly, apathetically weak. Well did I realize what my capture might mean to Elinor. More than ever was her disappearance a mystery to me; but weariness had affected mind and body as might some powerful anesthetic. I scarcely heeded the intentional roughness of the hands that swung me up from the ground and carried my unresisting body across the camp.

Scarce had I been tossed into the empty pen when my eyes closed. A battle might have been waging about me, and I would have slept through it all. This was not heroic, I know, but it was human nature. And, in the end, it served me better, perhaps, than could any other course.

For when I awoke, at dusk, I was myself again—weak from hunger, parched with thirst, but with only a slight stiffness marking the fatigues I had undergone. My custom of keeping myself ever in hard training now stood me in fine stead.

I raised myself on one arm. I was lying close to the wide wooden bars of the pen. Just outside bubbled a spring, and on its opposite bank squatted a man in sheepskin cloak. A rusty saber-hilt stuck out at one side of the garment, and across his knees rested a long rifle. He had not heard my slight movement, but was peering through the dusk toward the camp beyond, whence, I noticed, an unusual hubbub was rising.

I sank back again and took stock of my condition. My wrists were fastened together with goatskin thongs, and similar bonds tied my feet. My watch and scarf-pin were gone. So was my revolver. Small chance of escape, thus bound and with a guard on watch outside my pen.

Before my wits could center on any plan, I heard running feet.

"Well?" grunted the guard as some one came hurrying up to him.

Through my nearly closed eyes I descried the lad Mitri, who had tended me on my former visit to Gorgias.

"Well?" repeated the guard as Mitri halted before him, "what was the matter?"

"Ritojonyi has come back," answered the boy, "with news."

"What news?" asked the guard. "Oh, *he's* dead asleep!" as the lad glanced furtively in my direction, "and if he were awake he is as good as a dead man. Speak out! It's bad enough to have to stay here as guard while there is fun going on beyond, without losing the news. What is it?"

"Ritojonyi picked up the Americans' trail at their camp," answered Mitri, thus adjured, "and it led straight to Prince Vlasto's castle. He—"

But I had started up, dumfounded; and both turned to look at me.

"If you please, sir," said Mitri politely, "the chief posted me here to give you food and drink when you should awake.

"I hope you have not been awake long," he added. "I was sent on an errand a few minutes ago."

I said nothing, but accepted the proffered dish of cold scraps of meat and bread, and bolted down the distasteful fare ravenously. I knew that each mouthful meant a corresponding amount of renewed strength, and I was likely to need all the strength I could muster.

"The chief will be glad to hear you have eaten so well," commented the artless Mitri. "He told me to make you eat all I could."

"Why?" I asked, looking up from my empty platter.

"He says you'll last longer," was the reply. "Weak people don't stand torture very well, you know."

He gathered up the dish and pitcher and started away. The guard had released my hands, but not my feet, and now he replaced the thongs. I swelled my wrist-muscles to their utmost as he did so. When he had finished, I thrust my tied hands through the bars and plunged them into the spring.

"What is that for?" he asked suspiciously, pausing as he was about to step out over the topmost bar.

"I am washing," I answered.

He grunted lofty disapproval of such effeminacy, and resumed his former seat. Darkness was fast closing in. I withdrew my hands from the pool and quietly exerted all my strength upon the thongs. Goatskin, like all uncured leather, stretches directly after contact with water. My wrists, moreover, had been distended when the thongs were retied.

It was all very simple. A struggle, the scraping off of some of the wrist-cuticle, and one hand was free. To loosen the other was easy. Then I silently drew my feet upward and, after some trouble, unbound them.

Now for the guard.

"My collar—it chokes me!" I gurgled. "Loose it for me."

"Choke away!" he growled.

I obeyed, literally. Rolling toward the back of my pen, where he could not reach me through the bars, I forthwith gave a very lifelike imitation of a man strangling.

The guard had never worn a collar. To him, I reasoned, it would seem no odd thing that so useless and eccentric an article of apparel might suddenly tighten and seek to destroy its wearer. Also, if I choked to death, I could not be publicly killed by torture, whereat Gorgias would be displeased and would vent his displeasure on the person responsible.

So after listening with interest for a few moments to my gurgles and groans, the man rose, set down his gun and, with muttered profanity, clambered over the bars into the pen.

There, for all I know, he may still remain. For as he set foot to the ground, inside, I was upon him, bore him off his balance and hurled him to earth, keeping my thumbs close pressed into his windpipe. His head, as he fell, struck heavily against one of the pen's corner-posts, and he lay quite still.

But I took no chances. Tying him securely, I jammed a handful of leaves into his mouth and strapped a fold of his leggings across his lips. There had been no spectacular tussle. The whole maneuver had not taken many seconds. I was a strong man, a trained athlete, he an underfed peasant taken by surprise. There was no credit to my victory.

I had little time to waste. At any instant Mitri might come back. I tore off the sheepskin cloak and threw it about my own shoulders, drawing the hood over my head. Next, unfastening the saber's worn leather strap from around his waist I girt it about me, vaulted over the top of the pen, caught up his rifle, and was off.

I had a perilous night before me and could neglect no weapons—no precautions. At a slow, dawdling pace that infuriated me, I slouched across the lower end of the tiny valley and up the steep bank. Then, with head down and rifle tucked under my arm, I broke into a run, through the sheltering, blinding darkness.

From the moment Mitri had spoken Vlasto's name I had understood the turn affairs had taken. My only wonder was that I had not sooner guessed the truth. I recalled Vlasto's cryptic remark that he would see Elinor again very soon. Failing to win her hand by approved modern methods, the prince had fallen back on ancestral, mountaineer customs and carried her off—hence his interested queries of Jimmie as to our proposed route. As a concession to modern etiquette, he had borne along her family as well. Also, it would not have done to leave one of them to raise the alarm and bring down the much-despised official busybodies about his ears.

A weight was off my heart to know that Elinor was not in bandit hands and was with those who loved her. But, on second thought, I realized that Vlasto, if less openly brutal than the mountain outlaw, was no whit less deadly. He was quite capable of holding her and all her family prisoners, for a year if necessary, unless she consented earlier to be his wife.

It was all so ridiculous, so like comic-opera! But primitive facts often are, and Vlasto was as primitive, in his way, as the megalosaurus.

What I hoped to gain by running, as I now did, full tilt, toward his castle-rock, I did not clearly analyze. My obvious course, at first glance, was to inform the authorities at Athens. But what proof had I to offer that would lead the police to move? An American family had vanished. From a lad in a robber camp I had heard that a certain trail had been followed till it led to Vlasto's rock. What more? Could I, an unknown foreigner, convince the Greek police with testimony like this? It was out of the question.

No, I must play a lone hand, even though I had, as usual, not a single high card.

I had lost track of time, and my watch was stolen. By the few stars that peeped out in the black cloud-rifts, I estimated the hour to be somewhere near eight.

I came to a halt at the brink of a gorge. Opposite rose Vlasto's castle, perched on its high rock. The upper floors were dark, but the lowest was pierced by many twinkling lights. Down the slope I scrambled, slipping and sliding, the old saber clattering noisily over the stones and threatening to draw the attention of any guards who might chance to be on the battlements beyond.

Suddenly I felt water swirling about my ankles. I was in the little river that brawled at the gorge's foot. I waded till the water reached my shoulders. Then I struck out, and, weighted down as I was, swam across-current—no easy feat at best—for some ten yards. My knee then struck a ledge of rock, and once more I waded in the shallows to the farther bank.

Dripping, I emerged at the base of the steep, rocky hill. At the bottom of the gorge the darkness was pitchy, and I was forced to feel my way as I commenced the stiff clamber upward. Moving cautiously, stretching my hands up to find each new foothold, I wriggled, climbed, and crept up the rough face of the slant.

I could see by the decreasing blackness that I was making fair progress. I began to plume myself on my prowess as a climber, even while my breath came in gasps from the long-continued exertion. I stifled the sound and, holding the saber tight under my arm and swinging the rifle by its bandoleer to my back, moved as silently as possible. The scarcity of loose stones on this side of the slope made prevention of noise easier.

I came to a little ledge and stopped to rest. I looked about me and saw I must be almost on a level with the cellars of the castle; also that a quite visible path led upward, spirally, from the ledge on which I stood. Henceforth, I must cease to be mountaineer and turn spy, seeking some means of unobserved ingress to the place. For, once I should fall into the hands of any of Vlasto's servants, I might look for short shrift. And again I remembered, with absolutely no sensations of pleasure, that death-sign of Nikola's. Even should I win my way to Elinor—

I had recovered my breath and was about to recommence my climb. I stepped on toward the path, using less caution than before in the placing of my feet, for the way was clear. I was punished for my carelessness.

My toe caught against a jutting bit of shale, and I stumbled, almost falling off the ledge down the precipitous slope. To save myself, I lurched sharply in the opposite direction, throwing my whole weight inward, away from the incline, and thus dashing my body against the high slab of rock that lay back of the ledge.

Nor did the rock check my onrush. It quietly *yielded* to my shoulder's impact and I plunged headlong through the cavity thus formed, stumbled again over a second obstruction, and sprawled prone on my face and hands.

There I lay, marveling, dazed. But my position was not so comfortable as to warrant my retaining it from choice. My head was far higher than my feet; at intervals sharp edges seemed to cut into my body. Then I comprehended.

I was lying on the lower steps of a rough, rock-hewn stairway, leading up inside the rock. The slab against which I had tumbled was doubtless one of the rock-doors whereof I had often heard in the East—a slice of stone masking a cave, or other hill hiding-place, and so poised as to turn on a sort of pivot-socket when one side or the other is pressed with sufficient force.

Well, I had exerted the "force" and here I was—not in a cave, but at the foot of a flight of steps, worn smooth in the center, as I could feel, by the feet of countless generations. It had undoubtedly proved a handy byway to and from the castle in early days when houses were built honeycombed with secret doors, rooms, and passages.

That it led upward to some part of the building was certain. Equally certain that it would prove, probably, my best way of entering the castle unobserved. Once more, through no merit or fault of mine, fate had taken affairs into her own hands and used me as an unthinking puppet.

Getting to my feet, gripping the old saber and readjusting the rifle-bandoleer, I began to climb that endless flight of slippery, worn stone stairs. I traveled upward for what seemed an eternity, then came to level walking again.

Along a narrow, black passage I groped my way for perhaps fifty yards. Then, a sharp turn and I was standing in what, to my unaccustomed eyes, seemed a bewildering glare of light.

CHAPTER X.
At Grips With Fate.

THERE I stood, in the damp, black passage, blinking painfully at the sudden inrush of light that smote across my dark-accustomed eyes like a sword-blade. Then, bit by bit, I grew used to my surroundings, and my eyes focused. Yet even then I could not understand at once my situation.

The light, I saw, was not shining directly on me, but filtered through a substance of some sort studded with irregular apertures varying in size from a pin-head to a franc piece. I was evidently behind an arras or tapestry curtain on whose opposite side was a brightly lighted room.

By the time I had grasped this fact I noted, by the sounds of movement, the presence of several persons in the apartment beyond my screen. Yet, during that instant while I was recovering myself, I heard no spoken word. While I wondered at the silence it was broken.

"There is no need for this gloom," said a voice startlingly near by. It was Barzillah Clyde's, and instinctively it struck me as having an undercurrent which, despite its owner's plight, did not seem wholly sad. "There is no need for gloom, my dears," he repeated unctuously, as nobody answered his first consolatory words. "We are in the hands of Providence, and we must not despond. Remember how David of old—"

"David of old never got grabbed, in a family group, by a lot of peasants with skirts like ballet-girls', and lugged over miles of rocks to a measly old morgue like this!" protested Jimmie, a little farther down the room. "He never was ushered into a big stone-floored vault of a place with mortuary chapels opening off of it, and had a grinning jailer politely inform him that it was the family's suite till further notice. He—"

"Don't be irreverent!" adjured old Mr. Clyde, shocked. "We are in the hands of a wise Pro—"

"We are in the hands of Prince Konstantin Vlasto!" retorted Jimmie crossly.

"I recognized that majordomo of his—Nikola. He was the one

who met us at the gate and had us bundled into this drafty old joint. I knew him the first thing. So did you, dad," Jimmie went on more excitedly, "for you stopped groaning the moment you saw him. Ever since then you've been talking about Providence, and—"

"Don't, Jimmie," said Mrs. Clyde, and her placid voice had a note of fear in it that went to my heart—"don't let's dispute among ourselves, but stand together to bear this terrible suspense bravely."

"I didn't mean to growl, mother," said the young fellow more gently, "but it makes me sore to think that a bunch of Americans, in the twentieth century, can be snatched up bodily and yanked off into a gray jail like this, kept by an uncivilized Greek geezer—"

"I would not speak that way of Prince Konstantin Vlasto if I were you," blandly suggested his stepfather.

"Why not, I'd like to know?" shouted the angry youth. "He's—"

"For two reasons," resumed the smooth, unctuous voice. "First, because some of his people who understand English may be within ear-shot; second, because Prince Vlasto is likely to become your brother-in-law."

"My—what?" squealed Jimmie.

"Papa!" broke in another voice in the same breath—a voice that set my blood to dancing for all the grief and shocked surprise wherewith its tones were laden.

"Barzillah!" exclaimed Mrs. Clyde, "you surely aren't in—"

"We may as well be frank," the financier answered, unruffled, "and look the truth fairly in the face. Some days ago, in Athens, Prince Vlasto asked your hand of me, Elinor. And I must say he did it very handsomely. I will not deny that I was pleased with the idea of my little girl's becoming a princess, yet I would not then influence your heart. You rejected the prince. His is a strange, unconventional nature, and—if I may judge by what I have read of medieval Scotch romances and have heard of local customs here—I fear he has chosen this eccentric mode of inducing you to alter your decision."

"You can't mean it?" cried Elinor. "We are in the twentieth century, and—"

"And in ancient Greece, my dear. You must be brave. Remember—"

"Papa!" exclaimed the girl, dawning suspicion in her voice, "you speak as if you actually—actually—"

"I do not say I approve," purred Clyde in mild correction, "but we must take into consideration the difference between his customs and ours. He is an ardent wooer, you must admit. And the title of princess is—"

"Oh, please, *please* stop!" begged Elinor. "How can you speak so? Do you think for one moment that I will marry him—that I would marry any man who tried to bully me like this into accepting him? And, besides," she added, her dear voice ringing out clear and fearless, "last night I promised to marry Bruce Graeme. We—"

"Elinor!" cried Clyde and his wife together.

"Bully for you, Nell!" applauded Jimmie. "He's—"

What next would have been said or done I do not know, or whether I would have wakened sufficiently from my bewilderment to drop the unconscious, despicable role of eavesdropper. The creaking of a big lock at another end of the room checked all talk.

I could almost feel the simultaneous turning of the quartet's eyes toward the door whose opening was accompanied by a draft that blew through the ragged arras onto my face.

I leaned forward, pressing my eyes to one of the apertures, and all at once the scene became clear to me—the great, gray, low-ceiled hall, with its barred windows; walls hung with scanty, faded tapestry; long table, whereon rested the remains of the captives' evening meal; sparse furnishing of carved chairs here and there about the floor, and roaring wood fire at the lower end of the apartment.

Grouped about the blaze were the Clydes—Elinor with her back to me, her fragile body almost hidden by the huge chair-shoulder. Directly opposite, in an open doorway, stood the fat majordomo, Nikola.

He motioned to two rough servitors to clear the table. As, with unexpected deftness and speed, they did so, Nikola bowed low to Clyde and said, in halting French:

"His highness, my master, Prince Vlasto, begs leave to wait on your excellencies, if you will receive him."

"If we'll receive him!" snorted Jimmie. "*If* we'll receive him, eh? What else can we do? He's our jailer, isn't he?"

"His highness is your host and servant, *monsieur*," corrected the majordomo with elaborate politeness, as old Clyde vainly tried to suppress his excited stepson, "and he begs—"

Elinor had risen to her feet, and now stepped forward, quiet determination in every line of her dainty figure.

"Where is M. Graeme?" she asked. "Why was he not brought to this room with us? You captured him before the rest of us were awake this morning, did you not? Where is he?"

The Greek shrugged his shoulders, spreading out his palms apologetically on either side.

"I was commanded by my master," quoth he, with covert insolence under his humility, "to bring your excellencies whatever you might desire. But I cannot bring the American, Graeme, for we have not got him."

"He is not a prisoner like the rest of us?" cried Elinor, a catch in her breath.

"Mademoiselle jests. She is a guest—the most honored of guests—not a prisoner. But it is true the man you speak of is not here. We did not find him, though our men sought long. Even if we had, he should not be here."

"Why not?" asked Jimmie, evidently puzzled by this cryptic utterance.

"Because, excellency," replied Nikola with relish, "he was to have been put to death at once, with no delay or trouble. Those were the orders. But he—"

"Horrible!" gasped Mrs. Clyde, while even her husband lost some of his pink color. Jimmie swore long and loud. Elinor alone said nothing, but went white and swayed where she stood.

Forgetful of all else, I threw myself forward to catch her, should she fall. But the old arras stretched across the opening held firm. In the confusion my interruption went unheard. Before I could make a second attempt, Elinor had recovered herself, and, as footsteps sounded down the hallway behind him, Nikola's face lost its lurking, malicious smile. Stiffening, he drew to one side and announced reverentially:

"His Highness, Prince Konstantin Vlasto!"

Backing out of the room, he vanished, and on the threshold stood Vlasto. But not the Vlasto we had hitherto seen—instead, a very gorgeous being, clad from head to foot in white and gold. I recognized the costume at a glance. It was the full-dress uniform of a colonel of the Imperial Austrian Household Guards.

What Konstantin Vlasto was doing in such a rig, I could not fathom. Yet it was complete, from the splendid plumed, gilded helmet under his arm and the polished saber-scabbard at his belt, down to the golden spurs on his shining white leather boots.

He was the most magnificent sight, at the moment, that one can well imagine, his mighty frame and classic, high-bred, bearded face set off to wondrous advantage by the spotless uniform.

When I recalled my own soaked, muddy, unshaven aspect, I glanced involuntarily at Elinor. She had not given him a second look, but, back turned, stood gazing abstractedly at the floor. My brave, loyal love!

The moment's awkward silence incident on the prince's entrance was broken by old Clyde. In a nervously conciliatory tone he stammered:

"I—I did not know you were in the army, prince. I—I—"

"A colonelcy in the Household Guards of Austria is hereditary in my family," answered Vlasto carelessly, "as in other royal houses. I ventured to don it tonight, when I come in due form to beg the hand of your excellency's daughter in—"

"Hold on a second, prince!" cut in Jimmie. "When the *pater* said that's why you locked us up here, I thought he was guessing. She doesn't want to marry you, and she's engaged to a better chap. And even if she wasn't, she'd never marry a man who played a cad trick like this on us all. Do you mean to say you're going to keep us jugged here till she says 'Yes'? Because, if you do, we'll manage sooner or later to get out. And when we do, we'll cable for a Yankee cruiser to come here and blow your measly castle off this rock, and, if necessary, your three-for-a-quarter old country off the map."

"I have considered that," replied Vlasto gravely, "therefore I cannot afford to let any of you go until our marriage. After that, you will scarcely care to—"

"To sick Uncle Sam onto you? You look pretty big in that white-and-gold frescoing of yours, but you'll sing exceeding small when a party of Yankee marines—"

"I confess," said Vlasto, "I could not hope to hold the castle against a cruiser of your savage nation, with the barbarous modern weapons with which they so cruelly humbled Spain's grand old pride. But the contingency is not one to take into account. At present I have the honor to be your host, and—"

"Our turnkey, you mean! There, there, *pater,* I know what I'm saying! You're our jailer—our—"

"Your future brother-in-law, I trust," said Vlasto, with that same unruffled, courteous dignity. "In the meantime—"

The rotten old arras split from top to bottom under the slash of my stolen saber, and I stepped out into the room.

"In the meantime" —I caught up Vlasto's words—"you and I have a trifling account, prince, that may as well be settled here and now!"

I must have presented a weird enough figure as I stepped out among them and faced Vlasto, rifle in hand. Indeed, it did not require the gasp of amazement and the dumfounded looks wherewith my advent was greeted to tell me so.

Bedraggled, bruised, muddy, blood-flecked, unshaven, and haggard; still swathed in my vast, tattered sheepskin, the rusty saber sticking loose in my belt where I had thrust it after I cleft the arras, my awkward, old-fashioned rifle clutched in grimy, scratched fists, my eyes bloodshot and glaring—yes, I must have been a gruesome enough sight!

And opposite, his calm mask of a face actually deigning to express unbounded wonder, was Vlasto, clad in that gorgeous white-and-gold creation, so clean that a dust-speck would have felt lonely thereon. We were, I doubt not, as sharp a contrast, he and I, as ever man beheld.

Yet, what do you think? Elinor Clyde, with a little cry of utter rapture, ran forward and threw her arms about my muddy neck, and kissed my bristling face—not once, but over and over.

An hour earlier I would not have believed the time was to come when she could waste on me an unreturned embrace. Yet here I was, gripping the rifle at "present," with both hands, eying Vlasto as if he were the only being on earth. Not a word, not a caress, for the woman I loved.

Nor was my caution wasted. I had already observed that he stood between me and the only door in the room. Also, by the semitelepathy that is a trained swordsman's best friend, I read in his eyes the intent to summon his servants. If once they crossed that threshold, I was lost, and Elinor was forever in the power of the prince.

Do you wonder that I did not obey my impulse to drop the rusty gun and catch her in my arms? She, too, understood, for I heard her murmur:

"Don't let him harm you! You are all I have!"

The others stood stock-still in amazement. But Vlasto already had recovered that splendid calm of his.

"The adventurer!" he said coldly. "I hoped some of my men had silenced you before this."

"Your men, prince," said I in equal contempt, "are Greeks like their master, and, therefore, dolts. You surely did not believe a dull mountaineer like yourself could get rid of me, did you? Or that a rattletrap old castle such as your stupid ancestors built could keep out a wide-awake American?

"There is a United States war-ship at anchor in the southern harbor below the Piræus," I went on, lying with a certain rash, crazy purpose that had leaped into my brain during Jimmie's vehement conversation with his highness, "and unless you release these friends of mine you will find a detachment of her crew under your windows before many hours have passed."

"If you escape to bring them here," he finished, outwardly as calm as ever. Yet I fancied I could note a faint trace of doubt in his confident tone.

"*If* you escape," he repeated—"but you will not."

"No?" I smiled. "May I ask why?"

"Because this morning's delayed execution will take place in the courtyard, ten minutes hence," he answered, turning toward the door.

But my rifle was covering him before he had taken a single stride.

"Stop!" I warned him.

He glanced over his shoulder, with not one atom of emotion in his strong, beautiful face, then moved on undaunted, without so much as another backward look at me. He was sublime—a man without a taint of fear in his giant make-up.

But I had no time just then to admire courage. It was his life or mine; his life or misery for the woman whose happiness I placed above a hundred lives.

"Shut your eyes!" I called to Elinor. Then I pulled the trigger.

The hammer fell with a muffled, rust-choked click.

The rifle was not loaded!

CHAPTER XI.
THE GAME CHANGES WINNERS.

I DASHED down the useless old weapon, and sprang at Vlasto, bare-handed.

Lucky it was for me that the prince was moving toward the door with that stately, Old-World, measured tread of his, instead of at a twentieth-century pace.

As he reached for the big brazen knob, I was between him and it.

I think he had grown used to regarding me as a being from whom only the unexpected was likely to emanate, for though he, a second before, had me behind him with leveled rifle, and now found me barring his path with my empty, clenched fists, he evinced no surprise.

I braced myself for a struggle against a larger, heavier foe. But he halted, and stood eying me in quiet disgust.

"I do not wish to soil my hands on you," he said without a trace of emotion. "Move out of my way."

Now, I am athlete enough to size up a man at a glance, and I knew that, despite my six feet of stature and hundred and eighty pounds of muscular body, I would be as a child in the grip of this immobile giant.

I recalled, too, a tradition of his youth, current in the Athens cafes—how once a drunken soldier had lurched against him in the street, striking him and using an offensive epithet. Vlasto, according to the tale, had quietly stretched out both hands, caught the soldier by the throat, lifted him from the ground, and broken his neck at one grip of those powerful brown fingers. He had then fastidiously washed his hands and ridden away, unmolested, to the hills.

The memory of this gave me an odd feeling of constriction about my own throat. But my one chance of life lay in keeping Vlasto from opening the door.

The portal was thick and iron-studded, as befitted the entrance to the great hall of such a castle. Beyond, as I had seen when it was open, lay a long corridor. No ordinary sound could reach outsiders' ears so long as that door should remain closed. Here, then, I must play out the last and decisive hand in my game with this colossal foe.

My plan was laid by the time the last contemptuous word had left his lips. It was my only hope—a tenuous one at best, I admit—and I was resolved to act on it.

Shrinking quickly backward against the door, to widen the narrow space between us, I whipped out the purloined saber from my belt and struck him full across the face with the flat of the steel.

I remembered how of old the drunken soldier's blow had roused even Vlasto's iron nerves to fury, and I counted desperately on the same effect now. True, I might have plunged the rusty point of the sword into his throat; but it is one thing to seek to shoot down a man, as a last resort, and quite another to stab him, unwarned, while another chance of escape—be it ever so slender—offers itself.

So I struck the harmless blow. Nor was I mistaken in my hopes. He recoiled like a blooded horse under the lash, and instinctively flashed his own great saber from its sheath.

To such a man, a blow, especially in the presence of the woman he loves, is an indignity death alone can cancel. It utterly broke down the prince's monumental calm and led him, without second thought, to seize the first fatal weapon at hand for vengeance on the man he had but a moment before scorned to touch.

Scarce was his saber out when I slashed fiercely at him, that he might have no time to think better of the matter or to decide to leave my punishment, after all, in menial hands.

Vlasto guarded my slash with a quickness and instinct that showed me at once he was no novice at sword-play, and riposted with a lunge so rapid and fiery that I had to leap backward to avoid his point.

And thus began our fight—no mere farcical duel, but primal man's struggle for life under the eyes of the woman who was life's prize.

Back and forth we fenced, up and down the great hall, wheeling, circling, attacking, guarding—two strong men whose wrath but steadied their trained muscles.

From the first it was he who took the aggressive, seldom giving me scope to do aught but defend myself against the mad torrent of blows he aimed at me. Backward he forced me, by sheer weight; and more than once, by main strength, beat down my guard, so that I was fain to spring away out of reach of his crashing blade.

Yet the odds were less against me than an onlooker might have supposed. True, in reach, height, and brute strength, he was infinitely my superior. But, without conceit, I may say I ranked in those days as a premier swordsman even in company where excellence of fence was more common than otherwise. That I was his superior in deftness and practise, I saw when first our blades crossed. That that superiority could hope to offset his vast physical advantages over me, I was less sure.

Meantime, I fought on the defensive, husbanding my already taxed strength. By such tactics I had worn out many a man. But I felt that Vlasto was not the sort of man who wears out. Also, I feared lest my blade might prove as worthless as had its owner's rifle, and break in my grip, leaving me helpless against my more powerful foe.

Yet, in spite of all this, I was gloriously happy. I had my enemy face to face at last, on something like equal terms. And I fought under the eyes of the woman before whom, above all the world, I sought to appear at my best. Seldom is it given in this prosaic day for a man to wage actual physical combat for the girl of his heart—more seldom still to do so in her all-inspiring presence. I longed to glance toward her. Yet, for my life's sake and hers, I was too wise to shift my gaze for a fraction of a second from Vlasto's.

The blades clashed, whistled, whined, like sentient things, now grinding together in the engage, now striking sparks in a quick parry or moulinet.

Ever charging, his heavy saber dealing cuts and lunges that seemed beyond the power of mortal arm, Vlasto pressed me more and more hotly. Now and again, at rare intervals, I could catch his blow in time to riposte. But these swift return-thrusts availed me nothing until, guarding a sweeping head blow, I managed to slip, lightning-like, past his guard on the recover. Then I felt my saber's edge bite into something yielding, and a red splash darted out and widened on the white uniform on the giant's left shoulder.

I had touched, but only in a flesh-wound, that served to redouble Vlasto's rage and strength. Down came his weapon, beating mine to earth before it; an upward cut, and I was aware of a sensation like that of an icicle being drawn across my right forearm. I had sprung back in time to escape death, or even disablement; yet my sword-arm began to lose its pristine force. But for the folds of the sheepskin, which I had not had time to discard, his saber must have cut to the very bone.

Knowing I must soon tire, I changed my tactics. Turning one of his lunges, I forced the fight, taking the aggressive, and holding it by sheer swiftness and my greater skill at fence. Close I pressed, forcing him to break ground once again.

Then came the end, and in ludicrous enough anti-climax.

I was forcing the battle so fiercely that Vlasto had no thought for anything except my blade, that was ever turning, wriggling, and pushing its way through his steel wall of defense.

Yet I, being on the aggressive, noted something else. As we circled I caught a fleeting glimpse, out of the corner of my eye, of Barzillah Clyde. Seeing me drive the prince backward, the old reprobate apparently had come to the conclusion that I was winning, and that his own prospects of becoming father-in-law to a prince were dwindling.

Whether with this in mind, or with some strange idea of a peacemaker's duties; or if, indeed, he had lost his presence of mind, and was moved by some latent battle instinct left hibernating within him since his vaunted Civil War days, I do not claim to know. But this is what he did:

As I forced Vlasto for the third time to break ground, I saw Clyde snatch up a heavy stool, swing it aloft and aim a ponderous blow therewith at my head.

I leaped back, guided by the self-preservation instinct rather than any conscious thought. Vlasto, noting my sudden retreat, flung himself bodily at me with a frightful tierce lunge. My backward spring and his attack were almost instantaneous.

Down, driven with all the force of two pursy old arms, hurtled the stout stool. Down it whirled and, with a resounding crash, broke in three pieces over Vlasto's skull. My prospective father-in-law had quite involuntarily done me a wondrous good turn.

For, at the impact, the giant's knees doubled under him. The saber slipped from his nerveless hand and clattered on the stone floor. The huge, white-uniformed body fell in a huddled heap.

Clyde, mouth open, face a pasty green, stared with bursting goggle-eyes at the highly unlooked-for result of his interference. Even as I dropped my weapon, and knelt at the senseless prince's side, I was aware of a faint twinge of regret that so magnificent a man should have been struck down by such a cur.

Mrs. Clyde had quietly fainted in her chair. Jimmie and Elinor, up to this point too engrossed in the battle to notice her plight, now ran to the poor lady's assistance.

"No," I said grimly, in reply to a dumb look of inquiry in Barzillah's eyes; "he isn't dead. But you have stunned him pretty effectively. He won't come to himself for some minutes. And," I added, "we won't be here to see him recover. Is that your luggage, piled in the alcove there? Get some thick coats for the ladies and yourself. *Jump!*"

I fairly shouted the last word, and the dazed old man trotted obediently over to do my bidding. I made for the door, opened it, and looked down the corridor. It was still empty. No sound short of a gunshot could have penetrated that massive thickness.

I drew out the big bronze key from the opposite side, reclosed the portal, and stuck the key in my pocket. Then I bound up my grazed arm with a rough skill born of many campaigns. Mrs. Clyde was recovering, and could already stand alone. I dared delay no longer.

"Quick!" I ordered. "Wrap yourselves up and come. Please don't speak till I give you leave." For I feared lest other and occupied rooms might give on the secret passage.

I snatched a lamp from the table to light our way, and made for the slashed arras, the others meekly following my lead without a word—Elinor first, then Jimmie, supporting his bewildered mother, and old Mr. Clyde dazedly bringing up the rear, too completely bemused to protest or disobey.

Through the arras, along the passage, down the interminable flight of steps we plodded, single file, speechless. Elinor I could trust to go where I led; Jimmie, after witnessing that fight, would, I verily believe, have followed me blindly to the bottomless pit; the two old people, shocked out of all sense of individuality, trotted, sheep-like, wherever another might choose to direct.

Out on the ledge we came, the cold night air striking to our very vitals. There I halted for consultation.

"How did you get here to-day?" I asked Jimmie. "Across the gorge, I mean."

"Wooden bridge, about a quarter-mile beyond the castle," he answered. "We didn't see it till we got there. It's hidden by a spur of rock. Say, old man, you're the dandiest scrapper I ever—"

"Shut up!" I said. "We must go quietly, unless we want to get the whole hornet's nest about our ears. We'll follow the path upward till we strike a level place where we can cut across to the bridge without going too near the castle."

I passed an arm around Elinor's waist, and led the way with her up the winding path. She said no word, but, at a dark corner, she caught up my free hand and pressed it to her lips. Oh, it was good to have fought for this!

Jimmie and Clyde followed, Mrs. Clyde between them; and we thus began our long, tedious walk.

Before midnight we halted in a little protected glen, and there, with our coats, made couch and covering for the two women. Our next stop I briefly outlined to Jimmie, as he and his stepfather and I crouched for shelter under a jutting tablet of rock just beyond.

We would hurry on at dawn to our old camp. There was a chance that some of our horses might still be there, for Demetrius could not, alone, have driven them all back to Athens during the past twelve hours. We would mount and ride on, as quickly as possible, to the city, before Vlasto could recover, pick up the trail and overtake us. We already seemed practically out of danger, and I was elated at my own skilful handling of the whole affair.

To Clyde himself I spoke no word. He and I must have our reckoning later on. And at last, when Jimmie fell asleep, my time came. Catching the scared financier by the shoulder, I drew him quietly outside the rock shelter, beyond ear-shot of the rest.

"I saw your move to-night," said I, without preamble. "And I knew for whom you intended that dirty coward's blow. Now, listen: I am going to marry Miss Clyde. I shall not ask your leave, and I do not want your assistance. If you are wise you will not object. You might have trouble in making the world at large sympathize with your motives in trying to murder a fellow countryman who was saving your family from a savage mountain prince. So, I beg that you won't force me to tell the tale, and to call on your stepchildren for substantiation of my story. Is that settled?"

"I—I never meant to murder. I—"

"Probably not," I agreed. "You are not man enough for anything so vital. But others may not see it that way. For instance, those who remember how you indirectly murdered my father, Bruce Graeme!"

He collapsed in a gasping, shuddering heap, chattering forth bewildered incoherencies. I lifted him, none too gently, to his feet.

"I shall resume my rightful place at home," I said; "and, at worst, Miss Clyde will be under charge of a hundred times better man than her stepfather. As between you and me, our policy from now on is to be one of mutual forbearance. If it is not, it is you, not I, who will suffer by digging up the past. That is all. Go and get some sleep."

And alone I stood guard till gray dawn.

The sun was rising as—weary, footsore, inert—we reached the plateau whereon we had camped that first eventful night.

There stood the tents, the horses, and, to our astonishment, at a shout from some one on the rock above, men swarmed out to meet us.

Mrs. Clyde was first to note the presence of these men. Had I been walking in advance, as before, this story would have had a different ending. But I had dropped back some forty yards with Jimmie, to whom I was going over for the second time the details of a ruse I had thought out for utilization in case Vlasto should pursue and overhaul us before we could reach a place of safety. It is better to form emergency plans you may not need than to need such plans when you have not formed them. This particular suggestion had brought a grin of delighted appreciation to the boy's tanned face.

"By Jove!" he cried as I finished. "It would be the joke of the century. It's almost a pity we're not likely—"

Mrs. Clyde's exclamation, as she came into view of the camp, interrupted him. I quickened my pace as the fellows ran forward toward us. Then I halted stock-still, with a cry of surprise. For in the foremost of the men, whom I had deemed our returned muleteers, I recognized the white beard-bristles and scowling, unwashed face of Gorgias Padapoulos.

The old bandit was mounted on one of our own hired hill-ponies, I observed. His men were on foot. Before I could give the alarm they were upon us, swarming about us, a half-dozen rifles and revolvers leveled at our chests.

Here was the one contingency I had not taken into account—that Gorgias and a party of his cutthroats, disappointed in kidnaping Clyde, should have repaired to our camp to pillage whatever of value Vlasto's men might in their haste have left untouched. Yet it was the most natural thing in the world. How I had overlooked the chance I cannot tell, unless it was that Vlasto's dominating personality had for the time blotted out thought of all lesser obstacles.

"The game is up," I groaned in despair to Jimmie, partly turning to face the lad as I spoke.

To my unbounded surprise, he was nowhere to be seen!

But I had little chance or inclination to search him out amid the hillside of scattered boulders. For duty and will both drew me to Elinor. I ran forward and threw myself bodily between her and a man who was about to seize her shoulder.

Unarmed as I was, I knocked the fellow's rifle-barrel upward and sent him staggering. Then, with one arm about Elinor, I faced Gorgias. He had dismounted from the pony, which he left to graze on the sparse mountain herbage, and stood smiling sardonically at me.

"The old one with the round, foolish face is Clyde?" he asked me, speaking in guttural French that the rest of the captives might understand his coarse words. "It seems I have him by the heels at last without any outside aid. No sharing of ransoms, and no babyish oath not to catch the women, too, eh? Better than any blundering foreigner could have—"

"My friend," I interposed, speaking loudly and in French, with infinite coolness, "whoever you are, you seem to be laboring under a belief that we are your prisoners. You are mistaken. My friends here are recent guests of Prince Konstantin Vlasto. In fact, they just now came from his castle. Send one of your hunters to follow up their trail if you like. But I pledge you my solemn word that, within two hours at most, Vlasto or his servants will follow. And when they find, from the trail, what you have done, I leave you to imagine how the prince will repay the men who molest his guests. You know the guest law of the mountains, and—"

"You have been Prince Vlasto's guests?" Gorgias asked, wheeling on Clyde.

I could see my words had had an effect. Padapoulos knew as well as I that if he should harm a guest of the prince's, the old mutual rule of "live and let live" would be broken in such a fashion as to leave the existence of Gorgias's outlaw band a mere dead memory.

"You have been his guests?" repeated the chief.

"Yes," mumbled Clyde between chattering teeth.

"We were his prisoners," supplemented the tremulous Mrs. Clyde, with fatally generous intent. "We should be so yet, had not this gallant gentleman come last night to our rescue. To him we owe our escape. We are fleeing from the prince now, and—"

"So!" growled Padapoulos, his face falling, as he realized it would be safer for him to pick up an angry viper than to lay violent hands on prey which Konstantin Vlasto had marked for his own. His discomfiture was positively ludicrous. I drew a long breath of relief. Truly I was at last conquering my old enemy—Fate!

But Gorgias's aspect of chagrin underwent a sharp change as he encountered my smile of complacent triumph. Grim lines set hard about his mouth, and a light came into his angry eyes.

"So!" he repeated, deep down in his hairy throat, with slow, decisive accent, casting a look about the little knot of Americans. "That's how the land lies? You were the prisoners of Prince Vlasto, and this noble-hearted American hero bravely set you free? This true, honorable gentleman could not bear that any of you should suffer capture. He would not let his great and good friend, M. Barzillah Clyde, lose his freedom."

"Yes," said Mrs. Clyde enthusiastically, wholly missing the irony of the query, "we owe everything to Mr. Graeme. We—"

"You owe more than you guess," sneered Gorgias, his mighty voice rumbling forth, volcano-like, from the depths of his chest as he leered across at me. "He is modest and has forborne to tell you everything. I, who am his dear friend, will tell you."

It had come. And, for all the ready wit whereon I had been pluming myself, I could not find a way to meet it. So I stood still, looking him miserably in the face, while the Clydes glanced from one to the other, puzzled at his odd preamble, and the bandits, to whom all this French dialogue was shibboleth, shifted about uneasily, at a loss to guess the meaning of the prolonged conference.

"Did he tell you," began Gorgias, addressing old Mr. Clyde—"did this rescuing hero tell you that he sold you to me ten days ago, like so much mutton? Did he tell you why you came into the mountains? Was he too modest to tell that he had bargained to bring you to this camp and to tie a red handkerchief to that tree above there, to warn me you had come? Also, that I was to take you on this signal and to give him one-third of your ransom-money? Did he tell you all that? If not, you have failed to appreciate his full nobility of heart."

For a moment after he paused, snorting and glowing in pride at his own satiric powers, no one spoke. But Elinor moved a step nearer me and covertly slipped her hand in mine with a trustful, loving little pressure that caused me untold agony.

"If you have nothing more to say to us," she observed, addressing the chief as though he were some gibbering lunatic, "will you tell your men to stand aside and let us go?"

"You don't believe?" he shouted, sarcasm merging into a gust of wrath at her quiet ignoring of his charge. "You think I lie?"

"I *know* you do," she returned in the same unmoved tones, and did not even trouble to face his rage-distorted glare.

"It is the truth!" roared Padapoulos. "This American is a rogue; a man notorious for every swindler's trick. He—"

"Come, dear," whispered Elinor, "let us go. Don't resent what he says. It's not worth while. We—"

"He rode to my camp ten nights ago," vociferated Padapoulos, appealing to Clyde, "and volunteered to bring you into my hands on condition that I give him one-third the ransom-money. It is true. I swear it by St. Gorgias, by every holy relic! Look!" he cried in quick intuition. "Look at his face now. Let him swear I lie, if he can. Let him deny—"

I freed myself from Elinor's loving hand-clasp, and in the gesture I seemed to be tearing myself loose from everything of light and beauty and joy in all the universe. Moving away from her side, I faced the others.

"I do not deny it!" said I. "What this Greek tells you is true. I did as he says. There is no excuse."

I would not look at Elinor—would not let her inaudible moan of deathly pain reach to my heart. My back was to her, even as, in confessing, I had turned my back on all the once golden future. I walked across to Gorgias.

"I broke away from your bonds last night," said I. "Take me back if you will. I shall not try again to escape. Let these others go on their way. You dare not detain them, and you know it."

"I have a better notion," said he, the gleam of a positive inspiration lighting his seamed visage. "Fall in there!" he bawled to his men, and they closed about us all once more.

"Wha—wh—what are you going to do?" chattered Clyde.

Speaking once more in French, Gorgias replied, with a great bellow of laughter:

"I am going to earn the favor of the illustrious Prince Konstantin Vlasto by marching back to him his escaped captives! As for the noble Graeme, I had thought to torture him as a lesson to other traitors.

"But if I know Prince Vlasto's repute, he will deal with Graeme in much more interesting style than a poor commoner like me could hope to. The man who tried to rob the prince of his 'guests' is likely to taste some of the delights of the old torture–chamber where the early Vlastos used to bring their enemies to reason.

"Olà, there!" he added in Greek, "Marco! Pollos! Saddle three of the horses. Three are enough. The spy Graeme will walk. And if he walks too slow to keep up with the others, a knife-prick or two will hurry him. Now, then—"

He started, as he spoke, toward his own mount, which in grazing had strayed some twenty paces off. But, midway, a figure sprang up at his very feet, from behind a broad boulder, sent a smashing, staggering blow full into the unsuspecting chief's face, and at a bound was beside the startled pony.

It was Jimmie Clyde. Jumping into the saddle and beating the pony into a wild gallop with fist and heel, the boy shouted back at me over his shoulder:

"I'm off to try that trick you framed up! And I don't believe a word about—"

The rest was lost in distance, hoof-thunder, and shouts.

Two of the astounded brigands whipped up their guns and fired; a third flung himself on a barebacked mule and clattered off in lumbering pursuit. Padapoulos, wiping the blood from his eyes, swore horribly in his own melodious tongue.

"Who was that?" he raved, rushing at me.

"I do not know," I replied, in the same language. "Perhaps some tramping tourist."

But I took my place behind the three other prisoners in the line of march with a lighter heart. That I personally should escape death—perhaps torture as well—I did not hope.

Nor did I greatly care, now that Elinor was forever lost to me through my idiotic course in refusing to lie to her when a single word of denial would have saved me her esteem, her love.

But if Jimmie kept his head, and fate did not carry her hatred of me so far as to include my friend, the others still had a fighting chance for liberty.

CHAPTER XII.
An Uncle Sam Masquerade.

SUNSET is a poetical, inspiring sight. But to the man who views it, or any other beauty of nature, from behind bars, it has not a single redeeming feature.

At all events, the glory of sky and sea from a barred turret-window of Konstantin Vlasto's castle, some ten hours after our recapture, filled me with absolutely no poetic thoughts.

We had arrived in due form, under charge of our villainous escort. At the drawbridge we had been met by Nikola, the majordomo, who, doubtless seeing our approach from afar, was at the gate to receive us with a half-score of shaggy retainers at his back.

A babel of talk had ensued, at whose conclusion Gorgias and his gang had departed, bareheaded and bowing. The Clydes had been conducted with exaggerated courtesy within the castle, after which I had been led between silent men up a winding stone stair to a bare stone room in the turret, thrust inside, and left there. There I had remained ever since.

From the excited talk at the gate, between Padapoulos and Nikola, I had gathered that Vlasto still kept his bed, owing to an undescribed "accident," but that most of his servants and all his tenants had been scouring the countryside for the missing captives since long before daylight.

I had passed the weary, solitary day in communion with my own miserable thoughts. To my future I had not yet given any especial thought. That Vlasto would amply avenge my action of the night before was certain. The summons to my death or torture might come at any minute; or, in view of the semioriental cast of my captor's mind, the punishment might be enhanced by days of suspense.

Nor was it Elinor's fate at Vlasto's hands that greatly distressed me. I knew now that she would not consent to marry him, and that Barzillah Clyde would not have the power to force her into the match. Besides, I thought I had cause to hope for her ultimate escape.

It was my own selfish grief that filled my mind to the exclusion of everything else. I had been on the brink of a life so gloriously happy as to make the bitter, black years that were gone seem like a dimly remembered nightmare. My own confession had wrecked that hope, had robbed me of the only love I had ever known.

I tried to curse my folly in having admitted the truth of Gorgias's vengeful exposure. Yet in my heart of hearts I was conscious of a faint thrill of gladness. I had been true to my new, love-born resolve—I had been honest with Elinor. I had refused to let her believe me better than I was, to accept her faith with one stain of deceit on my conscience. I had given faith for faith, even though I had known that to do so would forever rob me of her trust and the love that I valued above life.

When in future she should think of me, she would remember, the first resentful bitterness past, that I had spoken the truth; that I had for once in my life avoided a lie—the lie that would have saved me in her eyes.

In the midst of these somewhat maudlin reflections I would now and then pull myself together and try to realize that this asininely honest creature was Bruce Graeme, gambler, trickster, and unscrupulous soldier of fortune. One little girl's honest eyes had surely wrought sore havoc with my brutal manhood, and I tried to resent it.

I could picture the scorn and horror that must have seared her flower face when she heard my avowal, there in the captured camp. I knew how she must now be loathing me, and how ashamed of herself she must be for having loved so vile a thing. But—

At this point in my wanderings I started up and rubbed my eyes. Then, with a cheer that reverberated from the cramped walls of my cell, I thrust my face to the bars and strained every nerve for what was passing below.

Beyond rose the hills, tumbled together as by some Titan hand, and in a gap glittered the distant ribbon of sea, under a sinking ball of red sun. The nearer dull monochrome of brown and gray had in a trice been thrown into still more somber gloom by contrast with an apparition that flashed out in the narrow, winding mountain road leading up to the castle.

There, catching the sun in its silken folds, flew a United States flag, borne aloft by a white-clad sailor! And, coming in martial step around the curve, behind the standard-bearer, marched a company of marines in spotless white. In their center trundled a small, gleaming brass field-piece. Ahead of the squad, drawn sword in hand, marched an officer, resplendent in blue and gold.

Up the slope trod this amazing cortége, the cannon rumbling and bumping along in its midst.

Was ever sight of Old Glory so welcome?

Nor was I the only spectator. A shout from another window, an answering cry from below, then general confusion. The battlements and courtyard swarmed with excited Greeks, among whom I at length distinguished Vlasto himself, his head bound in a white cloth, his dark face paler than was its wont. A babel of talk, of orders, queries, and aimless replies filled the whole place.

Meantime, coming on to level ground before the castle gate, the marines halted, swung their cannon about, and trained it on the great gate in decidedly businesslike fashion. The naval officer strutted forward, the incarnation of official self-importance.

"Ahoy, inside there!" he shouted. "Parley!"

More confusion in the courtyard. Then a word from Vlasto, and the smaller gate beside the main entrance swung open. The officer strode in, as unafraid as if the whole navy was at his back.

"Konstantin Vlasto?" he asked bruskly, as he came to a stop inside and the gate shut behind him.

"I am Prince Vlasto," replied Konstantin haughtily, with the slightest possible rebuking accent on the title. "Who are you, and what is it you wish here?"

"I am Lieutenant McKimmon, of the United States cruiser Arizona," replied the officer in very bad French. "Evidence was brought us at the Piræus today that four American citizens are held here illegally as prisoners by you. I am sent to demand their instant release."

"I am not accustomed to receiving 'demands,'" retorted Vlasto, with the lofty dignity that had ever won my grudging admiration. Pressing close to my bars, I could hear every word through the still air, and I thanked the luck that had made the original Prince Vlasto build those turrets broad and low instead of tapering.

"My country isn't accustomed to giving orders to kidnapers in any more polite form," snapped the officer. "I am instructed to demand that you deliver those four Americans over to me safe and unhurt, together with all their stolen belongings, within five minutes. Hurry, man! You've no time to waste."

Oh, it was delicious, this ordering about of the stately prince as though he were a cabin-boy!

But Vlasto made no move to obey.

"If I refuse?" he asked indifferently.

"If you refuse, the Arizona will steam opposite that opening there and bring her thirteen-inch guns to bear on your castle," was McKimmon's instant reply. "By night there will not be one stone of your building left standing on another. After which, a stronger force of marines will land, and—"

"I see no reason," commented Vlasto gravely, "why news of my refusal should ever reach your ship. You are my prisoner, officer. As for your handful of men outside, before they can reach the seashore—"

"As for my handful of men outside," interrupted the unperturbed lieutenant, "and as for myself, if we do not signal our ship by six o'clock this evening, the bombardment will commence at that hour. And," he added as an afterthought, "by the same time to-morrow morning you will be adorning the end of a rope from a limb of the nearest tree that will hold your weight. You say I'm your prisoner. Very good. I don't mind waiting. You have half an hour before six o'clock."

He seated himself on a stone block, and seemed to lose interest in his surroundings.

Vlasto's handsome face was a study. Immobile as it was, I, who knew the man, could read it. I knew the hereditary love Vlasto felt for the castle that so symbolized his own waning prestige and his family's mighty past.

I could see he was picturing the effects of futile resistance to this impudent transatlantic power—the battering down of his cherished ancestral home beneath the shells of those barbarous new-fangled guns; the ensuing rescue of his prisoners; the shame of having his tenants and vassals see in him a beaten, homeless, hopeless man; the hinted possibility of the last of the Vlastos meeting a low felon's fate at the end of a rope.

It was pathetic, this defeat of medievalism before the onset of hustling progress.

For defeat it was. After a minute of thought, Vlasto bowed with a haughty grace that held boundless superiority over his puny antagonist and that antagonist's whole commercial, up-to-date race.

He gave a curt order to Nikola. Then, with bent head, and hands clasped behind him, he walked into the castle alone, splendid in his proud submission to circumstance, superb in his disdain of the modern powers to which he was compelled by sheer lack of equal strength to yield.

Nikola, scowling and muttering curses, bustled into the building after him; and Lieutenant McKimmon, crossing one leg over the other, serenely sat and waited.

Ten minutes later we were outside the castle, riding triumphantly away down the road with a file of wooden-faced marines on either side, our luggage heaped high on the gun-carriage and rumbling along behind us, while McKimmon, sword in hand, strutted on in front of the procession.

Thus we marched in silence until that curve of the rocky road hid us from view of the castle. Then a strange transformation occurred.

One of the marines, utterly outraging all naval discipline, emitted a wild whoop of delight and fell upon McKimmon, hammering him enthusiastically on the back. At this demoralizing spectacle the lieutenant showed no sign of resentment, but grinned in appreciative reply.

"Well, Mr. James," asked he, "didn't I carry it off fine? I've a sort of sneakin' notion that a United States cruiser wouldn't quite have the right to smash holes in castles belongin' to a friendly power, or hang princes to trees, but your friend Mr. Vlasto don't seem to have studied up much on international law. Blest if I don't think I like bein' a naval lootenant even better'n my job as Mr. Clyde's sailin'-master!"

Jimmie, meanwhile, was paying little attention to this chuckling rhapsody. He had deserted the sailing-master, kissed his mother and sister, and was now pump-handling me in an ecstasy of glee.

"It worked like a charm!" he exclaimed. "I did it without a hitch. Got to the Piræus, took a boat out to the yacht, and put the whole job up to old Mac here. He was a trump. Rigged himself out in his dress uniform, and put twenty of the crew into their white parade ducks, and mounted the signal-gun on a donkey-engine truck. I wasn't going to be left out, so I borrowed a suit of ducks and spent most of the time, on the march, coaching Mac on his lines. Say, if I'd gone to the authorities they wouldn't have got the red tape untangled far enough to send word to Vlasto in a week. And by that time you'd—"

"Get in line again!" I exhorted. "There's a gap just beyond, and we'll be in view of the castle for a minute or so."

"By the way," Jimmie called over his shoulder, "there was one hitch, after all. We were half-way here before I remembered that every mother's son of us had the yacht's name on our caps. You'll find the letter-ribbons in a neat little pile under a rock farther on. Even Vlasto would hardly have swallowed the trick if—say, Graeme," he switched off in boyish appeal, "did I do all right? The idea was yours, but, for a kid, I worked it out to the queen's taste, didn't I?" Then he added, cut by the apathy of my response, "Why, man, you look as glum as if you were on your way to your own funeral. What—"

"I am," I said.

Then, to avert further inquiry, I went on:

"Just for the present the yacht will be safer quarters for all of you than Athens, especially if Vlasto happens to discover the trick. I advise you to go to the shore, signal for a boat, and get aboard as quickly as you can. To-morrow you'd better get your clearance papers and head for sea. You've probably all of you had enough of Greece for a while."

I turned in my saddle and looked back through the gap. There in the distance, pale against the flaming sunset sky, stood the gray castle. And on its battlements I made out a single dark figure, standing alone, hands clasped, head bowed, looking after us—Konstantin Vlasto, gazing his last on the woman he had loved, and whom neither by modern nor medieval methods he could win.

A turn in the twisting road shut him and his castle from our sight, and we moved downward, silently, to the sea.

The last of the boats ran up on the beach. Into one of them the crew were piling baggage; in the stern of another Mr. and Mrs. Clyde had already seated themselves. Jimmie stood by to help Elinor into a third before himself boarding it. Not once since we left the castle had she and I spoken to each other. I had not so much as dared to glance in her direction.

In the loneliness that was to come I wanted to remember those glorious eyes of hers as they had last looked into mine—abrim with love and deathless faith. That dear look, at least, I would lock in my heart for all eternity. I would not mar its memory by meeting the contempt that must now replace it.

There was a moment's pause, while the crews of the first two boats awaited orders to put off. Elinor, not comprehending the cause of the delay, asked, turning to me:

"Aren't we ready? Is anything left?"

"Nothing is left," I answered—"except—to say good-by."

"Good-by? To Greece?"

"To me—if you feel you can."

"You are not going aboard?" she asked in quick surprise.

"Surely," I answered with a mirthless laugh, "you did not expect I would carry my effrontery so far as that."

I raised my cap, not daring to look up, and, turning on my heel, started up the beach into the gathering night.

"Hello!" expostulated Jimmie, who had in nowise comprehended this brief scene. "What's up? *Nell!*" he went on in sudden remonstrance, "what are you doing?"

"I am going ashore," she replied calmly, and I heard the light fall of her feet as they touched the beach. I stopped, wondering, and looked back. But already she was at my side.

"What does this mean?" I faltered, wholly at a loss. "I don't understand. Aren't you—"

"Where you go, I go," she answered simply, slipping her hand through my arm. "I told you that the other night, sweetheart. Have you forgotten so soon?"

THE END

Appendix
Original source publication

This novel was serialized in four issues of *The Scrap Book*, the Second Section (that's important, for collectors) from February through May of 1908.

February 1908

Chapters I through III

Front text:

Author of "On Glory's Trail," "Their Last Hope," "The Scarlet Scarab," etc.

Wherein a Soldier of Fortune, at an Ebb in the Tide of Affairs, Confronts a Startling Dilemma of Love and Revenge.

March 1908

Chapters IV through VII

Front text:

Author of "On Glory's Trail," "Their Last Hope," "The Scarlet Scarab," etc.

SYNOPSIS OF PRECEDING CHAPTERS.

BRUCE GRAEME, American soldier of fortune, meets in Athens, James, son of the American millionaire, Barzillah Clyde, who has been largely responsible for the ruin and death of Graeme's father. After a quarrel at cards, the two young men become fast friends. The German Emperor is to arrive in Athens that night. In the crowded streets Graeme rescues from an insulting ruffian a girl who proves to be Elinor, James's sister. He also encounters Gorgias Padapoulos, a mountain outlaw, who dreams of kidnaping either the emperor or Mr. Clyde. Graeme becomes intimate with the Clydes, as does also an aristocrat, Prince Vlasto, his rival in attentions to Elinor. Mr. Clyde wishes to make an expedition into the mountains and asks Graeme if it is safe. The latter, slighted by Elinor, and with an idea of vengeance, says yes, and agrees to guide the party. Thereupon he rides out to the foothills of Hymettus to the camp of Padapoulos.

* This story began in THE SCRAP BOOK—Second Section—for February, 1908.

April 1908

Chapters VII through IX
Front text:
Author of "On Glory's Trail," "Their Last Hope," "The Scarlet Scarab," etc.
SYNOPSIS OF PRECEDING CHAPTERS.
BRUCE GRAEME, an American soldier of fortune, meets in Athens "Jimmy" Clyde, son of the American millionaire, Barzillah Clyde, who has been largely responsible for the ruin and death of Graeme's father. The two young men become fast friends. After rescuing from an insulting ruffian a girl who proves to be Elinor Clyde, Jimmy's sister, Graeme becomes intimate with the Clydes, and soon finds himself, much to his own surprise, in love with Elinor. He makes an appointment with her for ten o'clock one morning, and on going to keep it is told that she has gone riding with Prince Vlasto, a Greek aristocrat, who is his rival. Furious at the slight, he is stung into carrying out at once a plan for vengeance on Barzillah Clyde. After promising to guide the Clydes on an expedition in the mountains, he rides to the camp of a brigand, Gorgias Padapoulos, with whom he bargains to effect Barzillah's capture for a third of the ransom. The signal for the attack is to be a red handkerchief tied upon a certain blasted tree.

Graeme quarrels with Vlasto, whom he forces into a humiliating scene with Elinor, and Vlasto, in rage, withdraws to his mountain castle. On the first night of the camping trip, the Clydes stop, at Graeme's suggestion, on a little plateau beneath the blasted tree. As Graeme is waiting for the camp to fall asleep that he may go and put up his signal, Elinor comes toward him out of her tent.

* This story began in THE SCRAP BOOK—Second Section—for February, 1908.

May 1908
Chapters X through XII
Front text:
Author of "On Glory's Trail," "Their Last Hope," "The Scarlet Scarab," etc.

* This story began in THE SCRAP BOOK—Second Section—for February, 1908.

**Turn this book over for another complete novel
by Albert Payson Terhune!**

www.ingramcontent.com/pod-product-compliance
Lightning Source LLC
Chambersburg PA
CBHW070930190726
48292CB00004B/1179

As the Dice Fell

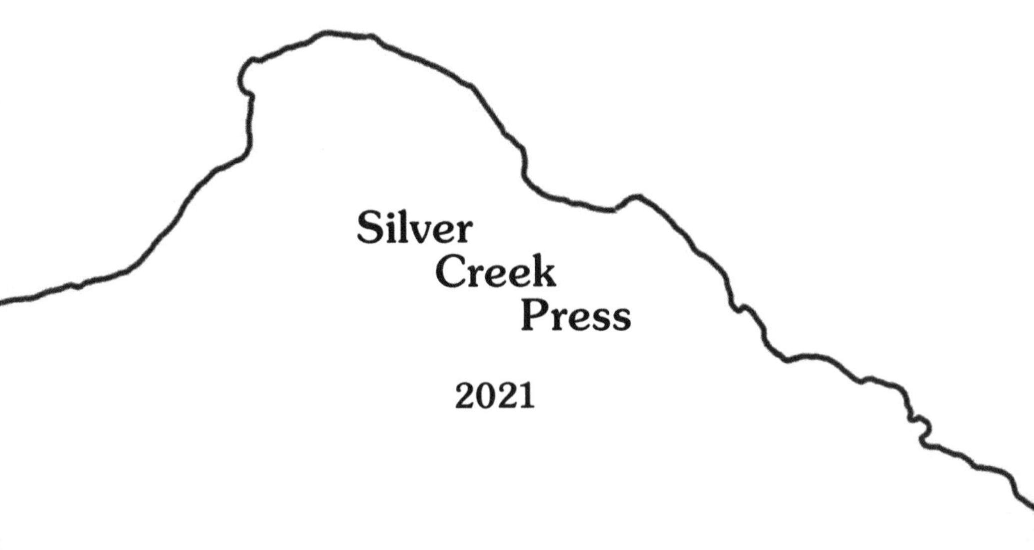

Albert Payson Terhune

SCP Tête-bêche
Book III

Silver
Creek
Press

2021

CHAPTER I.
I Fall In With Trouble.

I GLOWERED on him with a look that has often been imposed upon more warlike men than he, but he withstood my glare, and replied to it with something very like a grin.

"Master Gordon Clyde," quoth he, "the tale you have told me savors overmuch of the stage play for truth. Wherefore I made bold to laugh. And your scowl rebukes me right properly. Yet I meant no offense."

"No?" I snarled. "In other words, you call me liar and then vow you meant no ill. England may have changed much since I left it for the Italian wars, but I have not changed. So I beseech you to lead the way to the nearest bit of ground that will afford elbow room for sword-play."

"Is this a challenge?" he scoffed.

"'Tis the sequel among all men of honor when lie hath been passed," retorted I.

Again he laughed, lounging back on the ale-house settle and looking up at me in unfeigned amusement.

"Heigho!" he said. "Here be I, Sir Geoffrey Whitson, privy councilor to His Most Christian Majesty King James, and on my way to be lord chancellor of all England. And here be you, Gordon Clyde, down-at-heels soldier of fortune, defying me to mortal combat. I have all to lose and naught to gain. You have naught to lose and the rope to gain for breaking the king's edict against dueling. The fight you press upon me is no fair one. 'Tis as though I staked a gold guinea against a chipped penny."

"You will not fight me?" I asked.

"I assuredly will not," he yawned, making as though to rise.

"One moment!" I begged him humbly. "I arrived but to-day in

London, penniless. The clothes I stand in, my sword, and my honor are all I own on earth. I had thought I was richer. I—"

"If the gift of a handful of guineas—" began Whitson in lazy contempt, as he reached for his purse; but I stayed him with a gesture.

"I had thought I was richer by one friend," I resumed. "When I accosted you on Fleet Street here, a half-hour agone, it was with real joy, that chance had thrown me into contact again with an old school friend. And I bade you into this tavern that we might quaff a cup of ale for old days' sake. 'Twas not in the hope of bettering my fortunes. Yet, when you asked of my adventures in the foreign wars, and when I made bold to relate to you one of the simpler of them, you laughed at me as at a buffoon. You have doubted my word. You have from the first, to-day, treated me as though I were some drunken rustic clown and you a court noble. And now—"

"And now," he yawned, "I weary of the clown's antics, and wish to be seen no longer in the company of a disreputable swashbuckler. And so, good day."

As he rose I picked up the tankard of ale at my hand and tossed its foamy contents in his face.

Down over his curled and perfumed hair cascaded the torrent of ale. Yes, and down over his smoke-gray velvet mantle, with its shell-pink satin lining, and over his rich doublet and his slashed hose.

The fellow was no coward. Now that his scornful superiority was washed away by a cataract of bitter ale, he was quite another man.

Gouging the stinging liquid from out his eyes with one silk gloved hand, he whipped out his rapier with the other and rushed, bellowing, at me like a mad bull. I awaited his onset. Then, with a sharp twist of mine own blade I sent his jeweled rapier flying across the room.

Sheathing my sword I caught Whitson by the ruffled nape of his neck, propelled him gently to the door, and thrust him out into the mud-filled gutter, where, losing his balance, he sprawled full length, to the further detriment of his court clothes.

Swiftly he scrambled to his feet, meanwhile bawling:

"Watch, ho!"

And as swiftly a man who had sat smoking a long pipe in a far corner of the taproom leaped forward, flung an arm about me, dragged me back across the room again and out into another alley by

a rear door.

I struggled, but he cried earnestly:

"Run, man! Time enough later to argue. And better to do thy arguing under heaven's clear stars than in the bridewell."

As he spoke the man was ever dragging me along with him down the twilit by-street. He was stout, partly bald, far older than I, and scarce half as strong.

Yet, somehow I suffered myself to be carried along by his very earnestness and vehement fear for my welfare. It is sometimes so, when a man of strong purpose takes sudden control of a situation. Yet, by the time we had traversed a few hundred yards, mine own spirit asserted itself.

"Wait!" I ordered, "I will go no farther. Who are you that you should haul me hither and yon as though I were a prize bullock at a fair?"

Before he answered he paused, listening.

"'Tis safe enough!" he muttered. "We have thrown them off. They will have gone the other way."

"Thrown *whom* off?" I demanded.

"The city watch," he answered, "and such stray denizens of the Fleet Street taverns as may have cared to curry favor with a king's councilor by joining the hue and cry after you."

"After *me*? For what, pray? I did but resent a black insult. And I did it monstrous gently, I think."

"Now, Heaven save us from you in your ruder hours," he said in mock solemnity, "if that be a sample of your gentleness. Listen, sir," he went on more gravely. "If I understood aright from such scraps of your talk with Sir Geoffrey Whitson as chanced to drift to my corner of the room, you are but new returned from the Italian wars?"

"Yes," I made answer. "After eight years of campaigning."

"You left England then," said he, "during Queen Elizabeth's blessed reign? A reign when bold fellows were rewarded, not driven to cringe or starve."

"Have times so changed, then?"

"James sits now on England's throne, as you know. A strong man who swoons at sight of a naked sword and who turns his face away and trembles whenever he must hold blade in hand to administer the

accolade to a new knight."

"A king who fears bright steel?" I exclaimed. "And he the son of Mary Queen of Scots!"

"'Tis true. He hates sword-play and soldierships. About him he gathers a few court favorites who feign to hate brawling as much as he, and who cajole and trick him into doing their will in well-nigh all things. The chief of these same favorites is Sir Geoffrey Whitson."

"So? He had ever an eye to his own advancement, even at school."

"And," pursued the stranger, "when he tells the king that you have drawn sword upon him, this England of yours will be too hot to hold you."

"What then," I asked, "of the man who has just saved me—an utter stranger?"

The fellow shrugged his shoulders.

"I have no great love for the court of to-day, nor its courtiers," said he, "and—to be frank with you—I acted also through selfishness. For I was minded to put to you a few questions if you would have the patience and courtesy to reply to them."

I glanced at him in open curiosity. He was stout, as I have said; of full middle age, and clad plainly yet richly in black velvet. I should have taken him for a merchant but for the aspect of his face.

This was no smug merchant's visage, with its domelike forehead and deep, unfathomable eyes, and the myriad thought-lines that crossed and recrossed the calm, florid countenance.

What object could such a man have in rescuing from the noose an obscure adventurer and claiming the privilege of questioning him? What questions could he have to put to me—and why?

For an instant I glanced apprehensively at the black-clad figure moving along beside me in the twilight. For I minded me of a stage-play I had seen by Marlowe (a tavern brawler and a shrewd scrivener withal) called "Dr. Faustus." A play wherein the evil one tempts one Faustus to sell his soul.

It was well understood at that time—1606—that such things were quite possible; though nowadays folk are beginning to laugh at such fantastic beliefs. (In another century or so, mayhap, folk

will also laugh at witchcraft and at "demoniac possession.")

Yet I shook off the momentary dread. This man's face was as benevolent as it was wise.

"I will gladly answer," I said at last, "what knowledge of mine can serve you?"

CHAPTER II.
I Behold a Strange Monster.

"FIRST," began the stranger, "would you sate my curiosity as to the scene yonder in the tap-room? I heard but part."

" 'Tis simple," said I. "In early days Whitson and I knew each other at school. When he would have been expelled, and perchance jailed for an offense there, I came to his rescue. Later 'twas my sword that saved him from death in a street brawl. So when I met him to-day I thought to find a welcome. He treated me like a dog and—"

"And you paid off the score with usury," my companion laughed. "Man, your temper is peppery."

"When gold is low, honor must run high to make up for it," said I. "Indeed, 'tis for that same cause I find myself here tonight."

"An affair of honor carried you across seas?"

"Why, yes. One that sounds silly enough, I doubt me, in the telling. 'Twas in the Hungary wars a year agone that I met a soldier of fortune like myself. One Forgeron by name. I volunteered for service to enter the enemy's city by night and bear away certain information of use to our general. Ere I could go this Forgeron undertakes the mission. He succeeded and returns to camp, covered with a glory that should have been mine. I was laughed at for a laggard.

"I challenged him. We fought. At the first assault my sword broke at the hilt. I clamored that he either kill me or else wait till I could procure another blade. He said he had no more time to waste in foolish squabbling. And he rode away, leaving me once more a laughing-stock of the whole camp. A month agone I had sure news that he had sailed for England."

"And," broke in the stranger, wonderingly, "you threw over

employment and hope of high reputation in the foreign wars—all to hunt down a man you fancied had affronted you?"

"What better object could I have had?" I asked. "Employment is easily found again wherever sharp swords are playing. And reputation is but a bubble at best. But honor is another thing. I came to England to seek mine enemy. And I shall find him, never fear."

We had reached the Strand—as the ill-paved waterside avenue was called, whose mansions and lawns sloped down to the Thames. Beyond us lay the meaner "seafaring quarters," where sailormen foregathered. And thither we were moving. A thought struck me.

"It was surely not to learn my sordid little story," I queried, "that you risked your own freedom by helping me out of yon mess at the ale-house? What are the questions by whose answer I am to help pay for my deliverance?"

He hesitated. Then he said, apologetically:

"I chanced, as I told you, to hear fragments of your talk with Whitson. If I mistake not, you spoke of having wandered in far lands. In lands farther afield than the continent of Europe."

"Why, yes," I made answer. "I roved the sea for a time in a privateer and then in a merchant ship. I touched at Africa and once I sailed even to within a few score leagues of the Americas."

"Passed you the Bermudas?" he asked.

"Aye, and vexed waters they are that surround those isles."

"Is it true," he inquired, "as some do say, that spirits rule those waters, and that monsters do inhabit the Bermudas?"

"As to that," I returned, "I cannot say. Yet I have heard such tales, even though I saw no signs of life there. But the Bermuda waters can scarce be so vexed, I should say, except by spirits."

"And Africa?" he asked eagerly. "Saw you the fabled crocodile while you were there?"

"Several of them," said I, "on the mud banks of the river Nile."

"Then there are really such creatures. And is it true they weep like babes in order to draw compassionate folk near enough to be slain by the creatures?"

"I have heard tell so. It is told as fact among the Egyptians. But I confess I saw no such case."

"And in Africa," he pursued, "saw you or heard you of the strange

people whose heads do grow beneath their shoulders? Saw you the anthropophagi, the men that eat each other? Men say the hills in Africa be so tall they touch the heavens. I would fain know the truth of these things and of others like them that I have heard."

"And these," I marveled, "are the idle questions you wished to ask. Perchance you, too, seek to make me the butt of your laughter by drawing me on to tell travelers' tales?"

"No, no!" he protested.

"Because," I went on, "Whitson burst into great guffaws of laughter when I but told him I had seen, near the city of Naples, a mountain that did belch forth fire and smoke from its open crest like an oven. He vowed 'twas not possible. Yet I myself saw it. And when I protested 'twas so, he but laughed the louder."

"I have lived too long," said the stranger, "to be unbelieving of any marvel that this world can produce. Nor is laughter the argument of any save a fool. I do but ask concerning these marvels that when some fool mention of them occur in my plays, and who hears shall laugh, I may tell him what I say is true."

"Your plays?" I echoed." You speak of stage plays?"

"What else? I have in mind a play of a man who goeth to the Bermudas and there is able to rule the spirits to his will. And I have writ another wherein a blackamoor shall tell of his wild exploits by flood and field and mid the monsters of far Africa. I—"

"A man of your substance," I exclaimed, "to waste his days in petty scribbling? What wealth or fame can such trifling bring? Who honors a scrawler of idle tales and such like trash?"

I spoke in genuine scorn—the scorn of the man of action for the man of thought. But he answered me as though too great to feel my foolish contempt.

"Each man to his own. And the hero may at times stand in need of the scribbler. Just as Gordon Clyde, gallant soldier of fortune, just now deigned to accept help from Will Shakespeare, simple scrawler of plays. And if—"

But I heard no more. With a yell I had sprung from his side. And, sword drawn, I was rushing madly down the darkening street.

We had been nearing the seafaring quarter, where waterside taverns and huts crowd along the wharfs of the Thames, and where ride

at moorings the tall ships that ply from London to far ports.

As the stranger and I had strolled along, nearing this section, I had noted several men who turned in, one after another, at the door of a house somewhat larger than its squalid neighbors.

A lighted lanthorn hung above the door. By its glow, I had idly noted a thickset figure that had to me a vaguely familiar air, the figure of a man who was mounting the two low steps that led to the entrance.

As this man passed through the doorway the lanthorn-light touched his face. It was then that I had shouted and dashed forward. For the face, half disclosed in the flare, was the face of mine enemy.

It was Forgeron, who had bested and flouted me in the foreign wars, and from whom I had never yet been able to wring the satisfaction which should draw the rankling thorn from mine honor.

And now here he was, scarce a hundred feet away, this man I had crossed the Channel to find.

I had expected a long and tedious search for him. I had found him almost at once and by sheer chance. Wherefore, with drawn blade, I rushed toward the house into which he had vanished.

In a few seconds I had cleared the intervening space, well-nigh falling headlong more than once over cobbles and rubbish-heaps, and so gained the house.

Up the two steps I sprang at a bound. Still gripping my sword, I pushed open the door, which yielded readily enough to the pressure of my shoulder and swung shut behind me.

I found myself in a long passageway, at whose farther end was another closed door. From under this door flowed a stream of light, and behind the closed panels came the sound of many voices. The passageway itself was dimly lit by a lanthorn that swung from the raftered ceiling.

Now, I had for years lived and fought in hostile lands where my quick wits and quicker sword-blade alone stood between me and death. I had learned to dodge a trap as cleverly as can any wild animal. And if ever man was rushing into a trap, it was I at that very moment.

Here was I, alone, friendless, helpless, save for my sword. And I was pushing my way into a strange house in a rough quarter of London in pursuit of a man who, from his apparent familiarity with the place, was well at home there and was among friends.

8

In that day it was no safe thing at best to venture into unknown parts of London after nightfall. And in the case of armed intruders into a house the inmates were apt to kill first and to ask questions afterward.

Had I been in my senses I should have heeded all this, and should have kept clear of a mess that was to alter my whole future.

But what angry man is in his full senses? And the sight of mine enemy had fanned my rage to white-heat.

Into the house I burst. Now, down the passageway I was striding toward that farther door with the light and the many voices behind it.

On I went at top speed. Then, half-way down the passageway, I halted as though a cannon-ball had struck my chest.

There I stood, shaking, my mouth open, my gaze fixed, the sword dangling inert in my loosening grip. For the very first time in all my thirty-five years I was afraid.

Yes. *Afraid!*

For from the shadows of the passageway, where it had been crouching, arose a terrible thing.

It was a monster—a demon. Such a being as I had heard tell of in old wives' tales, but infinitely more horrible than the most daring imagination had ever conceived.

I had heard and I had read about demons; but up to then I had secretly doubted that such things existed. Now I knew.

Slowly from its crouching position on a floor-mat in the passage-way arose the thing. How shall I describe it as it appeared before me there in the half light?

It was half naked. Its body was of a coppery brown, and was painted with weird designs in red and blue and yellow.

Such few garments as it wore were of fantastically beaded and fringed wild-beast skins. Growing from the crown of its otherwise shaven head was a tuft of nodding feathers. Its eyes gleamed wickedly through the gloom. In one brown claw it gripped a decorated hatchet, which it raised with a slow, majestic movement, as if to bar my progress.

And I, not ten minutes agone, had been telling Will Shakespeare that I had never actually seen any of the spirits or fiends that were then supposed to people the waste places of the earth.

I stared blankly at the thing, my knees almost knocking together. For a full half-minute we stood thus, we two, in the gloom of the passageway. And the more I stared, the more unearthly the creature seemed. It was like a figment of some fever-dream.

Little by little my amazement permitted me to grasp certain details in its appearance. I saw it was shaped like a man, slender and wiry, yet powerful—yet unbelievingly tall. I myself stand well over six feet in height. Yet this apparition was a full head taller than I.

The features, too, were human, though cast in a mold I had never before seen. The cheek-bones were high, the nose aquiline, the lips thin. And the coppery cheeks were horribly painted in vivid colors, as were the forehead and chin.

My courage returned to me at last, as it ever does in moments of peril. I was confronted by a monster from the pit. Was I to turn and run—as I might long to do—and ever afterward be ashamed of myself? Or was I to risk certain death and keep mine honor intact by assailing the supernatural thing?

There was but one course open to me. Nerving myself and tightening my grasp upon my sword, I charged upon the creature. Yet I would rather have charged single-handed against a battery of artillery.

CHAPTER III.
I Meet Mine Enemy.

DOWN the passageway toward the monster I forced myself, blade uplifted. The creature, reading my intent, whirled his gaudy hatchet aloft. In another instant we would clash.

I fell to wondering, even in that tiny space of time, whether the coppery hue of his polished skin meant that he was made wholly of some metal? I had heard of such beings.

Should my first sword-thrust prove his body to be metal, I resolved to cast myself upon him barehanded and seek to wrench apart his copper joints.

Then, even as I sprang, and as he brandished his hatchet, the rear door at the end of the passage was thrown open. A blaze of light from

the room beyond struck through the dimness, and for the moment well-nigh blinded me.

I halted and drew back a pace, lest the monster should take advantage of the dazzling light in my face to attack me unprepared.

A man came out of the farther room into the passage. At sight of our belligerent figures he leaped nimbly between us, his hand on his sword-hilt.

"What is this, Aquia?" he rasped, wheeling on the monster.

Then, turning toward me, he went on sternly:

"Who are you? And what mean you by drawing blade on my servant?"

"I—I came hither," said I, still blinking uncertainly in the strong light, "to seek a man whom I saw enter this house. As I crossed the passage I beheld that demon."

"This *what?*" queried the man, puzzled.

"This fiend from the pit," quoth I. "He rose from the ground before me, and I—"

A laugh from the man interrupted me.

"A 'fiend,' eh?" he guffawed. "Why, 'tis my servant Aquia."

"You are a sorcerer, then," I asked, "that you make demons serve you? If—"

" 'Demons'?" he mocked. "Saw ye never a red Indian before? Scores of them have visited London in the past few years."

"Red Indian?" I babbled. "From the Americas?"

"From where else, man? This one came to England as servant to Sir Walter Raleigh, a traveler and courtier, of whom perchance you have heard. When Raleigh was thrown into prison Aquia took service with me."

I frowned in disgust. No man loves to play the fool. And the thought that I had been fear-stricken for the first time in my life at sight of a mere savage filled me with self-contempt.

"I came hither," said I stiffly, changing the topic, "to seek a man whom I saw enter—"

"So you said," answered the other. "If he be in this house, he is one of the gathering in yonder room. Shall I call him forth, or will you go in?"

"I will go in by your permission," I answered.

My old hatred for mine enemy flared up again, now that the momentary fear of the copper-colored apparition was stilled. For a full year I had sought Forgeron. And now he was in the room just ahead of me.

Brushing past the man who had accosted me, and whose figure—silhouetted black against the light from the doorway—still blocked the passage, I strode forward across the farther threshold.

I found myself at the entrance of a great, low-ceiled room that contained perhaps thirty persons, chiefly men. They were seated for the most part about tables, puffing at long pipes and with ale-mugs in front of them. In one corner was piled a mountain of portmanteaus and bundles.

'Twas the gathering of a ship-load of sea-passengers on the eve of sailing. They had doubtless come together at this place in order to go aboard a near-by ship as quickly as the tide should serve for departure.

But what struck me as strange in the group was the fact that they were by no means the sort of folk one would expect to see gathered for emigration. There were few—almost none—of the hardy, rugged tradesman or farmer or mechanic class that go aboard for such voyages.

Some of the men were gaily pranked out in tottered finery and wore long swords. Some were in rags, and had the faces and bearing of cheap criminals. Others were palpably "broken" fellows who had served long as Fate's useless playthings.

In one corner sat an elderly, plainly dressed man of strong countenance. Beside him, clad in a long cloak, whose hood half hid her face, sat a girl who, from her general likeness to him, seemed his daughter. These two held aloof from the noisy crowd of their fellow voyagers.

The girl was pretty. I noted little else about her at the time. For my eyes were busy seeking out mine enemy. From face to face I peered through the blue tobacco-clouds. But I could see no one who bore the slightest resemblance to Forgeron. Clearly he was not here. And I grew sick with disappointment. Well, if he were not in this room, he was doubtless elsewhere in the house. I would search, and wherever he might be hiding I would have him forth.

I turned on my heel to leave. There in the doorway stood the man

who had admitted me—the man who owned the red Indian as a servant. But now, instead of being blackly silhouetted and unrecognized, he stood in the lamplight's full glare.

And I knew him. It was Forgeron, mine enemy.

"Forgeron!" I shouted, drawing sword. "You remember me? This time our quarrel can be settled once and for all."

In his stern yet twinkling little eyes I saw perfect recognition. Indeed, I think he had recognized me at that first glimpse in the passageway. Yet he made no movement either to defend himself or escape. Instead, he stood with folded arms, calmly and amusedly surveying me.

Let me draw his picture for you in a mere thimbleful of words. For he was a man whose mark shall rest on history so long as his story shall endure.

He was of middle height, perhaps twenty-eight or thirty years old, thick-set and of enormous strength. His forehead was high and broad, though tanned brown by the weather. His brows were beetling and bushy above the sharp, fierce eyes.

A great sweeping mustache, worn French fashion, covered his firm, thick-lipped mouth. A monstrous bristling beard hid his lower face and jutted forth like a courtier's ruff.

There was about him, moreover, the indefinable air that bespeaks the born leader of men, and a certain boarlike truculence that seemed ever to be warring with a desire for laughter.

As I have told you, Forgeron made no move either to meet or to elude my attack. He stood unmoved, eying me with a quizzical half smile.

"You remember me?" I repeated furiously, standing ready to plunge into the combat on the very instant his sword should be out of its scabbard.

"I remember you well," he replied in that great harsh voice I now so well recalled. "You are Gordon Clyde, a gallant soldier of fortune, whom I would far rather enroll as a friend and a comrade than as a foe. It was for that reason I would not resume our duel in Hungary."

"You have no choice now," I cried. "Will you fight, man, or shall I strike you across the face with the flat of my sword, here in the presence of your own associates? Which shall it he, M. Forgeron?"

13

"My name is not 'Forgeron,'" he answered, as though patiently correcting a stupid child. "Nor am I *monsieur.* I am an Englishman, like your somewhat peppery self. 'Twas but for a *nom de guerre* that on the Continent I translated my British name into its French equivalent. Know you not what 'Forgeron' means? 'Tis the French word for 'Smith.' And I am Captain John Smith—all at your service. I—"

"It matters not who you are," I retorted, in no wise interested in his explanation. "You are the man who made me the laughing-stock of the Hungary camp. And for that you shall pay. Will you fight or—"

"Oh, I will fight!" he assented wearily. "But I would far liefer be your friend. If an apology will serve— No? Then be it as you wish."

He still made no effort to draw sword, and I waxed doubly impatient. The bulk of the emigrants had flocked close about us, eager to witness the fray.

"You challenge me, I understand?" remarked the immovable Smith.

"I assuredly do," I flashed. "Draw, man!"

"By the laws of the *duello,*" he resumed with the same imperturbable calm, "the challenged man has choice of weapons and of all other arrangements for the combat."

"I grant that," I fumed. "But to soldiers what possible weapon is there except the sword? And what time or place can be more suitable than this? The light is good; the floor smooth. Nevertheless, if you prefer other weapons and other arrangements, name them. I pledge myself to abide by them. All I demand is to fight you and to clear mine honor."

"I claim the privilege of the challenged party," said he gravely, "and I hold you to your pledge. Will you hear the terms?"

I nodded assent, still full of fury, yet puzzled by his odd calmness.

"At daybreak," said Smith, "I and these people set sail for the Americas—for Virginia."

"If you survive the duel," I corrected grimly.

"I shall survive," he replied. "It is a way I have. We sail with others—one hundred and five souls in all. Virginia is a tract of wilderness that stretches from the Atlantic to the Pacific oceans. No man knows just how far that may be. And it stretches from the French colony in New France—or Canada, as men now call it—to Spain's province of Flor-

ida. A goodly land and large withal."

"I am here to fight," I snapped. "Not to con a lesson in geography. What—"

"In a moment," he urged. "We purpose to sail thither in three tall ships, there to found a colony where Sir Walter Raleigh and the rest failed to establish one. We—"

"I care not what you propose," I interrupted. "The terms of the duel, man! Get to them!"

"I am getting to them," he answered. "On the table yonder is a dice-box. That dice in that box shall be our weapons."

"What jest is this?"

"No jest. Hear me out. The dice shall be our weapons and—"

"I understand!" I cried. "I recall, now, that I once heard of the custom, in Italy. The two foes throw dice. The loser is pledged to stab himself to the heart. Let it be as you say. Though I shall have preferred the joy of actual battle."

"You go too fast," Smith corrected me, as a little buzz of wonder ran through the group at my words. "I had not come yet to the terms of the duel. Merely to the weapons. We shall throw dice, you and I. Should I lose, you shall have the privilege of carrying out your threat and shall strike me across the face, here in the presence of all my following. To receive such a blow, unresented, will disgrace me forever. Are you content?"

In a thrice I saw how much keener than death would be the humiliation I might thus cause mine enemy. And my heart glowed.

"I am content!" I exclaimed. "And if I lose?"

"If you lose," he drawled, "I shall not strike you, but you shall hold yourself pledged to cross the seas as one of our company. Is it agreed?"

"I have no wish to go to that barbarous land!" I protested.

"And I," he retorted, "have no wish to be stricken across the face and thus forever degraded before my people. Yet—"

"Have done!" I broke in. "I accept! The chance of avenging mine honor on you is too strong to be missed."

The dice-box was brought. Smith and I seated ourselves at opposite sides of the table. The rest crowded eagerly about.

And our strange duel began. A duel which was to affect the future of a whole continent.

CHAPTER IV.
A Strange Duel.

IT was an odd scene. The low, crowded room, with its smoky ceiling and flaring lamps; the blue reek of tobacco; the tense, excited faces of the adventurers who pressed close about the board.

Smith and I, seated opposite each other, were outwardly the calmest men in the place. Our faces showed no sign of our inward thrill. Yet, each in his way, had as much as life itself at stake.

Smith was evidently the master of this odd assortment of voyagers. And, from my own knowledge of men, I foresaw how utterly he would lose his hold over the nondescript adventurers if once it were known that he had meekly consented to receive a blow in the face.

For, in those rough days, an unresented blow was a lasting and irredeemable disgrace to its bearer; no matter what the occasion of its receiving. Such a victim was forever looked down on and scoffed at by his fellows.

Oh, I had been wise when I had consented to stake all upon that form of vengeance against mine enemy!

On the other hand, my own case, in the event of my losing, would be little better. I was but thirty-five; of splendid strength and health; a veteran soldier who could always find fat employment whenever hard knocks were given and taken.

Many a soldier of fortune, not so well equipped, had risen to the very steps of thrones, or had, with their keen swords, carved fortunes and high rank upon destiny's tablets.

And now, I stood in peril of throwing away all these golden chances and of burying myself in that Virginian wilderness for life. A luring death, forsooth, and one for which I had scant desire.

I had ever a scorn for men who were content to turn their backs on home and kindred and to start colonies in heathen lands. Such a man, for instance, was that same Sir Walter Raleigh. He left career and court and spent the best days of his life trying to make savage Virginia an English colony.

He had explored it, taken possession of it in England's name, and had called it "Virginia" in honor of England's virgin queen, Elizabeth.

Yet his colonies had failed. And one of them—that at Roanoke—had even vanished from mortal knowledge as completely as though the earth had swallowed it.

And now Smith, it seemed, was not only a leader in one of these same crazy colony-schemes, but was angling to hook me into it. Small wonder I dreaded the outcome of our strange duel!

I seized the horn dice-box, rattled it sharply, and made my first cast.

The two yellowed ivory dice struck the table's hard surface with a double click like the cocking of a musket. They bounded and rolled along like a couple of live things. Then, they suddenly settled. And I read the numbers scored on the upturned planes of the cubes.

Two!

The lowest cast possible; a cast that gamesters make barely once in a hundred throws. Such was the luck that dogged me that night.

My foe could not throw a lower number. The odds were more than one hundred to one that he would throw a higher.

Already I seemed to feel myself aboard the west-bound ship. Through my disgruntlement there was but one gleam of consolation.

I remembered, all at once, what Will Shakespeare had told me of Whitson's influence with King James, and his prophecy that, after my assault on the courtier, England would be too hot to hold me.

Nevertheless I could have wished to go back to the Continent, where men were more or less civilized, even the worst of them; and where at least they did not wear feathers on their heads and have painted copper skins.

Smith picked up the dice, dropped them in the box, shook it and let the cubes fall lightly on the table.

Five!

Well, I was beaten in the first throw, but there remained two throws more. And, as ever, when the odds are against me, my fighting spirit rose to meet the crisis.

Smith courteously gathered up the dice again, put them in the box, and passed the box across the table to me.

I took it, with a nod of acknowledgment.

The chances of victory were now two to one against me. Yet I was cooler and less excited than at any time that day.

I rattled the dice and cast them.

Twelve!

Two sixes. The "Venus Cast," as an Italian scrivener once told me the ancients used to call it. The highest cast possible.

I permitted myself a smiling glance at Captain John Smith. He was as imperturbable as ever, and even seemed to be weary of the whole proceedings. I envied him his splendid self-control. Not to be outdone in calmness, I passed in the act of watching him prepare to throw, and stifled an imaginary yawn behind my hand.

Smith threw the dice as gently as before. I glanced carelessly at them, as though not one whit interested.

Nine!

I had won the second throw. We were even, mine enemy and I. We could start abreast on the final cast.

"Captain," I urged, arresting his hand as he made to offer me the dice-box, "we stand equal now on this. Therefore, I may speak as I could not when chances were against me. I have no wish to go to the Americas and there toil like a black slave in building a colony. Nor, I take it, do you desire a blow across the face. Let us have done with this silly gaming and turn to man's work. I have humored you by throwing dice for a fearful stake. Humor me, now, I pray, by meeting me hand to hand, sword to sword, foot to foot, in such combat as becomes brave men."

Smith raised his bushy brows in mild wonder.

"Since when," he asked coldly, "have 'brave men' begged off from the terms of *duello,* as they have already agreed to? Are you a coward?"

I leaned back in my chair and stared moodily across at him.

"I hate you," I said quietly, "and I want to meet you sword to sword, and quench that hatred in your blood; not to shake dice with you like a boon companion."

"You prefer your own game," he sneered, "and you fear mine. Are you really a coward?"

"You have twice asked me that vile question," I made answer, "and I have endured the insult for the hatred I bear you, and for the hope of forcing you to fight me. Once for all, you refuse to offer me the satisfaction I crave?"

By way of reply he shoved the dice-box toward me across the

board. I caught it up savagely.

"The blow across your ugly face," I snarled, "shall be one you will carry to the grave."

"Your position in the Virginia colony," he retorted with a cold smile, "shall perchance be scarce more enviable than that same grave. Throw, I beg. Unless you really fear to."

Down I cast the dice. One of them fell on the table almost directly beneath the box, and lay there. It was a six.

The other ivory cube bounded and rolled along the expanse of the table until I thought it would never come to a stop. To my overexcited nerves it seemed to be rolling foolishly along for an eternity.

On the very edge of the table, balancing almost half-way over, it halted in its flight. And I saw it was a six!

Twice in succession had I thrown twelve. It was a cast that could not be beaten, and could scarce hope to be matched. I had won! And the wave of relief that swept over my body showed me for the first time how keyed up I had been.

The cube, I say, hung balanced on the verge of the table-edge. And ere I could reach forth to pick it up, some one in the crowd that pressed so close about us, chanced to strike a knee or elbow against the table. The jar, tiny as it was, sufficed to knock the cube off onto the floor.

Now, by every rule of gaming, in that day, if one or more of the dice should fall from the board before being picked up, after a cast, the throw was declared void.

All present knew this, even as did I. Indeed, the cube's hazardous position on the table-edge had led to my swift effort to seize it ere it could fall. But I had been a fraction of an instant too late.

"A false cast," commented Smith indifferently, as he stooped to pick up the cube and to restore it to the table. "The luck is against you. You would have scored twelve—two sixes. By the rules you lose your turn, and the next cast is mine."

As he spoke he had let both dice drop into the box, and was tranquilly swaying the latter to and fro. Now he rolled forth the cubes onto the table, with a scarce perceptible motion of his wrist.

They lay almost as they fell, so slight was their momentum. I breathed freely once more as I glanced at them.

A three and a one—*four!*

A simple throw to beat. In fact, the chances were more than four to one in favor of my besting or equaling him.

It was with ease not wholly affected that I gathered up the fateful little dice and boxed them for my final cast.

Down they tumbled onto the board. And my heart turned sick within me.

Three!

A two and a one! With every chance in my favor I had achieved the improbable.

I sat back, letting the empty dice-box fall to the table. Then, in a moment, I was on my feet, master of myself once more, ready to submit to my fate.

"You have won, sir," I said steadily, bowing to Smith as I spoke. "I will go to the Americas with you. But there was naught in my pledge that should force me to be civil or obedient to you, or to forgive you the scurvy trick you have played on me. I wish you joy of the firebrand you have won for your colony."

CHAPTER V.

Captain John Smith—and Another.

CAPTAIN JOHN SMITH leaned back with a great, noisy sigh, as of a man who throws aside an irksome rôle, or who sets down a heavy burden.

"Faith," he cried, "'twas a tough won victory enow! And never have I so long kept cool my temper under such trying occasion. I was mightily tempted, man, to take you at your word and to try conclusions with you, sword to sword."

"Then," I demanded crossly, "why did you not do so?"

"Because," quoth he, "I am bounded to Master Bartholomew Gosnold to ship so many good men as may be, on this voyage, and, peppery and hot-headed though you are, you are one of the strongest and most energetic men I have met. The sort of men we shall need beyond all others in Virginia. I watched your career in the Continent wars.

You were a prize well worth my playing for."

While I sought for a surly answer, I felt a hand slip into the empty money-pouch at my belt. Glad to vent my rage on anything, I gripped the hand with lightning speed, ere it could be drawn away, then wheeled to face the thief.

He had wriggled up to me, unnoticed in the crowd, and had taken advantage of my momentary diversion of mind to try to pick my pocket.

The hand I grasped was jerked violently back, but it could not tear itself free of my grip. I found myself hanging like grim death to the wrist of a lean, sallow-faced fellow, clad in leather, and cursed with the shiftiest, red-rimmed eyes that ever I saw.

"Accept my humble compliments, Captain Smith," quoth I, monstrous polite, "on the class of men you have picked as my fellow colonists. This promising young pickpocket should add much luster to your fame in the new world. Are all the rest like him—and like your worthy self?"

Smith's swarthy face grew positively black and hideously distorted with wrath, as he saw what had happened. He paid no heed, seemingly, to my sneering words, but he strode up to the cringing thief, who shrank back in mortal fear before the lightning glare in the captain's eyes.

What might have happened I know not, but just then the door swung open and three richly dressed men swung into the room. Smith reluctantly turned from the pickpocket and moved forward with surly civility to greet them.

I took a step backward and seated myself miserably on a settle that ran along one side of the wall. Truly, I had made a precious fool of myself, and it was a goodly company of blackguards with whom I found myself.

Here, then, was the end of my bright dreams of martial glory! I saw the future stretching out before me, dreary and barren as a rainy sea.

"Do not judge us all by him," said a voice that was so soft as to seem to blend with my own silent thoughts.

I glanced to the right of me. I found I had unconsciously seated myself next to the girl and the stern-faced elderly man whose pres-

ence I had already noted on my entrance to the room. The girl was looking half shyly, half merrily, at me, from under the shadow of her dark hood.

"You spoke to me?" I queried absently.

"I bade you not to judge us all by him," she repeated.

"By Smith?" I asked. "Now, Heaven forbid! I would not so much malign any company."

"I spoke not of Captain John Smith," she answered, "but of Wat Croy, the man who sought to steal your purse."

"Oh," I laughed, "that mattered little. The purse was empty. Nor do I wonder at finding such a man on an expedition of this sort."

"We must take what men we can find," said she. "Men of substance and ability have too much at stake in England to cross the seas to a wild country. So, until the colony proves itself prosperous, we must e'en be content with such as will go. These are for the most part down-at-heel galloots, pardoned convicts, broken folk, and those whom King James's laws too cruelly oppress. Of such last are my father and myself."

"Yourself!" I echoed, roused to faint amusement. "You can scarce be eighteen. How can you have fallen 'neath the law's ban?"

"I go with my father," she said simply.

"And he?"

"He is Mark Errol," she replied, as though she spoke the name of one of the earth's great ones.

The name was wholly unfamiliar to me, yet I lacked the brutality to say so to her, just then.

"A man of his sort," I evaded, "can scarce find much to rejoice him in such company, and under such a leader as this fellow Smith."

"Why do you speak so of Captain Smith? He treated you fairly, and whatever his faults, he is the greatest man we have in all our hundred and five. He is the one man of all others who can make the colony a success."

"A success?" I retorted. "Naught can make it a success. North America will ne'er be settled. To the end of the ages 'twill ever be a desolate wilderness, peopled only by red Indians, and wild beasts, and forest demons. Each effort to colonize it has failed, and each will always fail.

"White men have never established a foothold there, and they never will. With South America it is different. That flourishes. It may one day be the land of a mighty nation. But North America, never! 'Tis a fit expedition for such a purpose. A company of tatterdemalions—barring your father and yourself—led by a windy braggart."

"Braggart?" she mused. "Yes, Captain Smith is assuredly a braggart. My father says so. And many of his boasts of past exploits do not ring true. In fact, when Master Will Shakespeare penned those five stage pieces, 'The Lives and Histories of Kings Henry IV and V,' some folk say he made the character of *Pistol* from this same Captain John Smith. But Shakespeare misread him. Boaster and full of conceit as he is, the man is gallant, and is a born leader."

"Those three men who came in just now, and with whom he is talking," said I, foolishly angry to hear praise of mine enemy from lips so fair—"who are they?"

"The stout man with the gray beard," she answered, "is Captain Bartholomew Gosnold, of the Godspeed. The little man with the red face is Captain Christopher Newport, of the Susan Constant. The dark, tall man, whose face seems always scowling, is Captain John Ratcliffe, of the Discovery. They are commanders of our three ships."

"Whatever they may be saying to Smith," I observed, "it seems to give him scant pleasure. See how he scowls and shakes his head."

As I spoke Smith turned from the three sea captains and pushed his way toward where young mistress Errol and I sat. But it was not to us he addressed himself.

He passed us and stopped in front of Mark Errol, the girl's father, who sat silent and wholly immersed in his own thoughts.

"Master Errol," quoth Smith, more gently than his frowning brow betokened, "I have black tidings for you. Captain Gosnold and the rest tell me there is a squad of the city watch at the door without, and that their leader holds a warrant for your arrest."

Errol raised his head, his somber face dull with apathy.

"I scarce expected to get scot free from England and gain a fresh start of life in an honester land," he muttered. "From the first I said 'twas too good to be true."

He rose. Smith held his big, hairy hand in sympathy.

"How they guessed your whereabouts," said he, "I know not. And

in another two hours you would have been safe aboard ship and off to the New World. I sought to persuade our three worthy shipmasters yonder to let us make shift to hold off the city watch by force till we could smuggle you aboard and up anchor, but they will not have it so. If prudence be a virtue, then those three fairly reek of virtuousness."

"'Tis the old charge, I suppose?" asked Errol.

"So Gosnold tells me. The watch-officer says the warrant accuses you of complicity with the gunpowder plot of two years agone, and—"

"Never did I take part in that foul conspiracy," retorted Errol, "nor was I privy to it. I have already told you how my effort to save one of the conspirators, whom I deemed innocent, brought this false charge on me. And now, after dwelling in hiding, like some felon, for more than a year, I must needs end my days in the Tower or on the block. Just when I saw light ahead! Good-by, sir, and take all my thanks for your great goodness to me.

"Dorcas," he went on, in a tenderer, infinitely sad voice, turning to the girl, and gathering her into his arms, "my own little lass, be brave. I wish—"

I moved back out of earshot. It seemed to me this parting between father and daughter was far too sacred for a curious outsider's ears.

But I could not take my eyes from Dorcas Errol. The hood had slipped back, and her face shone clear beneath the lamp-light. Never before had I seen such a look on human visage.

She was weeping. Not noisily or snifflingly, as do many women, but as a frightened little child might cry in the dark. Her great dark eyes were wide with dumb terror. Grief had stricken her radiant young face a ghastly white, and it was drawn and haggard, as from sharp illness.

I think, in some phases of life I am a fool. I can stare unmoved and watch the moistly picturesque weeping of most women. But when one cries like a frightened child, as did Dorcas Errol, or has in her face that look of dumb, hopeless, childlike horror, why, there is ever a silly something that grips fiercely at my heart and sends a lump into my throat and straightway prompts me to some idiot's action. And so it proved now.

What were these Errols to me? I scarce knew them. And if the father had run foul of King James's law, why should I concern myself?

I felt no interest in the somber, sour-faced old fellow.

Yet that look in his daughter's eyes, and her terror-stricken, silent sobs, all at once turned me from a sane man into an ass.

And, for good or ill, I took quick and imbecile resolve.

Gosnold, as Errol and Smith drew near the threshold leading into the passage, opened the door and beckoned in the watch-officer. Then, pointing to Errol, who stood apathetically waiting, his cloak wrapped about him, and his sugar-loaf hat pulled down over his eyes, Gosnold said:

"Officer, here is your prisoner. Bear witness to his majesty that we willingly surrender the felon into his hands. We are right glad to learn in time of his true character, and to be rid of him, for we want none but good men, and true, on this, our venture."

The officer nodded, and touched Errol on his cloaked shoulder.

"Mark Errol," he droned, like a child speaking its lesson, "I arrest you on charge of high treason against our lord, the king's high majesty, and against his sacred life. Come with me."

"No, no!" panted Dorcas, still clinging to her father's arm.

But I stepped between, officiously eager, and dragged her with seeming roughness to one side. Then I seized Errol by both shoulders and shoved him forward so suddenly that he collided with the officer with such force as to knock the latter bodily backward through the door and into the passage where his men awaited him. I noted with joy that the single candle in the passageway lanthorn had burned itself out, leaving the place in gloom.

Shoving Errol through the doorway ahead of me, I cried:

"I have him safe, Master Officer. Let your men seize and bind him, for I fear me he is a right desperate fellow."

As I spoke I released one of Errol's shoulders and slammed shut the door behind me. Thus, for a moment, we were all left in black darkness in the crowded passageway.

That moment sufficed me. While the officer, cursing me for a blundering, officious fool, had sent one of his men to fetch a torch he had left at the street door, I ripped the long cloak from Errol's back, threw it about my own shoulders, then snatched his hat and jammed it far down over my eyes.

All was done in a twinkling.

I had but time to thrust the struggling, uncomprehending Errol into an angle of the passageway wall, and whisper fiercely to him to crouch there and to hold his tongue.

Then the torch-bearer appeared with his light at the end of the passage. As he did so I dived forward, butting and hitting out wildly in clumsy effort to break through the little knot of watchmen and gain the safety of the street.

Instantly, as foreseen, my awkward attempt at escape was discovered. The officer and three of his men, seeing the supposed captive trying to get away, hurled themselves on me.

Down we went to the floor in a writhing heap. And when they dragged me to my feet and pinioned my arms, my sugar-loaf hat was jammed so far down over my face by a blow I myself had given it, that it hid my whole countenance from the mouth upward.

My own father could not have recognized me. My figure, under voluminous folds of the now torn cloak, was hunched to shorten my height and to give the air of an elderly, "settled" man.

The watch captain laughed gleefully at the clumsy efforts of his captive to elude him.

"One on each side, boys!" he ordered his followers. "And if he moves to escape, send your halberd points through the old traitor. Master Mark Errol," he went on mockingly, "ye have dodged the king's justice for over a year, but you cannot dodge the clutch of my stout lads. So come quietly or it will be the worse for you."

As he spoke, he and his men had been rushing me down the passageway toward the door and down the steps into the street.

I think they half-feared Errol's comrades in the room behind might attempt some rescue. For, at the noise of the turmoil in the passageway, the door had opened and excited, questioning voices had been raised.

Amid the babel as I was dragged down the steps onto the street, I had heard Dorcas Errol's voice raised in a cry of wondering ecstasy at sight of her father safe and sound.

And the memory of that joyous cry kept up my heart as I was propelled along the dark streets toward the Tower. It was my one comfort in a sea of self-contempt at my rash folly.

CHAPTER VI.
Out of Trouble and in Again.

LEST any should doubt the ease wherewith I had performed the ruse substituting myself for Mark Errol, let me say it was the very simplest sort of feat. Self-injuring maneuvers generally are, I find.

It had required but one instant of a swift action there in the utter darkness of the passageway, during which I had snatched and donned Errol's hat and cloak.

'Twas my futile rush for escape that had assured the success of my trick. For, when men are struggling in the half light with an escaping prisoner, they waste little time in scanning his features or in debating whether or no they have caught the right man.

Errol's long, old-fashioned cloak and his tall, parsonlike sugar-loaf hat were unlike most garments worn in that day. There had been none others like them in the room.

Thus, when a man thus attired had made a break for freedom, he had very naturally been seized.

Once out in the street, whose pitchy blackness was relieved only by the flare of the single torch borne by a man who walked ahead, the deception was still easier to maintain.

I uttered no sound as I moved along among my rough captors. I could see nothing, for Errol's hat, as I have said, was jammed down to my very mouth.

One thing only did I fear. I dreaded lest the fellow who was gripping my left arm should chance to feel my sword-hilt rubbing against his side.

Errol had been unarmed. I had seen the officer's quick glance stray to his side, to make sure of that. So, with my elbow I managed to keep my left-hand captor's body from pressing too closely to me.

When one cannot see his surroundings, a journey is ever doubly long. And our march to the Tower of London seemed interminable. Also, when one cannot see, the mind turns inward with added intensity.

And I, perspiring and half-stifled inside that miserable sugar-loaf hat, had ample time to review my situation and to rail at my folly in

rushing into such a predicament.

Twice that day had I thrust my neck into the noose. First, by my attack on Geoffrey Whitson, favorite courtier to King James. That assault alone, as I now full well knew, was enough to send me to the Tower for life or even to cause my beheading.

Having won free from that peril, through Will Shakespeare's help, and having been on the eve of showing a clean pair of heels to England and the law, I must now, forsooth, involve myself in a far worse dilemma and impersonate an old treason-hatcher with whom I had absolutely no acquaintance.

And all because a girl had chanced to look like a frightened child when she wept! What were Dorcas Errol or her tears to me?

How the miserable adventure was to come out, I did not know. Of course, the first official who knew Errol by sight would see that I was not he. But what fate would the law be likely to mete out to the man who had helped a traitor to escape?

We came to a halt, in answer to a challenge from a sentry. And I gathered that we had reached one of the Tower gates. There was a brief colloquy between the watch-officer and a guard-captain. Then we marched on a few yards (apparently into a courtyard, from the way our steps reechoed from high-surrounding walls), and thence up one or two steps. I was pushed through a narrow doorway.

A high, nasal voice in front of me demanded:

"Well, well, what's here, officer? What's here? A masquerade or a headless man? Take the thing's hat off that we may observe it."

A ripple of laughter followed his query.

"If it please your worship," said the watch-officer humbly, "this is a desperate traitor, who did conspire in the evil gunpowder plot, and whose body I have seized in pursuance of a royal warrant."

His men, as the officer spoke, were busy prying up the smashed rim and crown of the sugar-loaf hat from my head. Off it came at last with suddenness and then I saw I was in the office of the Tower gate, where presided the committing magistrate. He was a thin, flaxen-haired man in gaudy robes and lolled back in a chair behind a carved, black table.

Lounging about the room were several courtiers and other well-dressed men. I remembered, when I was in England before, it had

been the custom for well-to-do idlers to spend an hour or so in the committing magistrate's office of an evening to amuse themselves by watching the hapless prisoners who were brought thither for examination. And now—*I* was the prisoner!

I bowed to the magistrate, who took no heed of my salute, then stood awaiting the next move in the wretched game.

"What is your name, fellow?" demanded the magistrate in his high voice.

Before I could reply, the watch-officer spoke up.

"If it please your worship, 'tis Mark Errol, the—"

"Mark Errol?" broke in the magistrate. "I dined at Errol's house a score of times in the days before he turned malignant traitor to his king. Errol is full twenty years older than this man, and a head shorter."

"But, your worship," babbled the officer, "the name 'Mark Errol' be set forth clear and fair in this warrant. I know, for I be a man of learning as well as of substance and I can read. See it for yourself, your worship."

The magistrate brushed aside the proffered document.

"What care I about the name on the warrant?" he fumed. "This is not Mark Errol. You have blundered grievously, officer."

"*I*, your worship?" protested the indignant officer. "I be as zealous an arm of the law as may be found in all England. Aye, and as shrewd."

"You are an ass!" retorted the magistrate.

The watch-officer's fat face went purple with mortification. Then, observing that the magistrate's clerk was scribbling away at his notes, the luckless man cried in wild entreaty:

"Oh, master clerk, in your report I pray you write me not down an ass! That I should live to see the day that any clerk should write Jem Dogberry down an ass!"

A laugh burst from the bystanders. I glanced across at them, taking closer heed of their aspect than at my first general look. And there seated amid a group of gallants, I saw a familiar figure.

It was Will Shakespeare. His eyes were full of mirth, yet as he looked at me they filled with troubled pity. He could do nothing for me, yet his look of sympathy warmed my heart. I looked back at the magistrate.

"'Tis not Mark Errol," the latter was saying again, "but who is it?

And how and where captured you him, Dogberry?"

"At the house where the passengers for the Virginia voyage were gathered for departure, your worship," answered Dogberry. "'Twas there we had word he was hiding. And there, sure enough, he was. Behold him!"

"Silence!" roared the magistrate in the last stages of exasperation. Then he turned on me.

"Give an account of yourself, sirrah!"

"I was with some of the other passengers for the Virginia voyage this evening," I said quietly, "waiting to go aboard our ships. This fellow watchman entered the house to make an arrest. I chanced to pass out through the hallway and Master Dogberry and his crew seized me. They dragged me here."

Dogberry had been staring at me with his dull, near-sighted eyes.

"'Tis not the same man," he now broke out. "T'other was shorter and older. Yet I cannot have made a mistake. And—the fellow hath grown a head taller since he came hither."

Another laugh, and once more the magistrate cut in.

"You have the bearing and voice of a gentleman, sir," he said to me more civilly, "and I would not interfere with a volunteer for these colonies by which our gracious king sets such store. Yet, I can scarce understand—"

"'Tis simple," I returned. "These men seized me and brought me here."

"You suffered them to hale you—an innocent man—through the streets?"

"They represented the majesty of the law," said I right priggishly; adding with a grin: "Moreover, when a man's hat is bashed down over his eyes and mouth as you saw mine was, he can scarce talk convincingly. I could not raise my hands to remove the hat, for they pinioned my arms."

"He—he hath a sword!" cried Dogberry excitedly. "I take oath he was unarmed when we made the arrest. I noted that with especial care."

"He probably grew the sword during the journey," observed the magistrate. At which rare jest, his subordinates dutifully shrieked with laughter.

"But," went on the magistrate, "the fact that he wears a sword and did not know it nor was deprived of it by the watch, bears out his story. I fear, sir," he added, turning to me, "that you have been the victim of a grievous blunder. If there are any in London who can attest to your character I will gladly turn you loose and tender you the law's apologies for this inconvenience."

"By your leave," put in Master Shakespeare, rising and stepping forward, "I know this gentleman, and I am sure he is mixed in no treason plots. Will that suffice?"

The magistrate bowed assent; treating this mere scrivener of stage plays with as deep respect as though he were a man of importance; whereat I marveled.

"You are free, sir," the magistrate told me. "I grieve for your ill treatment. Also for the rents in your cloak. As for the hat's destruction, 'twas evidently a shocking bad hat at best and far out of style. So you suffer little loss there."

I thanked him and stood aside. I was about to depart when Master Shakespeare plucked me by the sleeve.

"Was it not rare?" he chuckled. "Was it not rare to hear yon clown of a Dogberry? Could I but put such a character on the boards, 'twould set the whole pit in a roar. I must talk further with this same Master Dogberry."

"'Twas monstrous good of you," quoth I, "to speak for me just now."

"Nay," he answered. "'Twas for mine own interest. At supper to-night I chanced to speak of you to my Lord of Shaftesbury. He hates Whitson and is powerful enow to protect you from him. He bade me, should I see you again, to offer you honorable service in his own household. There is much chance there for advancement. On the morrow you and I will wait upon his lordship."

I thrilled with joy at the idea. To find such employment was almost beyond the dream of a plain soldier of fortune. It was lucrative and offered fine chances of preferment.

To be a member of the great Shaftesbury's official household was the open sesame to wealth and rank, for the right sort of man.

In a thrice, my world was changed. From poverty and despair I found my feet set upon the high road to fortune. I felt as if all the gray,

old world were one glorious blaze of sunshine.

Then, athwart my golden dream came a black shadow. And at the shock, I could feel myself turn white.

My promise to mine enemy! I had pledged myself to sail to the Americas with Captain John Smith, to take up there the dreary, hopeless, grinding life of a Virginia colonist. I had made my solemn pledge to abide by the decision of the dice. And the dice had decided against me.

There was but one thing a man of honor could do. Had I been victor in that strange duel with Smith, I should have deemed him the vilest of curs if he had begged off or eluded payment and I knew he would have kept his pledge. Was I to prove myself less of a man than that swashbucklering braggart? There was but one course open to me.

"Master Shakespeare," I muttered—and my voice was dead with the deep despair that sanded my dry throat—"I thank you from my heart. But I have other employment."

I could say no more. And I knew my words must sound ungracious.

"As you will," he answered, plainly hurt at the rebuff.

And he strolled out of the room.

I wrapped the torn cloak about me, for the December night was cold, and prepared to set off to the meeting-place of the cursed Virginia expedition, secretly hoping that I might be too late and that the three ships might already have sailed.

As I neared the door, the threshold was blocked by several gallants who were sauntering into the magistrate's office. I stood aside to let them enter.

The first of the group was Geoffrey Whitson.

At a glance he recognized me. Whipping out his sword he cried:

"Guard! Arrest him! I accuse him, in the king's name! Seize him!"

CHAPTER VII.
MY HEELS SAVE MY HEAD.

IT is odd what sudden twists a man's mind will take. Half a minute earlier I had been berating my fate at having to turn my back on a bril-

liant career and bury myself in the Virginia wilderness.

Now, that same wilderness seemed paradise to me compared with lodgment in a Tower cell and the chance of a later acquaintance with the headsman's block.

Whitson, drawing sword and rushing at me, had yelled for the guard. In that small room, with a full dozen people in it, my mind and body worked at once and in unison. There was no time for me to get at my sword. Instinctively, before the cry of alarm was fairly past Whitson's lips and ere he could reach me, I had bounded forward.

I tore off my cloak with one wrench as I jumped. And with a single cast, I had hurled it at Whitson's face. The huge, torn garment covered his head and body like a clinging pall.

In practically the same movement I lowered my head and plunged into the little knot of men who were following Whitson into the room.

Unprepared for my action and not yet fully catching the import of the situation, they had no chance to brace themselves for the shock.

Like lightning I tore through the group, scattering gallants to right and left. I gained the small courtyard ere those in the room behind me could pass the staggering, sprawling men in the doorway and get at me.

The guard at the postern-gate leading to the street was just closing the portal after letting Will Shakespeare out. Before he could clang the door shut or turn around I was upon him like a catapult.

Knocking him to one side, I threw my whole weight and strength against the heavy and almost shut iron gate. The portal swung outward, under the impact, and I darted out into the night like a rat from a trap.

I had no time to shut the door in my pursuers' faces. And out after me they poured, pell-mell, swords drawn, yelling like a pack of hounds.

I sped past Will Shakespeare who had advanced scarce a half-score paces on his homeward walk from the Tower. By the light over the gate he glanced at me as I flew past, and recognized me. But there was no time for me to waste time or breath in shouting so much as one word of explanation. And on I fled.

Never again have I seen Will Shakespeare. Never again have I heard news of him. I have sometimes wondered if ever he kept his

intent of writing those dramas about the tempest off the vexed Bermudas and of the blackamoor who told of the adventures among the Anthropophagi, and if ever he portrayed my captor Dogberry's silly character in a stage play.

I am old now and I am not likely to learn more of Master Will Shakespeare or of his writings. For the events I am describing happened well-nigh fifty years ago, and the name of a mere scrivener like this Master Shakespeare is no doubt forgot by this time. Had he been a great general or a statesman he might perchance have been remembered by posterity.

And so, back to my story:

I plunged into the blackness of the unlighted street, with the full hue and cry after me.

The night was densely black. But years of night duty in the foreign campaigns had so accustomed my eyes to darkness that I could see easily, where these town-bred pursuers of mine could not.

Moreover, I was ever fleet of foot, beyond the average. So I swung along through the gloom at a tremendous pace, over the uneven street, easily avoiding the inequalities and holes and rubbish heaps; while those who followed me floundered desperately or stumbled and fell.

I dashed into a crooked alley, slackening my pace because of the increased darkness there; reached the next street, ran along it for a short space, then cut into a second alley that led toward the river. Cold as the night was, my exertions kept me glowingly warm.

By this time the sound of the clash had died away. I had shaken off my pursuers with ridiculous ease. And now I bent my hurried steps toward the docks and the house where Smith and his passengers had gathered.

As I turned out of the short-cut alley to the street before the docks, a shape rose out of its gloom before me; and the point of a half-unseen knife pricked my throat. "Stand and deliver!" ordered a voice.

I could have laughed. What, in the name of St. Nicholas, the patron of thieves, had I to deliver?

"Friend," I answered unflinchingly before the menacing knife, "I have an empty purse, a half-worn suit (without hat or cloak), and a serviceable, but not especially costly sword in a much scratched scabbard. I think you have hailed the wrong man."

As I had been talking I had managed, furtively, to raise my arm. Now, as I reached the end of my indifferently drawled words, I suddenly struck upward.

My blow caught the highwayman's arm just below the elbow, knocking the knife to one side. At the same instant my left fist caught him on the chin. Down he went, in a heap. I did not wait for him to recover, but cleared his rolling body with one spring and ran on.

Two minutes later I burst into the house from which, barely an hour before, I had been led by Dogberry and his watchmen.

The great room was empty. At my shout a sleepy servant appeared. He told me that all hands had gone aboard their ships a half-hour agone.

I ran to the docks which he pointed out to me. There, inquiry from a half-drunk sailor gave me the news that the last of the three ships carrying the Virginia colony had weighed anchor five minutes earlier.

For an instant my heart grew light. Assuredly, I had done all in my power to keep my pledge to Smith. If I had failed, despite my best efforts to reach the docks in time, the fault was not mine. I was absolved of my promise! Free to take high service under the Earl of Shaftesbury.

But the next moment my miserable sense of honor came to the fore again. And almost without volition I found myself racing at top speed along the river bank.

I remembered the section of London from former days. I knew that, a half-mile below, there was a sharp curve of the Thames.

And, by taking another short cut there, I believed I could reach the river at a point beyond the curve before the last of the three Virginia-bound ships should pass it.

So off I ran. And in another five minutes or so I had come, panting, to the spot I had had in mind. I stood on the muddy bank, straining my eyes across the faintly glimmering gray expanse of water.

The black bulk of a ship, moving slowly down stream with the tide, all sails set, was in mid-channel. Behind it, less than a furlong, came another vessel of the like size; while, fading away in the gloom far in front, I could barely make out the blot on the water that marked the third and leading craft.

Down the river, drawn by the ebb-tide and pushed on by the slight

wind that brushed their canvas, were the three Virginia-bound ships; slipping away from England in the darkness of a night which blotted out every vestige of land to scores of homesick eyes that should never look upon England's green coasts again.

Apparently I had reached the bank after the first of the three ships had passed. The second was abreast of me, and the third coming along in the rear.

There was no time for thought. Into the ice-cold water I dived and struck out for midstream. The freezing December water bit to my very marrow. It well-nigh shocked my heart and brain into lethargy.

For, remember, I was in a glow from my long, hard run. Yes, and I was tired, too. I had undergone much that day; and I was lately recovered from an attack of camp fever.

Yet, with all my strength I struck out; not waiting to remove my clothes, light boots, or sword. A mad feat, I grant you, and one for which I had no desire. Yet my honor and the memory of my unfulfilled pledge goaded me on with a lash of scorpions.

As I had feared, I reached mid-channel much too late to board the second ship, or to attract its crew's notice by my water-choked hails.

But I found myself straight in the path of the third and last vessel. She was coming on so slowly that I was well in front of her. I shouted. But no one answered. She seemed to carry no lookout. And her crew and passengers were evidently astern. Even in that moment, the circumstances struck me as odd.

I trod water and shouted once more. Then, all at once, her bowsprit was jutting directly above me, like the limb of some giant forest tree. And, 'twixt myself and the sky, I could see her battered figurehead silhouetted.

Just above me, and looping down to below the water-line, hung the bow-anchor chain.

I caught at it, when the prow was almost touching me, and passed my hand through one of the huge iron links.

Then, summoning all my remaining power, I clambered hand over hand up the chain. It was an easy feat for any agile man, for there was almost as good grip-hold as on a swaying rope-ladder.

But in my chilled, fatigued state I was almost unable to finish the simple climb. Again and again I had to pause, clinging to the big links,

chattering with cold and fighting for breath and fresh strength.

At last, after an eternity, my hands grasped the rail. One awkward, muscle-wrenching heave of my whole body and I had rolled over the rail onto the deck.

There I lay panting, gasping.

After a few minutes I got back my breath and enough strength to stagger to my feet.

I looked about me. Not a soul was in sight. The fore-deck was as deserted as a midnight churchyard. I could not understand. Was this the phantom ship of the Flying Dutchman that I had boarded?

The silence and horrible solitude seemed to beat in upon me like hammer blows.

CHAPTER VIII.
THE LION-TAMER.

I WALKED aft. For the first few steps the deck lanterns showed me no one. And again I marveled.

For folk newly come aboard ship are wont to scatter all over the decks and cabins, surveying their new quarters. And full two-thirds of this colonial crowd had never before set foot on shipboard, so would be doubly inquisitive.

A step or so farther and I was a trifle relieved of my apprehensions. There was a man on duty at the helm. And scarcely had I made out his figure when I saw another man at work up among the shrouds. But, except for these, no one was in sight.

A half-dozen strides brought me to the "break" and the entrance of the great cabin. About the doors of this a crowd of seamen flocked, intent on what went on within. I wondered at the laxity of discipline. It boded ill for good, sailorly work during the voyage. Then I elbowed my way into the cabin.

Under the hanging lamp stood Captain John Smith. His huge right hand gripped the shoulder of Croy, the shifty-eyed man who had sought to pick my pocket. All around pressed the passengers, eying the scene for the most part in sullenness or in open anger.

None observed my entrance, so intent were they all. As I came in, Smith was saying:

"And I gave fair warning that none but honest men were wanted on this voyage. You all know that. Yet, what find we? A common thief who preys on his own comrades. We catch him red-handed picking Master Gordon Clyde's pocket. There was no time to give the case attention ere we sailed. But now it shall be settled. Brothers, what is your verdict? How shall we punish him?"

A murmur arose. A murmur of discontent.

"Set him free!" called one man in the crowd.

"This is no law court," cried another. "We be all equal here."

"Who said that?" snarled Smith, whirling about and glaring from one face to the other, his eyes blazing, his teeth bared like the fangs of a wolf.

"Who said that?" he demanded again.

None answered. For his expression did not encourage argument. But black, rebellious looks everywhere greeted him.

"Since none has manhood to say a word for honesty," went on Smith, red with mortification, "I will e'en take justice into mine own hands."

Ere any could check him, or so much as guess his purpose, he had caught up the thief bodily, swung the fellow athwart his broad shoulders, as though Croy were a sack of meal and, striding out of the cabin, through the crowd, bore him to the rail.

"We cleanse our good ship thus!" cried Captain John Smith.

As he spoke he heaved the yelling, kicking, writhing pickpocket far out over the rail and let him fall with a mighty splash into the river.

The thief rose to the surface a few yards off, sputtering and floundering. Then, getting his bearings, he struck out for the nearer shore with a long, easy stroke that at once did away with any fears for his safety.

"So!" roared Smith, turning upon the muttering, yet cowed, group. "Let it be an example. And let none other merit throwing overboard. For, in mid-ocean, it might not go so lightly with the offender as within a furlong of the Thames's safe banks."

The muttering swelled and hands were laid covertly on sword hilts or knives. But ever, where Smith's fierce glance flashed, the mutterings

ceased and hands fell away from the hilts.

He reminded me, ridiculously enough, of a lion-tamer I once saw in Rome, who entered a cage of ravening beasts that longed for his life but dared not brave the light of command in his eyes.

Some men are like that. When their power extends merely to dumb brutes we dub them lion-tamers and pay our groats and pence to watch them risk their lives at the county fairs. But when the same power controls their fellow men we call them "born leaders" and obey them slavishly.

And, while this tatterdemalion crowd obeyed and cringed before Captain John Smith for the moment, yet I would not just then have given a clipped farthing for his chances of surviving the long voyage.

I did not envy him his position as their temporary leader. I have faced death more than once, and in no very attractive forms. Yet, I confess, I should have thought twice before trusting myself to be the hated disciplinarian of that gang of outcast cutthroats on a four-months' sea-trip.

It was as though the lion-tamer were compelled to spend four months, waking or sleeping, continuously locked in the cage with his murderous beasts and with no one to come to his rescue. In his sleeping hours something not wholly pleasant would be likely to happen.

Bitterly as I hated Captain John Smith, my heart at that moment went out to him in quick sympathy. For he was at least a man. And I felt as I might had I seen a human being harried by a pack of rabid curs.

The passengers, little by little, dispersed to their sleeping quarters and the ill-disciplined crew took up their stations of duty.

I looked in vain for Mark Errol and Dorcas. I learned later that they had sought their berths as soon as the ship had weighed anchor.

At last I left the dark corner where I had watched the scene of incipient mutiny and entered the cabin.

Smith sat there alone beside the table. His arms were folded on it and his head buried in them. I think he was realizing for the first time just what lay before him.

I walked up to the table. At sound of my step he raised his shaggy head, frowning, and glowered at me. Then, seeing who it was, his frown gave place to a look of amaze.

"How did you get here?" he demanded.

I pointed to my dripping wet clothes. He nodded, understandingly.

"But why?" he asked.

"Through no will of mine," I retorted sulkily, "you may be sure of that."

Again and more keenly he stared at me. Then, once more he nodded.

"I see," he said curtly. "I might have known. You are a man of honor, Master Clyde. I ought not to have doubted you would keep your pledge, had you been forced to swim the whole blue Atlantic to do it."

"I do not need nor wish your commendation," I returned surlily, my dislike of the man rising once more to the surface.

"I do not need nor wish to commend you," he sneered.

There was a brief, comfortable silence, during which I wondered what the outcome of the interview would be.

"I saw what you did for Errol to-night," said Smith. "I alone, of us all, saw part and surmised the rest. Why did you do it?"

"I do not know," I returned, uncomfortable under his sharp gaze. "The foolish impulse of a moment. The peril was slight. As soon as the committing magistrate saw me he knew I was not Errol. Convinced of his mistake, he set me free."

"H-m! You will merit the undying thanks of both Mistress Dorcas and her hard-shelled old father. I have had no chance to speak with them since then. But—as otherwise they will fail to understand the part you played in saving Errol—I shall explain it to them in full to-morrow morning."

"No!" I cried, hot with anger, in spite of the cold wetness of my clothes. "You shall not!"

"Very good," he assented indifferently. "If you prefer, I will not."

"You give me your word?" I insisted.

"Assuredly. But why—"

I could not explain to him how I dreaded being looked on in the melodramatic light of rescuer and of being overwhelmed with tearful thanks. So I but shrugged my shoulders and, to shift the topic we were discussing, said:

"I wish you joy with the ruffians and ne'er-do-wells you have shipped as colonists. They are rare material from which to build the welfare of a new land."

He winced under the coarse sarcasm.

"You are right," he agreed with something very like humility. "What I need is a band of sturdy, honest, God-fearing men. Tillers of the soil, builders of homes, good citizens. But such folk will not yet leave home. Nor even will they until home is made too hard a place for them. So I must e'en make shift to carve the colony with such broken and blunted tools as lie ready to my hand."

"Gamesters, thieves, broken adventurers, gold-seekers, ex-convicts, down-at-heel swashbucklers, and needy gentry," I supplemented.

"You have called their roll," he agreed quietly; "and in which category do you place your worthy self?"

"That is a hard question to answer," I said slowly. "First of all, I am a man who hates the whole venture and who, as you know, enters upon it with utter distaste. Also, I hate you and all pertaining to you. And should the opportunity ever honorably come, I shall slake that hatred."

He nodded, in no whit displeased.

"In the meantime," I went on, "you are a man alone among ravening beasts. And by the blood-kinship of man to man as against the lower animals, I shall stand at your side and aid you in all things. We understand each other now, I think. There is no further need of words between us."

He had sprung to his feet and, impulsively, had half-stretched forth his hand to grasp mine. I ignored the gesture and passed out of the cabin.

From the deck outside I saw him look after me for an instant with something like wistfulness in his ferocious little eyes. Then he sank back in his chair, and once more buried his head in his folded arms.

It occurred to me momentarily that I had behaved like a boor. And I was half minded to go back and take the hand of fellowship he had offered me.

I have since wished I had obeyed the impulse.

41

CHAPTER IX.
WHEREIN "GRATITUDE" IS QUAINTLY DEFINED.

IT was well-nigh a week later when Dorcas Errol and her father first appeared on deck. Mark had been desperately seasick, it seemed, and his daughter had remained below to nurse him. Thus it was that I had caught no glimpse of either of them.

But one blue-and-gold morning, when I was taking my usual brisk walk on the cramped little deck, I came upon them, seated in the sunshine in an angle of the cabin-wall.

I was more glad than I had realized. For the riffraff that made up most of our passenger-list were not of the sort wherewith a decent man might associate with any sort of mental or moral profit. These two were of a far different stripe. Already I had promised myself many a pleasant hour in their company.

During the past week I had been sadly at lack for society. I would not mingle with the worthless scum who were to form our wonderful colony. I would not associate more than I could help with Captain John Smith.

Hence, oddly enough, I had picked acquaintance with Aquia, the giant red Indian who was Smith's servant. The savage knew a smattering of English. And as I was the only man on board who did not mock at his strange aspect, he seemed to have taken a sort of liking to me.

I had resolved to improve the voyage by picking up from him something of his Indian language. It would serve to pass the tedious hours, and would prove of use to me in Virginia. Aquia, nothing loath, had consented. And our lessons had already begun.

'Twas a barbarous tongue. But I had ever had a knack for quickly mastering foreign lingo; so I hoped to make some sort of progress in Aquia's lingo ere the dreary voyage should end. This morning, as I caught sight of Dorcas and old Errol, it suddenly occurred to me that there were infinitely more agreeable ways of passing time on shipboard.

Sweeping off my hat with my very best bow, I advanced upon the father and daughter. They had not seen me until I was close to them. Then the look that sprang into the eyes of each could hardly be con-

strued as one of warm welcome.

I halted, irresolute, before that double gaze of utterly horrified contempt. Then, manlike, I rushed to my destruction.

"No doubt you have forgotten me?" I commenced, hoping that I had misread the look that I could not at all account for. "We met once before. I am Gordon Clyde—"

I paused. Mark Errol, quivering with rage and supporting himself upon his staff, had risen to his feet.

"You cur!" he panted, thrusting his face toward mine. "You man-selling, contemptible cur!"

Now, no living man of mine own age and strength could have lived to boast that he had spoken such words to me. But from an old and sick one I could not exact payment.

Moreover, Errol's odd speech struck me dumb. I had risked life and liberty for him. I had saved him from the headsman's block. And now—

"Were you not content," he raved on, "to play the blackguard and help in my arrest, but now you must pollute with your presence the air we breathe?"

Still wholly in the dark, I, nevertheless, choked back my choler and said:

"Will you kindly explain, sir?"

"Explain?" he rasped. "Explain to you, perchance, that you aided the minions of the law to make an unjust arrest? That you curried favor with the king by seizing me and thrusting me into the very arms of the city watch? That you dragged my weeping daughter from my embrace and delivered me over to the law? Explain? Faugh!"

I well recalled the scene he had described. But that—in the light of what I had done directly afterward—he could so grossly misunderstand my actions was more than I could believe.

"Pray, sir," I insisted, "since you have so accurately depicted my actions in that room where we met, go on and describe what befell after I had pushed you out into the dark passageway."

"Ah!" he cried, with a smile of sour triumph. "'Twas then that Providence mercifully overruled your evil intent. As you well may not know that I escaped your clutches, I will tell you, in order that you may see how miserably you failed."

43

"Yes," I assented drearily enough, "I have failed. And miserably. Go on, I beg."

"In the darkness there," pursued Errol, "of a sudden all was turmoil and confusion. I know not clearly what happened, for all passed so swiftly. But I opine that my captors quarreled among themselves. There was a scuffle. In it I lost my cloak and my beaver hat, and I was thrust by chance into a corner, while the fight raged on past me. The next moment the city watch had left the house. By a miracle I was saved."

"Accept my warm congratulations," said I dryly.

"But," he raged, his anger kindled afresh, "your own vile share in the arrest is none the less black. And for that I would I were a younger man that I might punish you as you merit."

"Mistress Errol," I cried, turning to Dorcas, "on my honor I am quite guiltless of this foul offense wherewith your father charges me. Will you believe? Will you let me explain my part in this affair of your father's arrest?"

But as I moved toward her the girl shrank back from me in horror as from some loathed reptile.

That gesture of hers, and the look that accompanied it, went to my heart like the thrust of cold steel. I had not thought mortal person could so hurt me.

Ere I could speak again old Errol was between us.

"Every word to my daughter from so low a beast as yourself," he mouthed, "is an affront. Be silent. Back to your kennel, dog!"

As he spoke he whirled his staff aloft and struck me full across the face with it. The force of the blow and his own enfeebled grip sent the stout oaken cudgel clattering from his hand to the deck. I snatched it up. Dorcas gave a little cry and made as though to throw herself protectingly in front of the raging old man.

I looked Mark Errol in the eye for a fully half-minute. And under my emotionless gaze, I saw his face change from fury to senile fear. Then I broke the thick oak staff between my two hands as though it had been a pine wand, and let the pieces fall clattering at my feet.

"Forgive my intrusion," I said gently, as I turned on my heel; "I shall not trouble either of you again."

CHAPTER X.
The Hour of Battle.

HAD I the prospect of Methusaleh's years and had my readers Job's patience, I might undertake to write a description of that voyage from England to Virginia. As it is, its incidents up to the hour of battle can be told in a mere handful of words.

The three little ships crawled over glassy seas or were buffeted like chips by the great winter gales. The passengers of our own vessel were first sick, then keenly interested in everything, then wearied and bored; and at length, by natural course, fell to plotting mischief.

Smith ruled them as though they were slaves. He had no legal right to do this, for the new colony's leader had not yet been named.

By orders of His Majesty King James, transmitted to "The Company," we were to sail to Virginia. Within twenty-four hours after landing there we were to open a sealed packet.

That packet contained the names of the men ordained by the king to be our president and of the men who were to form his council. None knew what names were written in the packet. None could know until we should land.

In the mean time we were normally under command of our three sea captains. But Smith, who had been the master spirit in recruiting the expedition, took on himself the temporary leadership. And he enforced it, by sheer strength of character, over the men who daily grew to hate him worse and worse.

For my own part, I kept my promise to the Errols. I never went near either of them again. But, curiously enough, I could not feel for them the wrath their stupid ingratitude and Mark Errol's blow deserved.

For the old man I had the pity one might have for a cranky, defective child. As for Dorcas, I found myself daily thinking more and more about her. And while this provoked me, I could not cease from it.

Left to my own resources, I plunged heart and soul into the wearisome task of learning from Aquia his language. When one has nothing else to do, and applies himself for more than four months to the acquiring of a foreign tongue, it is surprising what progress he can make. And in my own case, as I have said, I am ever quick at learning

languages. Ere that awful voyage was over I had mastered the dialect of the giant Indian's people.

Despite a few gales, we fared more than commonly well in the way of weather, until we were within a few days' sail of the Canary Isles. Then one morning as Smith was using a rounded mirror to signal to our sister ships, the glass slipped from his hand at a lurch of the vessel and fell to the deck, where it broke in fifty pieces.

A gasp of fear rose from the onlookers. They were an ignorant and crassly superstitious lot. And to them the breaking of a mirror signified fearsome ill-luck, not only to the man who broke it, but to all his house. And as Smith's "house" just then consisted of the ship, they loudly foretold disaster for us all.

Smith rebuked their fears; but in the midst of his harangue as to the folly of the belief in superstition, one of the crew gave a shout of terror and pointed to westward.

Five minutes before, the early spring sunlight had been cloudless and balmy above an almost unrippled sea.

Now, as by magic, out of the west had leaped a black wall streaked with lurid gleams. It was rushing down upon us like a live thing. No one who has not witnessed the swift upcoming of such a tempest in southern seas can imagine its aspect or the terror it strikes to the stoutest heart.

For a second everybody stared in mute horror at the onsweeping storm. Then the shipmaster howled orders that sent the sailors swarming up into the rigging like so many monkeys. There, in wild haste, they tugged and hauled at shortening sail—a task on whose prompt achievement all our lives hung.

A heavy-set man in a sky-blue mantle thrust himself forward from the crowd of passengers.

"Yah!" he screamed, shaking a dirty forefinger in Smith's face. "'Tis you we have to thank for this! You smashed the mirror and drew a curse on us all. If we go to the bottom, it is because of your—"

"Silence!" roared Smith.

But terror of the elements had robbed the man and his fellows of their lesser terror of their master. They pressed about Captain Smith, cursing him, reviling him, threatening him with eyes and fists and half-drawn blades.

The mastership that blazed in his little eyes had for once no effect on his followers. The fury of the tempest that was bearing down upon them was so terrible as to make mere mortal's rage seem a puny thing.

Like hungry lions about a man who sleeps at a dying jungle-fire, they edged closer and closer, and more menacingly toward the fearless but powerless captain.

In another moment, I think, the rush would have come—a rush that might have torn him limb from limb. But with a roar like that of a thousand pieces of artillery, the storm broke over us. It struck the ship as with the buffet of a huge fist. Over she careened, so sharply as to fling every one in a kicking, struggling jumble to the deck.

It was every one for himself. The waves swept the deck below the break before the ship could right herself again. Had the crew been five seconds less prompt in their work with the sails we must have turned turtle.

Then pandemonium broke loose.

The light of day was blotted out. Our ears were half deafened. The cordage sang like harp-strings. One seaman was blown out of the top rigging like a fly from a wall.

Men's yelling voices were inaudible in the uproar. The spume made everything invisible at a distance of a yard or so.

The ship shook and shivered and groaned like some sea-monster in anguish. From one side of the deck to the other we were tossed until the narrow decking-space was a shapeless mass of twisting, grotesquely writhing humanity.

In a few minutes the first force of the storm spent itself. The gale passed. But it was only the precursor of a three-day tempest, before which our three baremasted ships scudded impotently.

Hatches were battened down, and we were herded most of the time between decks like cattle. It was not pleasant. The air was vibrant with prayers, groans, and curses.

On the fourth morning the storm had somewhat abated, and we crawled on deck again. We could not see either of our sister ships anywhere.

The shipmaster ordered part of the canvas set and headed for the Canary Isles, where it had been arranged we should all meet in case our vessels should ever be scattered by a tempest.

In reply to an idle query, our shipmaster said:

"I dare not crowd more canvas on. We are not at the end of the storm. This is but a lull."

That was enough. Men glanced blankly at one another. Then the bulk of the passengers and several of the crew moved as by common consent toward the stern, and there they huddled for a time in eager, low-voiced converse.

I can read men a bit. That is why I am still alive. And if ever I read trouble, 'twas at that moment. I understood in part what the conversation portended. There was but one course for a decent man. I walked into the cabin, where I found Captain John Smith hard at work over a roll of maps and charts that he had spread out on the table. He glanced up as I approached.

"I am altering these," he said, too full of zeal to recall our cold relations one toward another. "Virginia now extends from the Atlantic to the Pacific and from New France settlement in Canada, down to the Spanish Floridas. It is in my mind to split it into two colonies, north and south, and to rename the northern one. Not to name it after a king who may die and be forgot, but after our own grand fatherland that can never be forgot. What think you, man, of christening the northern colony 'New England?' Is not the idea a worthy one?"

"Pardon!" I broke in impatiently, able for the first time now to stem the current of his enthusiastic speech; "but if, instead of naming colonies that may never exist, you will look to your own welfare, you are like to live the longer. Come!"

"What do you mean?" he asked, angry at the interruption, yet seeing me to be in deep earnest.

"Get your sword first and put on your helmet and breastplate," I answered. "Do it without delay. Afterward there will be time to question me."

It was characteristic of the man that he waited to ask no further questions. He went to the wall and snatched down his sword and helmet. Then, beckoning to Aquia, who had stood stolidly in one corner of the cabin gazing out at the clump of whispering men, Smith ordered the Indian to help him fasten on the heavy, dented breastplate. I talked briefly and to the point while these preparations went forward.

"The crisis has come," I said. "These ruffians of yours are no longer

content to snarl. Look at them out there. They mean mischief."

Smith looked. At one glance this ruler of men saw I was right, and at a stride he reached the doorway leading from cabin to deck. He was not one second too soon.

For, even as he stepped forward, the conference among the malcontents ended. As one man they moved forward toward the cabin in whose doorway Smith, sword in hand, stood glaring at them.

This time his weapon and his eyes did not check them. There was a hissing sound as a score of swords leaped from their scabbards. The big fellow in the blue mantle was in advance of the rest. It was evident he was spokesman.

Onward moved the men until their leader was barely two swords'-length from Smith. Then he halted and made as though to speak. But Smith spoke first.

"What does this mean?" shouted the captain, his rough voice booming forth like a cannon-shot. "Is it mutiny? If so, you will one and all wish you had not been born."

The blue-mantled man held his ground and replied:

"We have had enough of that, Captain Smith. We have endured your browbeatings and your bullyings long enough. The end has come. It is you who have brought ill luck upon this ship."

"A gang of blackguards like you and your fellows, Jerry Crowley," retorted Smith, "are enough to bring ill fortune on Westminster Abbey itself. If—"

"The breaking of the mirror," pursued the blue-mantled Crowley, unheeding, "brought a curse on this ship. Our lives have been in peril from storm and wave ever since. And the shipmaster says the storm is not yet past. It is you, Captain John Smith, who have brought upon us this curse. And while you remain on board we shall not know one safe hour."

"The shore is overdistant to swim to," jeered Smith, "and our consort ships are not in sight. I fear me you must e'en endure my fateful presence a while longer."

A confused howl of negation—furious, beastlike—rose from the crowd.

"We shall not endure your presence, Captain Smith," retorted the spokesman. "That is what we have come to tell you. You brought ill luck upon us. If you stay we will all go to the bottom. And—"

"The right men in the right place at last," commented Smith.

"And," continued Crowley, his voice raising, "to save our own lives we must sacrifice you."

(Do not think I overdraw this scene, I beg. History will bear me out. From the beginning of the world seafarers have been rankly superstitious. And again and again they have thrown overboard men who they believed brought misfortune to the ship. To search no farther afield for an example, let me recall the case of the prophet Jonah in Holy Writ.)

"You mean to hurl me overboard?" asked Smith in genuine wonder.

For reply they unanimously pressed closer. Again was their fear of him forgot in a greater terror—the superstitious dread that his continued presence would bring them shipwreck and drowning.

At their forward move Smith raised his sword-point, but gave no other sign of emotion. Indeed, his usual truculence was replaced by calm—a deadly calm.

"Before you can cast me into the sea," he drawled, "you must take me. Who first will court death by laying hands on John Smith?"

They gathered for a rush. I quietly stepped into the broad doorway to one side of Smith, sword in hand. Aquia, the giant redman, hatchet aloft, stepped to Smith's other side as unconcernedly as though about to serve his master's dinner.

We were three against twenty. The odds seemed overwhelming. Our position in the doorway, which we completely filled, gave us some added advantage. But I knew enough of hand-to-hand warfare to realize how slender was our hope of survival.

Well, it would be, at any rate, a soldier's death. And at the side of two brave men. One might do worse than die thus, with drawn sword, for the right.

And, happier than I had been for months, I threw myself on guard.

CHAPTER XI.
I Try My Hand at Sword-Play.

THE appearance of Aquia and myself beside Smith was an evident surprise to the mutineers. I think they had not counted on the

captain's receiving help from the few of the passengers and crew who were not in the plot.

Indeed, the non-combatants were huddled like scared sheep in a group near the farther rail, watching the proceedings with helpless terror.

I could make out Dorcas Errol's pale face and great frightened eyes. And beside her was her father, striving to force his way to the front of the knot of spectators.

Smith glanced quickly from one side to the other and noted our presence.

"Thank you, Clyde," he said to me under his breath, "you are a brave man. I knew I could count on you."

"Captain John Smith and you two others," cried Crowley, "I call on you to lay down your arms. You three will but die uselessly. Surrender, and Clyde and the Indian shall be spared."

"Oh, cease gabbling and begin your attack," snapped John Smith, "or do you want us to come out there and settle you? Ye are twenty. We are three. Yet we three be *men.* And—"

"No!" called a voice from one side of the mutineer group. "Ye are *four,* Captain John. I cast in my lot with you."

It was old Mark Errol. He had at last made his way through the non-combatants, and was shuffling rapidly across the deck toward us.

He had almost reached our side before his defiant words called the mutineers' notice to him. Then Jerry Crowley, who was nearest the old man, struck brutally at him with his sword.

I heard Dorcas cry out, but I was in mid air when I heard. For I had sprung forward and caught the heavy, descending blow on my own blade, at the same time clutching Errol by the collar and throwing him bodily toward the doorway.

Aquia caught the old man as he spun toward the threshold, and unceremoniously thrust Errol into the cabin behind him. Scarce had he done it when I was back, unhurt, in my former place at Smith's side.

It was a daring thing I had done. But its very unexpectedness, coupled with its lightning speed, had made it possible. I verily believe that less than two seconds elapsed from the time I left the doorway to the moment I returned to it after rescuing Mark Errol.

But the instant of action had been enough to snap the last thread

of hesitancy on the part of our assailants. Instinctively, and waiting for no word of command, the whole mass of them flung themselves upon us.

Then, for a minute or so, ensued some of the hottest work of my life. There was no time nor room for clever fencing. There was naught possible save to elude or beat aside as well as possible the bristling sword-points that came toward my breast, and to thrust with ceaseless and wondrous rapid insistence at my oncoming assailants.

I had no chance to note how my comrades were faring. It was all I could do to hold my own and to keep from going down under the onslaught. A sword-point pricked my shoulder, another my thigh.

"Clyde," shouted Smith above the clamor of battle, "stick to the point, lad. Never give 'em the edge. 'Tis the only chance."

"I am no novice," I yelled in reply. "Save your breath for fighting."

For I was already observing the needful warning he had called to me. A swordsman trying to hold a doorway or other semi-protected position against two or more adversaries must ever thrust with the point of his sword, and never attempt to slash with its edge, for the latter motion leaves his guard open and takes up too much time.

Every swordsman knows this, and it irked me that Smith should have deemed it needful to tell me; but, like many born leaders, he seldom gave others the credit for common intelligence.

After a minute the first rush slackened. Unable to force their way in the initial attack, our assailants gave back for a second and a more concerted onset.

As the pressure in front of me slackened ever so little, I glanced at Smith, who was using his blade as coolly and dextrously as if he were in a fencing-school. He plied his great sword with perfect ease. And I noted that, like my own, his weapon was red to the hilt.

The Indian, Aquia, was equally calm. His arm was slashed by a sword blade, and another cut had laid open his cheek. But his stoical features gave no sign of pain.

At our feet lay six men, dead or wounded. And more than one of the survivors carried marks of our handiwork.

I hoped, for a moment, that the mutineers would be scared off

by this proof of our power to defend ourselves. But, rapscallions as they were, they assuredly were not cowards.

These were men who not only lived by their wits, but who for years had held death off by their powers and courage with the sword.

And the difficulty of the task that now confronted them served only to urge them to further and more furious efforts. Their hatred was at boiling point. Their fighting spirit was up. The time when the power of a more masterful mind could quell them was past.

There was no hope for us. I hit on a bold plan. These men were gamblers and were wont to stake all on one throw. I would appeal to that instinct in them.

"Wait!" I cried, as they gathered about Crowley, arranging for a better and more carefully executed assault. "Wait! Crowley, 'Tis to you I am speaking."

"The time for speaking is past," he growled.

"You are these men's leader," I hurried on. "You voiced their alleged grievance. Are you man enough to take the weight of that grievance upon yourself?"

He looked puzzled. So did the rest. They did not understand.

"Will you hold back your pack of curs," I continued, "and meet me, man to man, hand to hand, sword to sword?"

"What?"

"Will you let us represent our two factions and let the whole quarrel rest on the result of our duel?"

A murmur of keen, wondering interest sprang from the group. I gave it no time to die down.

"If you men charge us again," I said, "you may or may not overcome us. But in any case you will lose many lives. You have seen how we can fight. On the other hand, if we beat you into submission you all will continue to snarl for the rest of the voyage."

Again I paused for the fraction of a second to let my words sink in. Then I resumed:

"Let us rather be true gamesters. Fight me, Master Crowley. If I win let your men pledge themselves to obedience. If you win, Captain Smith shall be delivered into your hands."

"Hold on!" cried Smith (speaking to me in Italian, that he might not be understood by the rest). "What are you doing, man? Offering

to deliver me over like a trussed pig to the butchers? Have I no voice in this?”

“If they attack again,” I answered, in the same language, “we are none of us likely to have 'voice' about anything. We should not have lived through the first charge had they not attacked in confusion and with no concerted plan. Next time they will be wiser and four or five of them will engage each of us at once. No mortal, outside a romance book, could live for one minute against such odds. What I propose to Crowley is our only chance.”

“Then,” Smith insisted, “it must be I, and not you, who shall fight him. This is my quarrel.”

“Should you step from this doorway,” I retorted, “they will fall on you in a body. No. Mine is the only course. Take heart. You know something of my sword play.”

Turning to the mutineers, who had been conferring excitedly together, I asked in English:

“Do you consent?”

“Yes!” they roared, Crowley among them.

It is human nature to enjoy watching an exciting contest between two well-matched men. It is gambler nature to enjoy the playing of a desperate hazard. Crowley evidently had the reputation of being a brilliant swordsman. Otherwise he could not have won his way to the mastery of such a rabble. I, on the other hand, was unknown to them as a fencer. From all these reasons I was not all surprised by the loud and ready assent to my proposition.

“Good!” I assented, stepping out into the cleared space in front of the doorway. “So be it. If I win, you men are to come to heel and conduct yourselves with due submission. If I lose, Captain Smith is yours. It is so understood?”

“Yes,” roared the mutineers again.

And Crowley, casting aside his blue mantle, strode forth into the open space to confront me.

The deck was slippery and uneven. The ship was pitching wildly in the groundswell of the storm. The pain from my two flesh wounds was sharp, yet I greeted right blithely this single chance of winning for us.

“On guard!” cried Crowley.

And our blades clashed together.

CHAPTER XII.

An Affair in Midocean.

THERE is a sort of "sixth sense" possessed by every expert fencer which tells him at first clash of the blades whether or not his opponent is a good swordsman.

Such a sensation, I am sure, came to both Crowley and myself as our swords crossed, there on the ship's rolling, slippery deck. Around us, in a semicircle, crowded the mutineers. On the other side, in the cabin doorway, still grasping their weapons, stood Smith and Aquia. The wind was fresh in our faces and whistled through the cordage above.

For a few moments my antagonist and I were content to feel out each other's skill and to look for openings of attack. It was he who made the first aggressive move.

Dropping the point of his sword almost to the deck, in the hope that mine would follow it, he brought the point up again with incredible swiftness and lunged for my throat.

It was a clever trick, but an old one, and I was ready for it. Instead of being lured into sinking my sword-point, I had thrust as his point dropped. Crowley sprang back and parried at the same time, but he was just too late to avoid me.

The point of my sword sank into the flesh of his upper chest, struck on a bone, and deflected. The wound was light, but painful, and it infuriated him.

Casting caution to the winds, and spurred on by a cry of derision from some of his followers, Crowley rushed to the attack with a strength and savage quickness that taxed my powers to the utmost. For a space I could do naught but defend myself, and was hard put to it to do even that.

Our blades clashed and ground together, whining and slithering like living creatures. This man, Crowley, was a swordsman of prowess. I, who have been accounted a skilled man at that art, could scarce do more than repel his assault.

But his own vehemence was fighting my battle for me. He was a strong man, and swift of motion, but his florid face and baggy eyes

showed that he had lived the wildest of lives. And that same mode of life was now beginning to tell against him.

His fierce exertions were making him breathe fast, and were, ever so little, slackening his speed, whereas my own lungs and muscles, hardened by the rigors of many campaigns, and kept in condition by frugal, temperate living, felt no distress under the heavy strain I was putting upon them.

Around and around each other we circled, he ever on the offensive, I defending myself, and at each chance of an opening seeking to reach him. I had no eyes or ears for the onlookers. All I could see was Crowley's ferocious countenance, and the lightning play of his sword. All I could hear was the clashing of our blades and the panting breath of Crowley. My wounds were bleeding but little, yet they hurt me cruelly.

Our swords threw off a shower of red sparks as I parried a terrific cut for my head. I slashed under Crowley's guard. He sprang back to avoid the cut.

His foot slipped on the slimy deck, and down he crashed on all fours, his sword flying out of his grasp.

Now, here (as Smith did not hesitate to tell me later) was where I played the fool. Had the situations been reversed, Crowley would have spitted me as foul as I lay sprawling and disarmed at his feet.

Moreover, with the fate of Smith resting in my hands as it did, I had no right to indulge any foolish notions of chivalry. My duty was to Smith and to myself. Not to this cutthroat blackguard whom accident had placed at my mercy.

I knew all this. And I despised myself for my silly squeamishness. But I *could* not bring myself to stab the man as he groveled helpless. I could not do it.

I stepped back, sinking my sword-point to the deck.

"Get up!" I ordered.

A gasp of utter and unbelieving wonder burst from the mutineers. A cry of disgust came from the doorway where Smith stood watching.

But Crowley had caught up his sword, and was on his feet by the time the words were fairly out of my mouth. I could see from the look on his angry, bloated face that he felt a surprised contempt for me. Then he leaped to the attack.

As the Dice Fell

Humiliated by his own awkwardness, mad at having been thus shamed before his followers, he flew at me in a frenzy of rage that half blinded him.

But this time I withstood his assault with less difficulty. Fury had dulled his keen skill; fatigue and the jar of his heavy fall had shaken his bovine strength.

In less than a minute I was on the offensive. And now for the first time during the duel, I was the aggressor. Little by little I drove him back, my sword barely missing its mark in more than one cut or slash.

I "touched" his shoulder, and a red spot widened on the white of his cambric shirt. My sword-point pierced his left arm in a lunge that was meant for his heart.

Backward ever I forced him. Nor, despite his wildest efforts, could he resume the offensive. His bolt was shot. His great body, strong as it was, had begun to pay the penalty for the life it had led. His breath came in sobbing gasps. His eyes were glaring and bloodshot.

He still fought ferociously. But I knew the end was not far off. So long as he stood face to face with me, and able to defend himself, I felt no shred of pity nor of compunction for what I was about to do.

At any instant, now, one of my lunges or cuts must penetrate past his weakening guard with sufficient force to end the combat.

Smith would be saved, and with him such future as might possibly lie in store for the Virginia colony, and for the Americas themselves. And I pressed my foe the more relentlessly.

I cut at his head, rising on my toes to give the greater force to my blow. He warded the stroke, yet so feebly that my blade came down upon his head glancingly, cutting away his leathern cap and staggering him.

I leaped forward to follow up my advantage. One more such blow would stretch him lifeless.

As I sprang my toe caught against the outflung, stiffening arm of one of the men who had been slain in the attack on the cabin doorway.

The ship rolled jerkily as I strove to regain my balance, and down I went on one knee. Luckily the fall was not enough to send the sword from my hand. But it shook me, sickeningly.

Before I could recover myself or make the first effort to rise Jerry Crowley was upon me. With a shout he had swung his blade aloft, and

was bringing it down with every atom of remaining strength on my head. The slash would have cloven my skull in two, had it found its mark.

But, as he struck, I flung myself sharply to the right. Down whizzed the sword, barely grazing my left shoulder, yet with sufficient force to benumb my whole left arm.

And, as the stroke sped downward, I thrust.

I was still on one knee. But I thrust upward and threw the rising weight of my body into the lunge.

It all happened in a second. Crowley was drawn forward by the force of his own blow. And my upward thrust's force was redoubled by the fact that he involuntarily came to meet it.

Through leathern vest, through flesh and through bone, my good blade bit its way. Yes, and its point stood out a full three inches behind the man's back.

Crowley gave a convulsive start, whose force tore the sword-hilt from my wearied hand. Then, for a second, he stood stock-still, his hands upraised, a grotesque look of amazement on his purple face, and my blade transfixing his powerful body from chest to back.

He stood there, I say, while all the spectators stared breathless. Then, slowly, as if his legs were turned to melting tallow, he began to sink. And he lay on a great, huddled, silent heap on the blood-flecked boards of the deck.

Panting, I stepped back to the doorway of the cabin.

"I will take your hand now, Captain Smith," I said, "if you are still minded to offer it to me!"

"Brave lad!" cried Smith, thumping me on the back in a fashion that may have been commendatory, but was assuredly most agonizing to my wounded shoulder. "Good, brave lad! I could scarce have done a neater job myself. But why did you spare him the time you had him down? You saw how he treated *you* in like case."

"Yes," said I, dryly, "I saw. And it made my task the pleasanter. I—"

"Trouble!" croaked Aquia, in the Indian tongue.

He pointed at the mutineers. While one or two of them were fruitlessly seeking to revive Crowley, and to stanch the wound in which my sword-blade still remained, the bulk of them were eagerly jabbering together.

A less keen judge of human nature than Aquia could have seen that their conference boded no good fortune to us.

"Well!" called Smith, harshly. "Your champion lost the fight. And you will abide by the terms. Back to your quarters, all."

Instead, they turned on us as one man, and again their blades flashed out. It was clear they had hastily decided to repudiate the agreement on which I had staked my life and Smith's.

Low gamesters as they were, they had not even sufficient manhood to abide by the turn of the fortune they themselves had invoked.

Possessed by the superstitious belief that Smith's continued presence on the ship would bring them disaster, they abandoned even such feeble hold upon honor that the average gamester is supposed to maintain.

Smith read their vile intent, as did I, even before their drawn blades gave proof of it.

"Your gallant fight was useless, Clyde," said Smith. "They mean to have me."

"And they have my sword," I growled. "I cannot help you hold the doorway against them on the next rush."

They had bunched themselves in rude military formation, and were preparing to charge. I could see this would be no wild, unarranged assault like the first.

We were doomed, we three men, of whom two were wounded, and one weaponless. Nevertheless I darted back and snatched up a three-legged stool from the cabin behind me.

With this rude weapon I took up my place in the doorway beside the two others. I hoped to strike some one before being killed.

"Charge!" bawled a skeletonlike gallant, with a shock of black, oily hair. He stood in the lead of the mutineers, and had evidently assigned himself to Crowley's vacated place as their captain.

"Charge!" he ordered, waving his sword.

And, in the same breath, even as we three braced ourselves for our hopeless defense, a hoarse, quavering voice from far to one side, called:

"Halt!"

So unexpected was the crack-voiced command, and from so unforeseen a direction, that all of us turned instinctively to look. Even the mutineer leader, who stood just in front of his compactly massed men.

And at what we saw, we every one stood aghast—dumfounded.

CHAPTER XIII.
I Am Forgiven—For Nothing!

ON the high-jutting little platform just beyond the "break" of the deck, a culverin (a small cannon) was situated. One stood at each end of the ship, as precaution against pirate attack.

The two culverins had been overhauled and reloaded that very morning. For the storm-spray of the past three days had soaked their powder.

Idly we passengers had watched dry powder and a bagful of slugs and nails rammed into them not two hours before.

Now, instead of pointing swiftly out to sea, the culverin above the "break" had been slewed about on its greased base-wheel, and was so tilted as to point at the direct center of the mutineer group.

To turn and sight the cannon thus was no great task for one man. But what took us so vastly by surprise was the identity of the man who had done it.

Crouching at the culverin's side, a lighted slow-match held just above its priming, was Mark Errol!

His thin, white hair waving in the wind, his somber face aglow, he seemed like some grimly grotesque caricature of Nemesis.

I had flung him out of harm's way from Crowley's threatening blade. Aquia had bundled him into the cabin like a sack of rags. But Errol had evidently crawled out by the other and smaller door at the cabin's far side, and had made his way unseen to the nearer of the two culverins.

In any case, there he was, with the cannon trained full on the mutineer group, and the sputtering slow-match within an inch of the priming's powder.

I speak, of course, only for myself. But I think we all, at that minute, recalled how large a bag of slugs, nails, and scrap-iron had that morning been crammed into the culverin's gaping mouth.

And I think we all realized just what hideous execution, that charge of assorted metal would inflict at close quarters. It would sweep the whole deck like the wind of death itself. And, straight in the path of the discharge, the mutineers were bunched.

By a common impulse, all at once they started to spring aside from the menace.

But ere they could move a step, old Errol's cracked voice pealed out again in menace:

"Halt!" he screamed, his husky tones scaling to angry falsetto. "The instant the first man of you stirs hand or foot I shall fire."

Quickly as the group could scatter, they knew the hail of death would be among them ere the swiftest man could bound from its path of devastation. And they halted; pallid, muttering, dazed.

For a moment the old man eyed them with an air of mildly malevolent triumph. He, the unconsidered feeble passenger, to whom none of the noisy throng had ever given a second thought, held all their lives in the hollow of his withered hand! A far greater man than he might have been pardoned for gloating.

But the pause was only momentary. Then Mark Errol spoke again:

"Captain Smith," he called, "I have these rascals safe at your disposal. What is your will? Shall I fire?"

"Not yet," answered Smith, grasping the situation at once, as was his wont. "There may be no need. Let me disarm them first."

He stepped from the doorway. I drew him back by main strength.

"Are you insane?" I cried. "If you go out among them they will kill you like a sheep, for they know he will not fire on you. Let me go instead. Errol hates me like the plague. And if they attack me, he will not hesitate to blow me and them to kingdom come."

I gave Smith no time to argue, but hurried out among the cowed mutineers. I snatched the swords from their unresisting hands, the dirks and knives from their belts; tossing the weapons back by the handfuls to the doorway, where Aquia gathered them and stowed them safely away inside the cabin.

It was the work of only a minute or so to disarm the entire lot. Then

Smith summoned the shipmaster who, throughout, had remained cowering among the noncombatants.

"Call up enough of your crew to take these men below," he ordered, "and have them battened down there until we reach port. Take them two by two. The rest of you," he added, to the helpless mutineers, "stand still! Errol, if one of them makes a move, fire."

Two by two they were led away, under escort of the cowed shipmaster and his sailors. When the last of them was gone, Smith followed to the hatchway and called down it:

"You will be glad to know the priming plug was fastened into the touch-hole of the culverin. Errol did not know enough to remove it. He could not possibly have fired. That is why I bade him wait. You were all as safe from death as if you had been in St. Paul's Cathedral. Brood over your own heroic courage while we batten down the hatch above you, you vipers with extracted fangs!"

Two days later we reached the Canary Isles where, at the agreed meeting-place, we found the two other ships of our expedition awaiting us.

There was a great conference. The mutineers stated their grievances, and Smith roared his. Gosnold, Ratcliffe, and Newport sat in judgment, a judgment palpably swayed by the bulk of the three shiploads of colonists, whose sympathies were all with the mutineers.

Some were for hanging Smith from the yard-arm; some for executing him as soon as we should reach America; some for marooning or sending him back to England.

Gosnold pointed out that none of these pleasant suggestions were feasible. For, according to royal orders, no step of drastic justice could be taken until the colony's officers were appointed. And that could not be done until we should reach Virginia.

Then, by the king's command, we were to open the sealed packet that contained the names of the officials appointed by his majesty to rule over us.

As a compromise, Smith was placed under a sort of "honorable arrest," which did not affect his freedom or personal authority, until we should reach Virginia. And, this arranged, we sailed onward.

I foresaw more trouble the moment we should land. If Smith's name were not included in the sealed packet's list of officials (and

there seemed no reason to believe it would be), the officials would probably seek to curry favor with their colonists by ordering him to death or to banishment.

And thus the new colony would be deprived of the one man who could possibly save it from utter failure.

If, on the other hand, Smith's name, by any chance, should be among the officials, he was safe. For, desperate blackguards as many of them were, the colonists would not dare defy the king's authority, nor lay violent hands upon one of his chosen officers. Such an act would bring swift and relentless punishment upon the offenders.

I was seated on a coil of rope on deck the night after we left the Canarys, pondering on these things, when a shadow came between me and the moon.

I looked up. Dorcas Errol stood before me. It was my first glimpse of her since the battle. For, by Smith's orders, she and her father had kept to their own quarters, lest the mutineers' sympathizers might seek to harm them.

She had come silently along the deck. As she paused in front of me, I fancied she mistook me for some one else.

Knowing how distasteful my presence had been to her, I rose, and started quietly to move away; but, with a light hand on my arm, she checked me.

"Master Clyde!" she said softly.

I hesitated. She laughed a little, in embarrassment, as she looked up into my bewildered face.

"Please do not go," she continued. "There is something I must say to you. And, oh! 'tis so hard to say! Pray make it easier by seating yourself again, and looking out to sea or anywhere at all except at myself."

Dumbly I obeyed her. I sat down again, wondering vastly what had caused this odd change in her manner. She seated herself near me. And for a moment she was silent. Then—

"Master Clyde," she began timidly, "I have sought for days to speak with you. And—and now that the chance has come, I be monstrous frightened and uncertain what to say."

"If it pains you to say something that is on your mind," I suggested, awkwardly enough, "why say it? Unless, indeed, I can be of service to you."

She caught at the idea expressed in my hesitant words.

"Of service to me?" she repeated. "You can be. Will you tell me something?"

"Gladly."

"That night—the night we left England," she began, hesitatingly.

"Yes," I answered.

"I saw you push my father out into the hallway, into the very arms of the city watch. Why did you take from him, among other things, the silver chain he wore about his neck?"

"I did not!" I stormed, springing to my feet, ablaze with indignation.

"You took naught from him?" she insisted.

I did not answer.

"Captain Smith says," observed she, "that you are a man of honor. Do men of honor break their word? You promised me, but now, to reply to my questions. What did you take from my father that night?"

"His hat and his cloak," I replied sullenly.

"And why? Had you none of your own?"

"I beg you will pardon me if I answer no more questions," I retorted, bitterly. "Believe, if you like, that I stole them to buy liquor or for any other purpose."

"Suppose," she pursued, "that I prefer to think you played the hero rather than the thief? Suppose that these poor wits of mine have been working hard over this mystery, and that at last they pieced out the whole truth, except as to how you impersonated my father and fooled the city watch? Suppose—"

"Don't! I beg you to say no more about the affair. You and your father were convinced that I thrust him into the hands of the law's officers. Let it rest at that!"

"Suppose," she persisted, "that having pieced out the entire story except as to the matter of your disguise, I had put to you just now a question or two that seemed insulting, in order that I might learn the rest of the truth, would that have been an unworthy act of mine?"

"Mistress Errol," I began in dire confusion.

But she interrupted me.

"Master Gordon Clyde," she said, and the tears seemed very near her voice, "I have done terrible injustice to a brave, self-sacrificing gen-

tleman. And so has my father. We misjudged you and insulted you. You who had risked your life for us. What atonement can we make?"

"Oh, I beg you, speak no more about it," I implored. "It is not meet that any woman should humble herself before a man like me. I—"

"For weeks I had tried to hate you," she went on, "and to tell myself you were unworthy my lightest thought. But ever, in spite of me, came a voice whispering, 'You are wrong!' I—"

"Please!" I cried, but she hurried on.

"Then, on the day of the mutiny, when you saved my father again from death, and when you risked your life fighting for Captain Smith, whom you hated, why, it came to me all at once that you could not be the blackguard we had deemed you. Even my father now agrees with me. I—I—oh, 'tis so hard to confess one has been wicked and unjust! Pray make it easier by glowering at me, or berating me, or—"

"Or asking you to forget the whole wretched misunderstanding," I supplemented. "The happiness you give me by no longer deeming me a scoundrel is tenfold reward for everything."

I had leaned toward her in my eagerness. A very blessed and heaven-sent breeze blew a strand of her lovely hair across my face. Its caress thrilled me to the very soul.

And, all at once, I knew that my whole heart was tangled in that mesh of moon-kissed hair, and that never, never could I hope nor wish to untangle it.

She was speaking again.

"You will let us be friends?" she asked, half timidly, half appealingly.

As she spoke she stretched out her hand toward me. I took the little palm between my own two big hands, and bent down reverently to kiss it.

Such a salutation was frequent and commonplace enough in those days. Yet the touch of her cool, soft hand in mine went through my whole being.

"Friends?" I repeated stupidly, *Friends?*"

"It is so dull on shipboard during the long days and evenings," she said, talking fast to hide a sudden embarrassment, "and it will be good to have some one with whom to talk. You will talk with me sometimes?"

"Sometimes? Every moment that you will permit."

"And you will forget our cruelty to you? Our wicked injustice?"

"Forget it?" I answered. "Forget it? Never while life lasts. Does one forget the key that opens paradise to him?"

But being still just a little sane, I said this to myself. Aloud, I mumbled something stupid.

CHAPTER XIV.
LAND HO!

A LOW-LYING, sandy coast on either side. We had passed into the great bay of Chesapeake, and Smith had named its two bordering capes after the two sons of King James—Henry and Charles.

We had found safe anchorage, after a storm off, another point of land, and this, for its anchorage and the security it afforded our wind-battered ships, he named Point Comfort.

And now we were nearing the great, muddy river on whose banks we planned to form our little colony. We had left England early in December of 1606, and now we were in mid June of 1607.

Folk nowadays prophesy that in a few years ships will be able to cross from England to the Americas in five or even four weeks. Personally, I believe in no such wild forecasts. In any case, our own roundabout journey had consumed nearly six months ere we touched at Point Comfort.

And a dreary time it had been, the first part of it. Small wonder I had managed to learn from Aquia the Indian language during the endless days of the voyage.

But since we had left the Canarys my language-study had suffered sadly. And time had flown on golden wings, for daily I was with Dorcas Errol.

Her sour-faced father had even deigned to growl some halting apology to me, and a still more halting speech of gratitude for my services toward him, and little by little he had taken me into his confidences, and a genuine friendship had sprung up between us. For Dorcas's dear sake I would have endured a far more crotchety comrade than old Mark Errol.

This afternoon as we moved into the yellow current of the great river, away from the blue, dancing stretch of water behind us, Dorcas and I leaned over the rail, side by side.

"To-morrow we will land," she was saying. "What a voyage it has been!"

"A golden time for laziness," I answered, "that I shall never forget. It will be sweet to look back on, amid the endless toil that awaits us yonder."

"You still hate the idea of turning colonist?" she asked. "I thought you had become reconciled to it."

"I have," I said, "for now the toil means something to me. It means—home! I have never known a home, Dorcas."

She did not answer. Emboldened, I went on:

"After our town is laid out and the treaty made with the savages, and our crops are planted, I want to find somewhere in the wilderness a spot of land that shall be mine own. Shall I tell you of it?"

"Yes."

"A sloping lawn, running down to a lake, a forest behind and about it, with great, gentle hills coming down almost to the water's edge, and on the brow of my lawn a house. My house—and one other's. *A wife's!* And when I come home from my day's work of turning the wilderness into a fertile farm, she will be waiting at the door, in the sunset, to welcome me and to make me forget the labor of the day in the joy of seeing her. A strange dream, is it not, for a broken soldier of fortune. Does it interest you?"

"You know it does," she murmured.

I drew nearer to her side.

"Dorcas," I went on eagerly, "do you know who the woman is whom, in my dreams, I see waiting for me in the glory of the sunset at the door of my cabin? She is the one woman in all the world to me. Shall I tell you her name, or have you guessed it?"

I know not what she would have replied, nor could I guess it from her face, which was so far averted as to leave me but a glimpse of one very small, very pink ear. At that wondrous moment, as mischievous luck would have it, who should come a clumping up to us—actually looking as if he thought we would be glad to see him—but Mark Errol.

"Lass," said he, "we cast anchor in another hour, they tell me. Get

our goods packed and ready."

Meekly, after the manner of daughters in that day, she hurried off to obey. I looked at Mark Errol as calmly as I could, but of a certainty if he could have read the murderous thoughts behind my stolid, weatherbeaten face, he would have jumped overboard or climbed up a mast in sheer terror.

For weeks I had been rehearsing, and improving, and twisting that proposal speech of mine, and now, just when I had got it finely under way, the father must needs break in upon it and spoil all.

Yet I picked up heart, for I had also rehearsed for weeks a formal yet eloquent address wherein I was to entreat Mark Errol for the honor of his daughter's hand.

I had intended to deliver this second speech after I should have won the maid's own consent, but now it seemed a pity that so much good courage should go to waste, so I resolved to unburden myself of the formal request while Mark Errol and I still stood there by the rail together.

I fear me that luck was not with me on that day, for even as I cleared my throat and assumed a conciliatory smile, prior to plunging into my entreaty for his daughter's hand, Mark Errol, who had glanced about him nervously, bent toward me and whispered:

"Lad, you have a level head, and I can trust you. Moreover, it is needful that I confide in you that you may be on guard to aid him in case trouble should follow what I have done. Yet to me it seemed his one salvation, and the colony's as well."

I growled something under my breath which, luckily, Errol did not hear. I knew not what this confidence might be which he was trying to tell me, nor did I care. I knew only that his interruption had sent my own well-rehearsed speech scattering to the four corners of my brain.

"Lad," he went on, "in Gosnold's strong-box is the royal packet which we are bidden to open within twenty-four hours of landing. It names our officers who are to rule over us here, in the king's name."

"Yes, yes!" I retorted impatiently, "I know. It is known to all. What about it?"

"Simply this," he answered, after pause in which he seemed to be fighting back some confession that had sprung his lips. "Simply this,

lad: When it is opened look out for excitement."

"Zounds!" I exclaimed in vexation. "Was this the 'confidence' you were about to make?"

"No," he returned surlily, "it was not. On second thought I have decided that all I needed to do was to set you on your guard. These colonists are wont to act hastily."

"And you mean they will clamor for the new crown officials to hang Smith?"

" 'Tis possible."

"Officials or no officials, Smith shall not die while I can draw sword."

"How devoted and loyal to him you are!" approved Errol.

"On the contrary," I contradicted, "I am not devoted to him at all."

"But—"

"But he is the one man who can save this tatterdemalion colony from ruin. I may not love the helmsman of a ship, but while that ship, in storm, depends for safety on the helmsman's wise hand, I will do all I can, for my own sake, to protect him."

"A great man!" muttered Errol. "A great man!"

"I thank you right humbly, sir," quoth I, blushing violently and deeply gratified at the praise.

"I refer to Smith," he snapped, and his words were like a dash of ice-cold water.

"Oh!"

"To Smith. 'Tis a wise choice. He will guard her and make her happy."

"What are you trying to say?" I demanded, vaguely uneasy. "What is a 'wise choice'? And—"

"My consent to Captain John Smith's plea for Dorcas. Has the lass not told you?"

I could not answer. I stood, mouth agape, staring dully at him.

" 'Twas yesterday," prattled on the old man, "that Captain Smith broached the topic to me. It seems my lass has found favor in his eyes. She—"

I interrupted with a wordless gurgle of horror that I prudently changed to a cough. He went on:

"Captain Smith told me he intends to settle down for life here, as

colonist and planter. He wishes to marry, and Dorcas is a winsome lass, though I, her father, do say it. Captain Smith made full courteous request for her, and I granted it."

"But she?" I blurted out, trembling. "What of her? Does she consent to such—"

"Master Clyde," reproved Errol, "in my home I have ever been master, and ever shall be. My daughter has been trained since birth to obey. I did not ask her consent. I gave it. And she, as a dutiful daughter, realizes that I have acted for her best and highest interests."

Still I stared at him, wordless, dumfounded. There was a roaring in my ears as my beautiful air-castles fell in fragments about me. Oddly enough, in all my thirty-six years no other woman had ever touched my heart until I had met Dorcas Errol. She was the ideal which my heart had craved.

And now, I knew full well, through all the black years to come, all other women would be to me as shadows. Once more had mine enemy, Smith, scored against me. And this time with a blow that took all the joy out of life for me.

I could not speak. I turned on my heel and walked away, my heart as heavy as lead.

At a flat, marsh-bordered slope of green we landed. Here our colony was to be founded. Smith would gladly have sought the higher, healthier ground farther up the river, but he was overruled by force of numbers.

After months of sailing, the colonists would not hear of wasting more time in voyaging. To them the site of our colony seemed fair and healthful enough.

And here, in the early summer of 1607, was sown the seed that was to blossom into the first permanent colony in North America.

There were dozens of fantastic names suggested for our embryo settlement, but at length Smith's own suggestion was adopted, and, in honor of England's king, the place was called by us "Jamestown."

Scarce were the ship-loads of adventurers landed when they went apparently mad. Some were for rushing straight off through the hostile, trackless forests, westward, toward the Pacific Ocean. It was commonly reported in those days that the Pacific's shores were yellow with

pure gold.

Thither the adventurers resolved to go at once. They seemed to fancy that the Pacific was at most a half-day's journey westward from Jamestown.

Others snatched up spades and mattocks and eagerly began to dig in the soft, black waterside earth, tearing each clod of dirt apart with shaking fingers, in search of gold nuggets.

Still others pointed at the yellow waters of the great river and learnedly declared that the quantities of gold along its banks gave it that aureate hue.

Gold! Gold! *Gold!* GOLD!

That was all the crack-brained idiots thought of, talked of, dreamed of. It possessed their souls like a frantic mania. When one of them dug up a few shiny particles of mica the rest actually drew knives in rabid dispute over their possession, deeming the bright stuff gold dust.

Yes, it is true, all of it. And I have not told one-tenth. Such were the men on whom we relied to build a lasting colony here; to settle and to populate the New World.

Around them were miles of black forests, alive with savage beasts, and with far more savage Indians. Ere our scanty store of ship's provisions should be exhausted we must work day and night cutting down trees, reclaiming and plowing forest land, and sowing our crops.

Ere winter should come we must build warm homes and get the skins of wild animals for cold-weather clothing. Sooner than that, we must erect fortifications against the warlike Indians of the interior, who any day might swarm down upon us.

And, with this mountain of pressingly needful work looming up before them, what were our choice gentlemen-adventurers doing? Digging with their finger-nails for gold and planning treasure journeys to the Pacific coast!

Smith raged among them, purple with fury, shouting insults and commands, exhorting them madly to return to their senses, to get to work, to make at least preparations against attack.

At first the gold-maniacs paid no heed. Then, upon their craving for wealth, intruded the fact that their tyrant was once more harrying them. They ceased their treasure hunt and rushed as one man to Gosnold with the demand that he open at once the king's list of officials

for the colony.

Their intent was plain. So soon as these officials should be named, the adventurers would force them to put Smith to death. Thus, legally, they would accomplish what the mutiny had failed to give them.

As the king's commands were that the packet be opened within twenty-four hours of our landing in Virginia, Gosnold could find no excuse for refusal.

He brought forth his strong-box, unlocked and opened it, and drew forth the parchment, fastened with the royal seal. It was discolored and limp from sea-water that had soaked in during the storm. The seal came open almost at Gosnold's first touch.

Around him crowded the gentlemen-adventurers, faces cruel and eager, hands on hilts, ears strained to catch the wording of the list.

Smith alone, seated on a sea-chest, to one side, gave no sign of interest.

But I noted that his knuckles were white from the tight grip on his sword-hilt.

I moved carelessly across the cleared space until I stood beside him, and I motioned secretly to Aquia and Mark Errol to follow me.

Slowly, reluctantly, Gosnold unrolled the damp scroll. Then, as he glanced at it, his face changed, and I half drew my sword. Presently he read aloud, all listening breathlessly:

"By the command and the good pleasure of His Gracious Majesty, James the First, of England and of Scotland, to his well-beloved subjects in Virginia. Greetings and these:

"It is herewith ordained and commanded that the following President and Council shall rule over you in my name, and with royal authority—"

Gosnold paused. The silence was tense, alive with meaning. Then he read on:

"President of the Virginia Colony—Captain John Smith!"

Gosnold got no further. A groan that rose to a howl burst from the adventurers. Their tyrant, from whose power they had hoped to be freed in one stroke, was now their legal ruler; the choice of their king.

To raise hand against him was to court death. All England's mighty authority was behind him. Henceforth John Smith would be as secure among these blackguards who hated him as in the Tower London.

My sword slipped back into its sheath. There was no work for it.

My eye fell by chance on Mark Errol, and the look in his face struck me with a sudden suspicion.

Our eyes met and he moved across to me.

"I can trust you, now that the thing is done, lad," he muttered low. "I did it at Point Comfort when the ships lay at anchorage there. Gosnold slept. One of my keys fitted his strong-box. A hot knife-blade lifted the seal. Five minutes' work with erasing-knife and a quillful of ink completed the affair. The handwriting was easy to copy. Smith's name was not on the king's list. But for me the council would now be signing his death warrant."

"To work! howled Smith, "and a hundred lashes on the bare back of the first man who speaks the word 'gold'!"

CHAPTER XV.
INTO THE UNKNOWN.

THROUGH the dense, untrodden forest we moved in single file. Aquia, genius at trail-making and woodcraft in general, led the way. Close behind him followed Smith. And I brought up the rear.

We three were traveling alone through a wilderness where never before had white man's foot trod. We were bent upon an errand that meant either death to ourselves and the colony or else the saving of both.

For we were nigh unto starvation. We had been too short a time in Virginia for our first crops to reach the hour of harvesting. The provisions we had brought from England were well nigh exhausted.

Our men, who had been able to live by their wits in taverns and gaming-rooms of London, were unable to use those same wits for the snaring of wild beasts or the finding of edible fruits and berries here in the American wilderness.

Hunger's skeleton face grinned uncomfortably close to us all. Small, marauding bands of Indians, too, had kept us nerve-racked and sleepless.

Smith at length decided that there was but one course left to us. Powhatan was king of all the Indians in that region. Aquia told us the

savage monarch held court in a great village far to the westward.

Smith resolved to visit Powhatan, and to try to make with him some sort of treaty which should not only insure us against further depredations from his wandering war-parties, but should provide us with food as well.

It was barely possible such a mission might succeed. It was far more probable, as Aquia pointed out, that Powhatan might kill the envoys, and then, at his leisure, destroy the colony, for he was known to bear no love for the white man since the day that one of Sir Walter Raleigh's followers had shot his youngest son.

The chance we were taking was a desperate one. Still, slender as it was, it still was a chance. And it was our only one. We were three thousand miles from England, and at a time when no reenforcements or food could reach us for many months at best.

So Smith had called for twenty volunteers to accompany him to Powhatan's village. Of all our swash-bucklering company only Aquia and myself had offered our services. The rest took one look at the forbidding vastness of the forest, known to be peopled with wild beasts and savages, and believed to be peopled with forest-demons as well. Then, unanimously, they refused to go with us.

Thus it was that Smith and Aquia and I were pressing westward without guard or escort, risking our lives for the welfare of a crowd of men who would not stir finger to help us.

For days we had traveled, Smith's compass and Aquia's general sense of the direction of Powhatan's village being our only guides. Thanks to Aquia we had moved along a route not likely to be frequented by war-parties. And we had kept close hidden, traveling with almost ridiculous caution.

To-day, as we crossed a half-blotted out-glade in the thick of the forest, an arrow whizzed from out of the dense leafage beyond us. With a tinkle it smote Smith's steel head-piece.

We whirled about. Not a sign could we see of our assailant. Nor could we see Aquia. He had vanished as if in thin air.

Whether he had dropped and then glided to a thicker part of the bushes, or whether the earth had swallowed him, we could not tell. But he was gone.

There was something uncanny about it all. A minute earlier we

three had been plodding along safely and weirdly in single file.

Now our guide had vanished in the twinkling of an eye, leaving Smith and myself standing there, waist high in the rank undergrowth, the hot sun beating down upon us, while death lurked invisible behind the surrounding wall of leaves.

It is one thing to face peril hand to hand. It is quite another to stand helpless before a foe you cannot see. I know of nothing that so racks the nerves. It is the same dread magnified a thousandfold that makes little children fear the dark.

Smith and I did not stand supinely waiting. Instead, on the instant, we were back to back; our heavy muskets cocked and leveled; our eyes seeking vainly to pierce the barrier of foliage for a glimpse of our hidden foe.

The stillness was absolute. Even the myriad tiny forest noises seemed hushed as we watched tense and breathless. We were both veteran soldiers and accustomed to night alarms and surprises of all sorts. But not to standing in the peaceful sunlight trying to guard against an unseen enemy.

Suddenly the stillness was split by an unearthly shriek. From the long grass twenty feet away from us a savage in full war-paint sprang up into the air, his arms outflung, his face distorted.

In the brief moment that he hung thus 'twixt earth and heaven we could see that his skull had just been cloven as by a hatchet-blow.

Then he crashed noisily down into the undergrowth of the glade. And the noonday silence poured back upon us, until I could hear the throb of my own heart.

What did it mean? The bushes and grass of the little glade had shown no sign of motion. No rustle had reached our ears; we had seen no swaying of leaf and grass blade, as from the passing of some moving object.

Yet, from a spot in the glade which we had traversed not two min-utes earlier, this Indian warrior had leaped into air, and bearing the mark of a death-blow which must have been delivered at the very instant before he had sprung up. Who had killed him?

It was so unnatural, so weirdly impossible, that I felt a little chill of horror. The savage must have stolen forward from the woods since we had passed that point in the glade. Yet how had he done so, unnoted

by us? And what nameless thing had met him there in the grass and stricken him dead?

Again the wilderness silence brooded over everything. We scanned the undergrowth about us. It was moveless. This suspense was terrible.

"I cannot stand this any longer," cried Smith, and his voice was hoarse. "I am going to charge!"

"What? Where?"

"Into the forest. I feel as if a million unseen faces were grinning at me. Come! Let us make an end of this!"

Something like a great whizzing hornet buzzed through the glade. And from the branches of a great live oak at the clearing's edge a red, painted figure tumbled heavily to earth like a shot squirrel.

As the Indian fell headlong from his impenetrable nest of leaves I could see the shaft of a war-arrow sticking between his shoulders.

He fell into a clump of bushes. The crackle and thud echoed through the stillness. Then the hush came back, broken only by an occasional convulsive kicking or quivering of the arrow-pierced body in the undergrowth at the foot of the great tree.

And to my overtense mind came back a fragment of a psalm text:

"The terror that walketh by noonday!"

"Charge!" panted Smith. "It is better to be shot down than to stand watching the handiwork of unseen death!"

CHAPTER XVI.
I Enact a Strange Rôle.

WE had been standing on guard, back to back, our muskets raised and ready to fire at the first glimpse of our hidden foes.

Now, at Smith's nervous command, I ranged myself at his side. We sprang forward together through the waist-high grass, toward the thick woodland in front of us.

We had scarce traveled three yards in our plunging flight ere we crashed to earth. Together we fell, as by a signal. We did not stumble. We did not lose our balance on the uneven ground. But, simultane-

ously, our feet were jerked back from under us, and we sprawled heavily on our faces.

Ere we could either of us make the first effort to rise a score of strong, lean hands gripped and pinioned us. The seemingly empty glade swarmed all at once with naked savages.

They seized us, burying us beneath sheer force of numbers, binding our wrists and ankles with green withes. There was no question of a struggle. By the time we struck the ground, face downward, they were upon us.

We were lifted up bodily, like trussed pigs. Then I was able to look about me. We were surrounded by perhaps thirty Indians. That they were a war-party was proven by the nature of the paint on their coppery faces and lithe bodies. They grasped hatchets and bows and knobbed clubs. But they made no move to injure us.

And from this fact I understood the worst. We were reserved for torture. A big, fierce-eyed young man, who seemed to be their leader, a sub-chief, grunted an order. Several of the braves ran to two different points of the glade, and returned bearing among them the bodies of the two Indians we had seen so mysteriously slain.

And now the dull, stolid expression of the savages' faces changed to puzzled wonder as they marked the hatchet-stroke and the arrow-wound. From the two dead Indians to ourselves they looked in bewilderment.

I understood. They saw that neither of us carried bow and arrow nor hatchet.

And they could not guess how their comrades had met death, for doubtless this was their own territory, and free from incursions of any hostile tribe. In all this sea of misunderstanding it comforted me a little to find that others were as puzzled as I was.

But the American Indian spends little time in fruitless speculation over anything. In a few moments the sub-chief gave a second grunted command.

We were slung upon the backs of our four warriors in no gentle fashion, and the march westward was recommenced. Our muskets, which had caused some excitement and conjecture to our captors, were borne along by one of the braves.

And thus, for perhaps two hours, we were carried. At the end of

that time we came out upon an open space on the edge of a brook.

There was a fire burning, and over it a buck was broiling. Three or four Indians ran forward to greet us. The place was evidently this war-party's temporary encampment.

Smith and I were tossed down uncomfortably near the roaring fire, while our captors withdrew out of ear-shot and conversed together in slow guttural tones.

"What next?" I asked of Smith.

"The torture," he answered quietly. "I am sorry, Clyde, that my throw of the dice should have led you to such an end."

"I am not in love with the idea of death," I replied with forced lightness, "and I confess the thought of torture turns me sick, but I shall at least die beside a gallant man, and one whose example will keep me from showing these red beasts how keenly their torment hurts me. And so, old comrade, good-by, and good luck! Here they come."

The pow-wow was over. Two parties of braves set to work driving thick cedar stakes into the ground, about thirty feet apart. Others collected brushwood and began piling it near these stakes. Several Indians approached us, picked us up, and placed each of us beside one of the stakes. They loosened our hands, but left our feet tied.

Smith's stake was at the rear of the clearing, close to the network of forest undergrowth and trees. Mine was within a yard or two of the camp-fire. Suddenly, as I watched the torture-preparations, the craving for life surged up in me like a mighty wave, and with it came the unnatural calmness and clear thought that are mine in moments of fiercest stress.

The sub-chief chanced to be passing where I sat. I looked up at him and laughed. The Indian seldom laughs, save in mockery, or at the sight of suffering. To laugh in a redskin's face is an insult. So much I knew from Aquia.

The sub-chief halted and scowled down upon me. I met his glower with a veritable roar of laughter. Every eye in the camp was turned upon me.

The sub-chief's hand sought his hatchet. At the gesture I laughed louder than ever. (I wonder if any man since the birth of time has laughed with less mirth in his heart?) He paused, irresolute, angry. Then, in turning to his followers, he sneered:

"You have heard how the white fool can laugh. Soon you shall hear how he can howl."

He nodded toward the stake as he spoke.

"That is why I laugh," I cried in his own tongue.

Even the stolid savage looked blank at my easy use of their language, and I mentally blessed the tedious weeks I had spent in acquiring it.

"I laugh," I hurried on, "to see your preparations for burning us. Idiots! Do you think the fire is built that can burn me? I am fire's master. It will spring from the earth or at the sky at my bidding. Do you not know manitous when you see them?"

Boastful talk? Yes, in faith worthy of Smith's own worst bragging. Yet it caught and held the savages' attention.

"Look!" I declaimed. "I will make good my words. Whence shall I call forth fire? From the ground beside me?"

I reached across to the camp-fire's embers and caught up a smoldering coal in bare hand. It burned my palm horribly, but I gave no sign of pain.

"From the damp ground here fire shall spring at my call!" I bragged.

And with a mystic gesture I struck the earth with the little piece of red-hot ember I held.

At my action a burst of yellow flame flared up in a sizzling puff, and a cloud of dense smoke drifted away through the still air.

A miracle? Not at all. I had covertly emptied from my pouch a handful of gun-powder upon the black loam. The touch of the fiery coal had done the rest. Perfectly simple, as you see. But these savages had neither seen nor heard of gunpowder.

At the flash and the puff every Indian had sprung backward. I gave the impression no chance to pass. Raising my powder-blackened hand, and waving it dramatically in front of the sub-chief, I shouted:

"You seek further test? You shall have it. I shall now make fire burst from your face. A flame so fierce that it will blot out your eyes and burn away your flesh. Behold!"

But with a very unstoical yell of alarm the sub-chief jumped back, shielding his face with both arms.

"Coward!" I scoffed.

He stared down at me, irresolute.

"These foolish bands at our ankles!" I raged on. "Could I not burn them through at a touch? Could I not smite you all dead by calling upon the invisible manitous that serve me? Even as, at my orders, my invisible ones slew your two comrades back in the forest yonder?"

Another gasp and a start of dismay, as each Indian looked nervously about him to ward off possible attack from one of my unseen "spirits."

"In the hot nights," I continued, "you have seen the flash of my fire and heard the sound of my voice. You called it lightning and thunder in your ignorance. You have seen next day a great pine-tree blasted and prone. You thought it a lightning-stroke. It was my blow."

This last flight of imagination, I saw, was well-nigh too much for even these savages' credulity.

"You doubt?" I asked sternly. "Behold the proof."

I reached forward and picked up one of the two muskets that had been laid near the fire. A great buzzard, attracted, I suppose, by the smell of cooking meat, was winging heavily toward us. I pointed out the advancing bird.

"Watch!" I commanded.

I raised the musket and took swift aim. The target was not a difficult one for so good a marksman, yet when I realized all that depended on my shot my hand well-nigh shook.

The forest quiet was rent by the roaring report of the musket. The flash lightened up the shadowy clearing. The buzzard fell with a bump to the earth, torn half to pieces by the heavy charge of shot I had fired into him.

Four or five of the natives fell prone on their faces. Others incontinently bolted for the woods. One or two of the bravest stood poking at the shattered buzzard and murmuring guttural appeals to the Great Spirit for protection.

"Is it enough?" I demanded of the sub-chief.

"It is enough," he croaked from between ashen lips.

He knelt and undid the thongs from my ankles, but I noticed he made no move to free Smith.

"My fellow manitou," said I, "is as great as myself. Witness the test. He can hear the words whispered by the leaves and the tree-bark."

I picked up a strip of birch-bark from the fagot pile. On it, with the

charred end of a stick, I wrote in English:

"Give this man the kerchief from your neck."

Handing the bit of birch-bark to the trembling, frightened sub-chief I said in a low tone:

"Whisper to this bark the wish that my friend may give you the scarlet cloth that binds his neck. Then carry the bark across to him."

Sheepishly, yet as if not daring to refuse, the savage held the bark to his lips and mumbled the wish under his breath. Then he crossed to where Smith sat alert and watchful, and handed him the scrawled message.

Smith glanced at it, then held it to his ear. Presently he nodded, as if hearing something. He dropped the bit of bark and unwound from his throat the neck-cloth.

He reached out his arm to the savage, proffering the handkerchief. But the sub-chief, who, of course, had never heard of writing, shrank back from it in terror. He was convinced.

Was it more incredible that gunpowder and chirography should have fooled these sons of the forest than that I, at first sight, in London, should have mistaken Aquia for a demon?

"You will wonder," I went on, "why two spirits like ourselves allowed you to capture us. We did it because we demand your escort to your king, Powhatan. To him, King of the Indians, we come as envoys from the King of the White Spirits. Take us to him!"

CHAPTER XVII.

An Adventure in the Moonlight.

IT was on the evening of the second day. Through the forest we had traveled westward, escorted by the copper-skinned war-party. No longer did they lay violent hands on us or threaten us. But they accorded us the fearsome respect—and hatred, I was sure—that they might have bestowed upon a brace of invulnerable rattlesnakes.

They supplied us with food and gave us the warmest bough-beds by the camp-fire on chilly nights, but not one of them would willingly touch us. Nor would they lay hands on food we had tasted, nor come

near the bough-beds on which we had slept.

They avoided us as though we had the plague, yet waited on us as if we were emperors.

I became aware presently that there was never a moment when one or more of the savages was not watching us closely. When one or the other of us would stray beyond the camp, during the evening rest, there were always several of the Indians who unobtrusively formed a cordon on either side of us.

We were honored, shunned, and closely guarded. It was a combination I could not understand. In fact, the white man who can understand the Indian's nature is not yet born, and never will be.

The restraint and watchfulness began to tell upon my nerves. Smith stolidly bore it, and was but glad of our chance to reach Powhatan in safety. But I saw, or fancied I saw, something sinister in every move and every look of our escorts. When I said so to Smith he laughed at me for a fool, after which I kept my fears to myself.

On the second night the weather turned of a sudden warm, for the moon was full. I turned my back on the couch prepared for me by the fire and walked to the camp's farthest edge. There I threw myself down beyond the radius of the firelight, and shaded by the foliage from the moon's rays.

At once an Indian arose from beside the fire and crossed to where I lay. Seating himself on the ground a few yards from me, he folded his arms and stared at me.

This was abominably annoying. I rose and walked several steps into the forest, again lying down on a moss-bank. I was scarce settled there when I looked up to see the same Indian calmly sitting near, his beady, black eyes fixed on me.

Realizing the uselessness of remonstrating or of seeking more secluded quarters, I stretched my arms, yawned right prodigiously, and made as though to compose myself to slumber.

In a few minutes my snores were shaking the woodland stillness. Yet ever under my upflung arm, my eyes were a little open, and I watched the savage who was watching me.

It may have been an hour, it may have been two hours that I watched him. Then his shaven, top-knotted head began to nod. It had been a long, wearisome day's march, and he was tired.

At last I saw his chin sink on his breast. Of this I gave little thought. Any sitting man may simulate sleep by nodding his head. So it was his shoulders that I watched. When I saw the shoulders relapse and slope inertly downward at the corners I knew the man was sound asleep.

Why I had kept such cautious watch on him I myself could scarce have told, but I suppose it was in an unconscious effort to prove warier than he, and to outpoint him in this game of vigilance.

Now that I had succeeded, and my guard was actually asleep at his post, while I remained still wakeful, another thought came to me. Would it not be a rare joke, would it not greatly enhance my repute as a manitou, could I steal off unseen and unheard into the forest, and then calmly walk into camp again at dawn?

My eluding of Indian vigilance surely would give our captors a new respect for me. The idea appealed, as will any silly notion to a man who is living in the monotony of the wilderness.

Silently as an Indian, without the rustle of a leaf or the crackling of a twig, I rose from my mossy bed. The savage did not stir. His shoulders were still relaxed. Without noise, I stole away, farther into the forest. For a furlong or more I crept on still as death, through the dark leafage. Then I stepped out into a moonlit space between two mighty pine-trees.

A figure motionless as a graven statue stood there awaiting me. It was the Indian I had left asleep back near the camp.

What had awakened him, and how long he had been close to me in my furtive march I did not know, but I felt like a schoolboy whose clever truancy has been detected and balked.

I stood there for a moment, speechless with mortification. Then I strode forward.

"Be off!" I growled. "What d'ye mean by spying on me like this? Be off, I say! Back to the camp!"

He inclined his shaven head reverently at my command and stirred not one inch. I sprang at him, full of petty rage, and resolved to enforce my commands by physical strength.

Then I halted and involuntarily recoiled a step in sheer amazement. Some one had just stepped from out of the black depths of the wood and now stood between us in the vivid glow of moonshine.

It was a woman.

She glanced at me in open-eyed curiosity. Then her gaze fell carelessly upon the savage. She made a curt gesture. The Indian bowed to the ground, his hand to his forehead. Then, with a sudden backward movement, he glided silently out of sight.

And the woman and I remained facing each other.

I had had time to improve on the first quick look. Now I saw her clearly, flooded as she was by the southern moonlight.

She was tall, slender, infinitely graceful, more in aspect like some woodland sprite or naiad than like mortal. Her black hair, rippling and glossy, was unconfined. It fell below her knees. Her eyes were huge, dark, fathomless.

She had a bearing that, nothwithstanding her evident youth, was nothing less than regal. Her face was that of an Indian, but without the harsh outlines and ridiculously high cheek bones of the savages I had seen.

The features were delicate and sensitive, with a nameless, wistful appeal in their expression. Her complexion, while richly dark, was not coppery like those of the other redskins. She was clad in a mantle of white deer-hide, soft as velvet, and decked with many old beaded designs. Her little feet were enclosed in white deer-skin moccasins. In one graceful hand she bore a bow, and a quiver full of arrows was slung across her shoulders.

"Diana!" I muttered, involuntarily; "Diana of the olden myths! And come to life again here in the Americas! Verily the moon goddess walks the earth as in the days of Endymion."

She listened with eager, child-like attention. But it dawned upon me that she could not understand one word of my foolish rhapsody. So I spoke again, this time in Indian dialect.

"Who are you?" I breathed, still lost in wonder.

"I am the princess," she replied, in a perfectly self-possessed voice, and as though wondering just a little at my ignorance in asking such a question.

Her voice was soft, with a girlish, unspoiled quality that was singularly sweet. "The princess?" I echoed, blankly. "Of—of what?"

"Of America," was the quiet response.

"I might have guessed it," I answered, seeking to humor her; yet still half under that strange spell which tempted me to kneel and do

homage to this utterly delightful forest deity.

"And you," she went on evenly, "are one of the two 'white manitous,' who came as envoys to the king?"

"How did you know?" I cried in astonishment.

"Your escort sent on a courier to tell the king," she answered. "The courier reached us to-night at the set of sun. I was curious to see you—and for another cause. So I walked forth to meet you. 'Tis but two hours' march to the king's palace."

"The king?" I repeated. "You mean Powhatan?"

"Yes."

"Oh," I exclaimed. "And you are his daughter, perhaps? That is why you called yourself the 'princess'?"

"Assuredly. But how did you chance to be so far from camp. We were told you came heavily guarded and could not escape. Yet I found you here with but one single watchman. My father will be angry when he learns how lax a guard has been kept over you. With the magic powers you possess, you might have escaped?"

"Escaped? Guarded?" I echoed. "Then I was right in my fears. We are not going to your father under an escort of honor, but we are being taken to him as prisoners!"

"Yes," she assented. "Yet you go the more comfortably, because of the tricks you played on the warriors. They are ignorant. They take you for manitous. My father is very wise and, of course, knows better."

I stared at her in dumb dismay. We had hoped to impress old Powhatan with the belief that we were white gods, and that the members of our colony were also deities, and thus work upon his superstitious fears to force him into a treaty.

And now, this girl's word showed that it was we and not the wily old king, who were being duped. I think she read something of my consternation in my face, for she continued:

"You see, in the other years, my father journeyed to the sea coast. There was a ship there, full of such men as you. My father saw them play with the black grains that flash fire, and saw them use the sticks that spout flame and death. And they showed him that it was not magic, but a trick. So, when the courier told what you had done, my father understood."

"Oh?"

"Yes. He understood all save the way you caused the death of the two warriors by arrow and hatchet. For the courier say neither of you had such weapons."

"No," I said, "we had not."

"But my father is in wrath," she went on, "for one of the slain braves was his nephew, and the white men in the earlier years slew his son. So you are both to die."

She spoke with no show of regret. It was as though she stated a simple fact, and I could not at once frame a reply. I could not understand this singularly childlike, yet self-possessed girl who spoke thus of death. But she was talking again.

"Why did you come here?" she queried.

On the tip of my tongue was the pompous lie that Captain John Smith had prepared for Powhatan, but to this clear-eyed forest nymph I could not lie. I said simply:

"The story is long. I will put it in few words. Across the sea is our home, the land is crowded and the laws are harsh upon the poor. So, many of us sailed across to the Americas, to build here new homes where we might be free and where every man might have a fair chance at livelihood and happiness. We have built rude homes on the bank of the great river, but we are starving and your people harry us. Therefore, my leader and I came into the wilderness to beg your father for food and protection."

She had listened eagerly, and for a moment she did not speak. Then she said wonderingly:

"You and your leader did not know you were coming to certain death when you journeyed to my father? You did not know he had sworn to avenge his son by slaying every white man he could find?"

"Yes, princess," I answered. "We knew it. I had it from an Indian, the same who taught me your language."

"You knew you faced death? Yet you came willingly."

"Not willingly, princess, but because our comrades were starving."

"You faced death that they might live?"

"They are our comrades, the men for whose lives our leader is responsible, and we hoped there might be one chance in a thousand that your father might grant us peace and food. On that chance we came."

She made no reply, but stood gazing at me in silence from out of those great, impenetrable eyes of hers.

"There is still time to escape," she said at last, as though suddenly making up her mind. "I will go with you to your camp. At my command the warriors will let your leader go free, then you and he may gain the coast again ere the war-party my father will send in pursuit can overtake you."

"Ten thousand times I thank you, princess," said I, "but it cannot be."

"Why not?"

"Our men are starving. If we return empty-handed, they will die. My leader is wise. He may yet be able to move Powhatan's heart to aid us. If not, we shall at least have done all that mortal man can do. Our Master has said: Greater love hath no man than this—that a man lay down his life for his friends.'"

Again there was a long silence. Then she asked:

"This leader of yours? The courier described him as a mighty, noisy, hairy man. Could not he have come alone on this mission? Did you so love him that you wished to share his peril here?"

"I love him not at all, but none of the others would come."

"They were afraid?"

"It seems so."

"And *you* were not afraid?"

"Why, yes," I laughed, "I was very much afraid. But some one must come. He could not come in safety alone."

"He is not your friend, yet you are risking your life for him? Why?"

"Because he alone can save us from destruction. It is his genius that has saved the colony thus far, and if the colony is to live, it will be by his splendid efforts. Should he die, all must perish."

"You are brave, sir," she cried, taking my hand impulsively, "and you are good. What I can do for you and for this great leader of yours shall be done. But, oh, count not on it. My father hates the white men. Maybe I cannot save either of you."

She was gone! Gone, in the twinkling of an eye. The earth seemed to cover her. Without a sound, she had left me.

"Princess!" I called.

But the woods above gave back the echo of my voice. I turned back

toward camp, my head in a whirl.

I had not gone two steps when the Indian who had followed me from camp rose up before me out of the thicket. There was an ugly light in his little eyes.

"I have heard," he croaked. "No manitou, but a mortal. Yet I alone know except the princess, and he who slays a manitou, will win high fame. It can be said you attacked me in the forest and I slew you in fight, overcoming your magic by my courage."

He had drawn the hatchet from his belt, and now crouched like a wild beast, for a spring. I was weaponless. I had even laid aside my hunting-knife when I lay down to rest earlier that night.

Yet I made shift to sell my life as dear as might be. As he leaped at me, I ran in and grappled with him.

Yet he wrenched free one of his hands and whirled the hatchet aloft above my defenseless head. There was no time for me to tear loose from him, ere the blow should fall. Down swirled the hatchet, its blade gleaming evilly in the moonlight.

But it did not reach my head. Instead, it fell tinkling among the mossy stones at my feet. I felt the savage's lithe body relax in my grasp. I let go and he sank lifeless to the ground.

From between his shoulders protruded the feathered shaft of a war-arrow.

And even in that moment of wonder, I noticed that the weapon was far heavier and larger than were the dainty arrows that had filled the princess's quiver.

CHAPTER XVIII.
WE BEHOLD THE KING.

I MADE my way in a roundabout journey back to camp, leaving the fallen Indian where he lay. I was so accustomed, by this time, to surprises and to things I could not in the very least explain, that the savage's strange death left me almost callous.

My brain was full of my odd meeting with the princess and with forebodings of our next day's interview with Powhatan. That an Indian

had sought to murder me and that an arrow flying out of the darkness had stricken him dead, would have roused me a few days earlier to all sorts of speculations and to a fruitless search for the unseen archer.

But now I was surfeited with adventure and with mystery. In the wilderness one experiences things that would be impossible in the haunts of men. Small wonder that savages, the world over, believe the forest wastes to be peopled by spirits!

Back to camp I went. I arrived there in the first dim gray of the morning. The fire was out. Smith still snored beside it. But the Indians were beginning to stir. They eyed me wonderingly as I strolled toward them.

There were quick-exchanged whispers. Then a brave left the camp. He "picked up" my trail as a hunting dog picks up a scent. And off he set, over the route I had traversed.

I crossed over to where Smith lay. Waking him, I told as briefly as possible the things I had learned that night and the adventures that had befallen me. He listened with keen interest. But when I told of the forest princess's vanishing, his worried face broke into a grin.

"Lad," he said, "you dreamed it. I have seen these Indian squaws. They are flat-faced, shapeless, hideous. Not in the very least like the woodland nymph you describe."

"I have seen them, too," I answered. "But I also saw this maiden last night. The moon was bright as day, and she was as I have described her. Nor was I dreaming. I have never been wider awake."

"But you say she vanished without a sound?"

"Assuredly. I had turned my eyes away for an instant. When I looked back, she was gone."

"You did not hear her go? There was no noise of twig or leaf? Impossible! A dream, I tell you."

"Was it a dream when Aquia vanished from beside us, in broad daylight, when we were ambushed back here in the glade?" I retorted. "It showed what an Indian can do. They appear and disappear as suddenly and as soundlessly as serpents or foxes."

"But—"

"I was not dreaming. I was wide awake, and no dream ever knew so sane a conversation as I held with the princess; no, nor so wise a warning as she gave me."

Smith smiled in that exasperatingly superior fashion of his. I could see he did not believe a word, and that he was quite satisfied in his own mind that I had dreamed the whole experience.

Once he had formed a conclusion (which he ever did with startling quickness and usually with equally startling correctness) nothing on earth could shake him from it.

Yet I was about to try again to convince him, when, of a sudden, an Indian burst into the clearing. He was the man who had "picked up" my trail.

At a glance I knew he had followed that trail to the place where his slain comrade lay. I knew it even before he called out tidings in a scared, excited voice to his fellows.

Some ran to verify the tale and to bear the dead man back to camp. The rest stared at me in horrified loathing. Yet none of them dared raise hand or voice against me.

The morning meal was prepared and eaten hastily and without words. Then camp was struck and we set forth at a rapid pace along the brook's edge.

The Indians walked in front of us, behind us, on either side of us. But they would not willingly come within arm's length of either of us.

"You saw the savage brought back to camp," I said to Smith. "Does that seem to you like part of my dream?"

"No," he answered. "The man no doubt attacked you, as you say. And a marauding Indian of another tribe shot him from ambush. You were doubtless roused from your odd dream by the attack, and that is why you failed to see whence the arrow came."

"We were not dreaming that day in the glade," I insisted, "when we saw one Indian tomahawked and another shot by invisible hands."

Smith made no answer, but trudged on, his brow furrowed. Presently he said:

"It was not like Aquia to desert me."

Now for the past two days we had harped ceaselessly in our talks upon Aquia's strange defection and had come to no sensible conclusion about it. So I saw no profit in reopening the subject. I did not reply. Smith continued, a moment later: "Could he be following us unnoticed? Could it have been he in the long grass, that day, who killed the two Indians? And, last night—"

"We have gone over that point before," I said wearily, "and we decided it could not be. These savages keep as close a lookout for spies as if they were in hostile country. You remember how they scoured the neighborhood of the glade that day for the trail of the unseen slayer. And you saw them hunt the trail again this morning after the Indian's body was found."

"Yes," agreed Smith thoughtfully, adding with a chuckle: "It was clever of me, when they asked what had become of the tall Indian who had marched with us, to tell them he was our servant-spirit and that he was still at our side, invisible."

"It was clever," I acquiesced, "in that it doubtless kept them from continuing their search for poor Aquia and tracking him down. Have you thought how you are to conduct the negotiations with Powhatan?"

"I have it all planned out," he answered confidently. "Do not fear. As I told you back in London, I have been in a thousand death-perils, and I have ever a habit of surviving them."

It was an hour or so later that we came out upon a great clearing in whose center rose a hill. The slopes of the hill were honeycombed with huts, caves, and skin-tents.

On the summit stood a great, irregular-shaped house, a single story high; thatched of roof, and walled with unhewn logs. Around this huge building stood a veritable forest of gaudy totem-poles.

"The house of the king," curtly grunted the sub-chief in reply to my question.

The plain at the foot of the slope was swarming with Indians of both sexes and of all sizes. All were staring eagerly and wonderingly at us. Upon our approach they raised no clamor. But in dead silence they made a wide path for us among them—a path that ran straight to the hill.

With our escorts we entered this lane in the crowd. I glanced keenly to left and right, but could see no sign of the princess. No, nor of any savage whose bearing or dress could be recognized as King Powhatan.

So complete a stillness in so large a throng of people was positively uncanny.

A plump redskin baby, perhaps two years old, toddled forward from its mother's side unnoticed, and came toward us, its little, dark

face alight with interest in our strange appearance.

I smiled and held out my hand toward the youngster, whereat the stillness was broken by a cry of horror from the mother, who clasped her protesting baby tightly in her arms and ran from us, shrieking.

This trivial happening hurt me. I had not minded the angry silence of the natives, but their belief that I could or would harm a little child was unexpectedly painful.

"We seem highly welcome guests here!" I commented bitterly to Smith.

"'Tis the way of savages," he replied encouragingly, "to greet honored guests in silence."

"I have never heard so," I contradicted.

"Pooh, man," he scoffed. "Never pull so long a face! One would think you were scared."

"I am," I answered frankly. "And if you were as scared as I, you would be running away."

His jaunty confidence and calm assurance in his own lucky star, annoyed me. Then I reflected that two white men marching to probable death, might be better employed than in bickering like cross children. So I choked back further ill-feeling, and we proceeded on our queer march.

We had reached the hill and were mounting its slope between the huddles of native dwellings, toward the great house on the crest. As we came out upon a little plateau on the hilltop we found ourselves at one end of a short avenue bordered by totem-poles and leading to a wide, rough-hewn doorway which was curtained by an arras of sewn panther hides.

As we reached the doorway, the curtain was drawn aside from within. We entered, followed by the sub-chief. The rest of the band remained outside in the totem-lined avenue.

We found ourselves in a large, low hall, whose sides were hung with weapons, animal-skins and utensils of various sorts. At first glance the place was not wholly unlike many an English country house's assembly-hall; except that it was dirtier and quite devoid of decorative taste.

There were perhaps a score of men standing about the room on either side of a rude dais at its farther end. They were in more or less

gaudy attire. I guessed them to be sub-chiefs and councilors.

On the dais itself sat a very splendid figure. He was very tall and of great breadth. The scalplock of his otherwise shaven head was nearly white.

His lean face was seamed with war scars and crisscrossed by a thousand wrinkles. Yet his aspect was not one of age. And his fierce eyes blazed with a quenchless fire. There was, moreover, a stateliness and cold dignity about the man that must have struck every beholder.

He was clad in a mantle whose groundwork seemed to be the dyed and softened hides of animals. Over this were sewn countless fox-tails. About the throat was a necklace of polished wolf-teeth.

Rude, massive circlets of dull, yellow metal banded the bare arms. The feet—and the incongruous effect was laughable—were incased in a pair of worn-out, down-at-heel, much-patched, old-fashioned English jackboots.

Such, at a glance, was Powhatan, self-styled "King of America," and probably the wisest, most powerful chieftain in all the Western Hemisphere.

On either side of the copper-hued monarch stood a half-naked savage who gripped a knobbed war-club, and who had a way of gazing eagerly at the king as looks a dog who waits for its master to throw a stick.

Smith, as ever, took the situation in his own hands. Walking quickly down the long room, between the rows of silent courtiers, he halted in front of the dais and, in his broken Indian dialect, cried:

"Hail, Powhatan! Greetings from the white manitous across the big water to the emperor of all the red men—greetings!"

To my surprise, Powhatan rose from his seat, his grim face breaking into a smile, and advanced to the edge of the dais.

"Brethren, hail!" he said in his deep voice. "You are welcome. All I have is yours."

Powhatan came down from the dais and led us to seats of honor near by.

"I have long awaited you," he went on, "and it warms my heart to see you."

He signaled to a group of women who crowded one of the small curtained doorways behind the dais. They disappeared. I tightened

my hold on my sword.

But in another moment the squaws were back again carrying in to the room wooden platters piled high with venison and wild fruits.

As the platters and earthen cups full of some brownish, sweetish drink were set before us, Powhatan asked:

"Why have you honored my poor hut by journeying so far to it?"

This was Smith's opportunity. He rose impressively and began his oration. He told in flowery diction how he had journeyed from the home of the manitous, far beyond the rising sun; how he sought to honor America and bless its natives by conferring our presence upon the wilderness land and by founding here a colony.

He went on to say that he had persuaded his fellow white spirits not to wipe the Indians from off the face of the earth, but to be friendly and merciful to them, in token of which, he said, he had journeyed in person to Powhatan to consent graciously to a treaty of alliance, to receive the Indian king's allegiance, and to accept from him all the food he could spare.

It was a fine speech—had it been addressed to the inmates of a madhouse. But at every glance toward Powhatan's face I read a wisdom as great as mercy was scant. And I wondered why he listened to the oration with such an air of credulous courtesy.

As Smith paused for breath, I muttered in English:

"Keep your sword held where you can reach it with ease."

"Pshaw!" Smith sneered, in the same undertone. "Your dream and your croaking fears were moonshine. This welcome proved it. We are carrying all before us. I know Indians."

"You will know them better ere we are out of this," I muttered.

"Brother," interposed Powhatan suavely, "you say you are manitous. Is it indeed true?"

"True?" echoed Smith indignantly. "Can you doubt it? Ask your men how we struck flame from out the wet ground, how we spoke with the death-voice of thunder and lightning, how we made birchbark to talk! Ask how our invisible red manitou servant slew three of your warriors who dared to raise impious hands against us. And, if further proof be lacking, ask yourself how I, who came from across the big water, can speak your language as I do."

"Yet," politely argued Powhatan, "I should scarce have thought an

all-wise manitou could speak it so very badly."

Smith reddened, and glared suspiciously at the king. But old Powhatan's face was a mask of mild courtesy.

"I doubt you not," continued the king, "nor for one moment did I doubt you. Yet, for my people's sake I wished you to declare your powers before them all, that none might henceforth doubt. Manitous you are. Masters of us you are. And we rejoice to serve and obey you. Will you deign to feast?"

Smith sat down with a great sigh of relief. At that instant there was a sudden commotion from the outer doorway. And a truly terrible creature whirled screeching into the great room.

At sight of the apparition my hair began to rise. Even Smith's stout nerve was visibly shaken.

CHAPTER XIX.
In the House of the Foe.

AT first glance one could not tell whether the thing that had dashed into Powhatan's great audience-hall was bird, beast, or human.

It was perhaps four feet in height. Its head was the head of a wide-jawed wolf. Its body was one mass of outstanding feathers of a hundred hues that flapped and slithered at every fantastic step the creature took.

The horns of a stag jutted out between the narrow shoulders. The hands were skinny claws with unbelievably long carved nails.

It spun about like a tee-totum, uttering shrill screeches and pounding on a queer little drum that was slung from its neck.

Then, on second glance, I saw the awful thing was human. The wolf-head was a sort of helmet, under which peeped out a hairless little face, fleshless, withered like a mummy's, and seemingly a thousand years old. The stag horns were but affixed to the feather mantle. And all the dozen other grotesque details of the tiny figure were matters of costume.

On noticing this I felt a wave of relief. Yet so deadly, and so full of crazy hatred was the little monkeylike face that I could scarce endure

to look upon it.

And now I remembered a tale long since told me in an idle moment by Aquia in reply to some of my queries as to Indian customs. He had described to me the weird "medicine men" that attended on the great chiefs, and had told me with perfect sincerity instances of their supernatural powers.

From Aquia's description of such persons' attire I at once concluded, and rightly, that this fear-inspiring manikin was Powhatan's medicine-man.

Had I doubted it, the veneration in which he was very evidently held by all the Indians in the room would have convinced me. They looked at him as at a god.

He whirled about like a wind-tossed leaf, scarce touching ground in his flying gyrations, until he halted of a sudden directly in front of Powhatan. Then I saw he was foaming at the mouth as though in an epilepsy (which I believe he was). He clawed at the king's bare arm with one clawlike hand and with the other pointed wildly at us.

"Kill!" he squealed shrilly. "Kill! Kill! Kill!"

I confess, a chill crept down my back at the concentrated venom in the little madman's cry. But Powhatan listened with unchanged face, though the warriors and councilors along the walls of the room broke into an instantly checked mutter of excitement.

"Kill!" shrieked the medicine-man again.

There was an ominous rustling as men felt for their weapons. But Powhatan, with a single stern gesture, enforced peace.

"Later," soothed the king. "Later we will hear all. Be at peace, O prophet. Leave us for the time."

But the little man, with a wolfish snarl tore away from Powhatan's kindly touch. Twisting horribly in his fit, he again pointed to us:

"Kill!" he yelled. "Kill now! It will be too late if—"

He fell to the ground and writhed in convulsions. His eyes rolled back into his head. The foam-flecked lips grew stiff. Then, all at once, he grew rigid. And from between those stiff lips a voice issued.

It was not the shrill falsetto wherewith his scream of "Kill! Kill!" had pierced our eardrums. It was a solemn, deep, sonorous tone that filled the hushed room like an organ-note.

"Too late!" breathed the voice, "too late! Their feet are on our

shore. Never again shall they depart. The hour of sight is upon me. Hear your doom, O my children. Hear it!"

A moment more of that dreadful hush. Then again the voice reverberated through the great room:

"I see men—millions upon millions of men—white men—from all over the earth. They pour in upon our shores like storm-waves. They fill the land. They sweep westward. And before their march, the wilderness vanishes as frost breath in the sun. The land shakes beneath the white man's tread. Its waters are swarming with his great canoes. The ground and the fire and the lightning serve him like slaves."

He choked, then broke out again:

"O my people! Lords of the forest and the mountain. You are scattered like chaff. You are slain, you are robbed, you are hunted fugitives, beggars, and at the last you are swept from the face of the world. It is doom! Doom!"

Like a deep bell he boomed out the last word. Then the rigid body seemed to dwindle and the stiff limbs relaxed.

"The hour of sight is past!" whispered Powhatan, his lips dry, his words tremulous. "Carry him to his lodge and tend him until he wakes."

Reverent heads lifted the limp little figure and bore it from the hall. Powhatan, by a supreme effort, regained mastery of himself. At his commanding glance the warriors and councilors slunk back to their places.

"My brothers," said the king, turning to us with grave courtesy, "will you feast with us?"

He seated himself at Smith's side. An attendant, at a gesture from the king, led me to a wide block of wood on which food was set forth. I seated myself and made as if to eat, though Heaven knows I had scant appetite.

Smith, on the contrary, had quite recovered his spirits. He chatted gaily, even boisterously, with the dusky monarch. But I sat still, my eyes furtively sweeping the room and dwelling unnoticed on each other's face.

The air was tense with impending trouble, even as before a furious thunder-storm. Not a face around me showed emotion or excitement. Not a voice, save Smith's, was raised. But a drunken man might have

felt that mysterious tension.

Soldierlike, I took in my position. Just back of me was a sharp angle in the hewn logs. Here a strong man might well hold his own for a moment or so against attack. And I noticed the spot.

My straying eyes suddenly fell upon a face that appeared through an opening in the small, curtained doorway behind the dais. And I recognized it at a glance as the face of the "Princess of America."

Unobserved by the rest, she stood there, behind the curtain, her eyes upon mine. I was about to rise and bow, when a forbidding glint in her big, dark eyes checked me.

So, too unostentatiously to attract the notice of the feasting Indians, I continued to gaze at her. And I began to see she was making with her eyes some sort of signal to me.

Her glance would rest first on my face, then shift commandingly to a spot a yard or two to one side. There was a horror of appeal in the look.

And presently I understood it. For some occult reason the princess wanted me to leave my seat and to move to that spot indicated by her gaze. Moreover, she was terribly eager that I make the move without delay.

Not waiting for further proof of her wishes, and affected by that look of anguished pleading, I leaped to my feet and at a single step I was in the spot to which her eyes had assigned me.

As I stepped back there was a crash overhead. Through the thatched roof a monstrous boulder tore its way.

Down it crashed—a ton or so of weight—so close to me that I could feel the wind of its passing.

It struck the block where I had just been sitting. And it smashed the stout slab of wood into splinters, driving the fragments and a part of its own mighty bulk deep into the hard-packed earth of the floor.

Had I held my former place a half-second longer, I must have been crushed not only to death, but out of all semblance to a man. Truly, that look of agony in the princess's wondrous eyes had not been without cause.

My sword flashed out. My back was clapped to the angle of the wall, where none could assail me from behind. The heat of battle flamed up in my heart. Also a rage at this smooth-spoken savage king's treach-

ery, and this sin against the sacred guest law of the wilderness.

Had Powhatan ordered us slain as we neared his village, or had he sent orders to our escort to fall upon us and kill us in our sleep during the march it would have been quite another matter.

But he had greeted us with the "peace sign" (the palm held upward and outward in front of the brow) when we drew near. He had hailed us as brothers. He had promised us friendship and had broken bread with us. And now he had sought to murder me by treachery.

Even in that hurried moment, I understood his motive. While he knew we were not gods, yet he did realize that the white men possessed many "magic" arts unknown to him. And he feared lest some of these same inventions might save us, and perhaps harm him, were we put on our guard.

Ever since the days of Jael and Sisera, the most approved fashion of throwing an enemy off his guard has been to feed him. The whole plot was quite clear.

At my sudden leap backward from the feasting board and the almost simultaneous crashing down of the vast stone through the roof thatch, the whole room was in an uproar. As by magic a ring of fierce-eyed savages pressed about me, hatchets or war-clubs in hand. I stood, sword raised, ready to cut down or transfix the first foe who should be daring enough to venture within reach.

Smith had sprung up and had whipped out his great sword with one hand, while with the other he had drawn his hunting-knife. Nor did he wait to be attacked. At a bound he was confronting Powhatan, his sword-point at the king's throat, his arm drawn back for a thrust.

"At the first blow—at the first move," he yelled to the buzzing roomful, "I shall drive my sword-blade through your vile king. Now, who strikes first?"

There was a pause of consternation, of irresolute bewilderment. It was Powhatan who spoke. Unruffled in his regal calm, and no more heeding the deadly steel at his throat than if it had been a summer fly, the monarch said in cold rebuke:

"Is this the 'friendship' the white manitous come so far to proffer? Do you call me brother, and eat of my food and then spring at me like an angry wildcat because one of the roof-stones has rolled from its place?"

Smith's hot anger seemed to merge ever so little into perplexity. Powhatan continued:

"Or did your manitou magic cause the great stone to break loose from its fastenings and fall among us? Was it further proof of your powers? If so, it is the most wondrous test of all, for that stone has abode there with its three fellows, on the thatch corners ever since my dead father reared this house."

His manner of contemptuous, lofty reproach would have utterly convinced me that a common accident and tight-strung nerves had betrayed us into our exhibition of dread, had it not been for the memory of the princess's unspoken warning as she had looked at me from behind the deerskin curtain.

As for Smith, he was wholly convinced. Back went his great sword, clanging into its scabbard, and his knife into his belt.

"I crave your pardon," he said, sheepishly enough, extending his hand to the king, who gravely accepted it.

The two resumed their seats, but I called across in English to Smith:

"Here! Over here as fast as you can move. Together we may hold this sheltered position for a minute or two, before they destroy us."

"Sit down," retorted Smith, in wrathful scorn. "Will you shame us both? They will deem you a coward. Sheathe your sword and sit down. 'Twas but an accident. The stone slipped its socket and fell through the roof. That is all."

"A stone as large as that," I answered, "would be visible from the plain below. Powhatan has just said there were four such on the roof; one at each corner. I saw none as we approached."

"You did not notice," rejoined Smith. "He would not be fool enough to lie about a thing we could disprove the moment we leave this house and look up at the roof."

"Smith," I cried, "he does not mean that we *shall* leave this house—alive."

"Will not your follower conquer his fear so far as to lay aside his weapon and partake of the new food that I have ordered brought to him?" queried Powhatan of the captain, looking with scornful amusement at my unchanged attitude of watchful defense as he spoke.

"No," I called back before Smith could reply. "If I must die I will

die like a man, not like a trapped hare."

Smith reddened with mortification at my apparently timorous conduct, but turned again to Powhatan, and took up the thread of a boastful tale he had been telling when the mishap occurred.

My ring of enemies had stepped back and were no longer paying heed to me. Yet I noticed they did not return to their former positions in the room. They still remained lounging, between me and Smith.

Nor could I see the princess's face now at the curtain. She had evidently done what little she could to save us and had retired ere the final tragedy should be enacted.

Sword in hand, I maintained my watchful guard, for I knew we were about as safe as though we were in a panther's lair. And I waited each moment for the storm to break.

"Yes," Smith was declaiming in his broken dialect, to the politely interested king. "Three champions were they of the Turkish Soldan, and they challenged every cavalier of Sigismond's army to single combat. One by one did I meet these heathen Turks, and one by one did I leave them dead on the field, whereat our whole army—"

He got no further. Of a sudden a score of hands seized him. Nimble fingers wrenched away his unheeded weapons from his belt, and tripped from behind by some cunning wrestler, Captain John Smith plunged headlong to earth. In a trice he was tied and helpless.

CHAPTER XX.
Under the Breath of Death.

You will ask why I did not spring to my captured leader's aid, and perform prodigies of useless, suicidal valor in an attempt to rescue him.

I did not do it, for two reasons. First, the whole attack, capture and binding did not occupy three seconds of time. Second, because, at the instant the secret signal for the onset was given by Powhatan, no less than a dozen armed savages formed a human wall in front of me; their brandished weapons menacing my head.

I could not move forward. To throw myself upon the warriors who

confronted me would mean that they would at once close in upon all sides of me, and that I should have a half-dozen or more hatchets sunk into my back ere I could strike a blow.

No, though I was doomed, yet my only hope for momentary safety was to stick to my semi-sheltered position and to hold off the enemy, as long as might be, with vigorous sword-play.

As to Smith, I could not hope to reach him, even by sacrificing my life in the effort. His own overconfidence and his disregarding of what he considered my cowardly advice had brought him to his present straits. And I could do naught for him.

Though the ring of savages threatened me, they did not at once attack. They contented themselves with holding me at bay; doubtless awaiting further orders from their king.

Thus while half-consciously keeping watch for the first sign of their onfall, I was able to see something of what was going on in front of the dais.

Smith, wriggling powerless in his bonds, lay prone upon the ground. Powhatan, a gentle smile on his cold dark face, stood gazing down at him. Then he stepped back on the dais and spoke a word of command.

Three or four warriors swung Smith into the air as though he were a truss of hay, and dropped him on the dais at Powhatan's feet.

The king glanced down at him again and said:

"Well, white man, is this the end of your lies and your boasting? Can you call on no magic now to save you? Surely it were a slight thing for so great a magician to free himself."

Smith made no reply. But the face he raised to that of the sneering savage above him bore no sign of fear.

"Your death," continued Powhatan, "was ordained when first I learned of your approach. My war party believed your idle talk of magic and they feared it. Therefore they spared you. But I am not a child to be fooled with tricks."

He paused as if to give his captive a chance to reply, but Smith did not speak, neither did he for a single instant abate the glare of cold fury that blazed from his little eyes.

"You are a brave man," vouchsafed Powhatan, "for a white-face, and you have given me entertainment this day. Wherefore, you shall

die at once and not by the torture. Your follower yonder will afford us sport enough when we wall him into that corner later, and listen to his screams of hunger and suffocation. Yet if you have the courage, he has the wit. It is sad the two qualities could not have been combined in you, then you might have escaped death."

"I shall escape death," returned Smith, speaking with a quiet certainty, at odd variance with his wonted bluster, "I shall not die."

Even the stolid Powhatan looked surprised.

"I shall live," went on Smith coolly, "to see my life's work succeed. How I shall do it, I do not know, but I do know my destiny, and it is too strong to be turned aside by a gang of redskin savages."

"You speak as one who is certain," scoffed Powhatan, "but I fear none will agree with you."

"I ask no one to agree with me," Smith replied with that same lofty assurance. "But, in this, mine hour of peril, it is borne in upon me that I shall not perish until this land, to which I have devoted my life, is given into the hands of the white man. Until England's foot is so firmly planted on these shores that never can her colonists be driven hence."

He spoke rather to himself than to the glowering savage; and in the last part of his strange prophecy he lapsed unconsciously into English.

"In another tiny space of time," said Powhatan, grimly, "ere the shadows of the sun can move a hand's breadth, this last of your many vain boasts will be as dead as the breath that spoke it."

Smith did not answer. He did not seem to have heard. His truculent, ruddy face was aglow with some mystic light that appeared to spring from within his gallant soul.

"It is in my mind, white man," said Powhatan, after an instant's pause, "to speak to you what is in my heart; that you may bear the message with you into the spirit world."

Again he paused; then resumed:

"When first the white men touched these shores—more than two hundred moons ago—I and my people were eager to be their friends. We crowded down to their ships at the mouth of the Great River. We brought them gifts. What was their return for our welcome?"

Even before he spoke the next words, I well remembered the treatment accorded the simple Indians by the first futile colony which Raleigh vainly tried to establish on these shores.

"They greeted us with mockery," went on Powhatan. "Some of us they tortured and slew because we could not tell them where to find mountains of yellow metal. Some of us they plied with a fiery liquid that stole away our senses. And as we lay helpless, they robbed us. Some they beat and sought to enslave. Are these the breed of men whom we wish to see living as our neighbors? When once they come here and abide, it will mean naught but dire ill to my people. And they shall not abide here!"

His suavity was gone. He was now the outraged ruler of an outraged race: His eyes flashed as he added:

"I had an only son, whom I loved as I loved none other on all this earth. In a gust of anger I sent him one day from my presence and from the lodges of my people. When I repented me of my wrath, I caused search to be made for him that he might come back and one day inherit my throne. My messengers returned with dust on their heads."

His harsh face twitched, and he hurried on.

"They bore me word that my son, fleeing from my wrath, had gone to the white men on the coast, and that they had slain him and cast him into the sea. With all my braves I marched to the coast to avenge my murdered first-born. I found the great canoes of the white men had long since sailed away. But a village of them was left. Where is that village to-day? And where are its men and women and white-faced children? They, one and all, followed my son in torture and agony to the spirit world, where presently you shall follow, boaster."

Well did I recall the colony whose fate Powhatan had described. It was that sent out by Raleigh under Captain White's command. The colony during whose few months of known life, little Virginia Dare, the first white child in North America was born.

And that colony's fate had ever been a mystery. For when White returned three years later with supplies, it had vanished.

"Bear my greetings to those slain white folk in the spirit land," cried Powhatan, "and kneel there at the feet of my son."

He stepped back. Raising one arm he signaled to the two guards who stood on either side of the dais with uplifted war-clubs.

At his shouted word the two club-bearers rushed forward, chanting a weird death song. Their sticks were whirled high above their

heads, above the helpless head of the bound captive who lay before them

In another instant the descending clubs would have dashed out Smith's brains. Yet he did not flinch. He scarce seemed to note the impending slaughter. On his face still glowed that strange light from within.

Then it was that something flashed forward, from the curtained doorway, past the king and between the two executioners.

It was the princess.

Not heeding her father's stern shout of rebuke, she threw herself upon Smith's prostrate body. With upraised hands she waved back the executioners.

The whole maneuver was as sudden as lightning. Even the swift-witted savages were wholly dumfounded by it. The two club-bearers hesitated, checking their weapons in the very act of downward flight.

Powhatan was the first to recover himself. Striding forward, he reached out to draw his daughter away from the man whose body she was shielding. But she eluded his grasp.

"No!" she cried, her sweet voice fearless and imperious. "It shall not be, I say. The man is guiltless. He has done us no harm. He and his comrade came here, braving certain death, to save their friends from hunger."

"Back!" grunted Powhatan fiercely. "What has my love for you brought you to, that you seek to baffle my authority? Back!"

Again he made as though to seize her, and again she shrank aside, clasping Smith about the neck, and so protecting him with her slender young body that the guards could not strike at him without striking their monarch's adored daughter as well.

"You will let him live?" she pleaded. "I ask it. I, who have never before asked a gift of you. I ask his life."

Having heard something of the contempt wherewith Indians were said to treat their women, I looked for an explosion of rage from Powhatan, and for possible death to the heroine who so fearlessly defied his authority.

And indeed the mad wrath in the old king's eyes made the supposition plausible enough. But even as I looked, the rage melted into sullenness, and the sullenness into something very like the smile a white parent accords sometimes to the audacious impudence of a dearly loved child.

The two guards, their clubs still held ready, were looking to their

master for orders. Powhatan spoke a gruff word of command, and the executioners fell back to their former posts at the sides of the dais.

The princess sprang up with a little cry of delight and threw herself at her father's feet.

"You will give food to their starving people?" she pleaded.

"Shall I give warmth and shelter to the rattlesnakes that seek refuge under my hearthstone?" he snarled. "Shall I feed and succor those who will repay me by maltreating my people?"

She had slipped a knife from her girdle and was cutting away Smith's bonds. Powhatan made an angry forward movement as if to check her; then stepped back again, with that same half smile on his cold face. Smith freed, rose to his feet, and stood confronting the princess.

"For what you have done, maiden," said he, his deep voice shaken with emotion, "my heart and my life lie at your feet. You have saved a life I do not overmuch value. But you have saved it for the good of a cause that I value above all else. Unborn generations shall bless your name, for you have not only saved worthless Captain John Smith, but America as well."

In spite of his braggart words, his tone held no taint of his wonted boasting. He spoke from the very depths of his soul.

"You talk as though you were free," interposed Powhatan, apparently glad to have found some one on whom he could impress his recently defied authority. "You are not. I have spared you, for the foolish love I bear my daughter, Pocahontas, as I should spare a wounded wolf she wished to protect. But shall I let you and your comrade go back and guide your white-face village to success? A thousand times no. Here you shall remain. If not death, you shall at least know slavery. And for all your lives."

CHAPTER XXI.
THE TERMS OF POWHATAN.

THE princess made as though to speak. But her father checked her.

"Here you two white men shall remain," he repeated. "And you shall be the sport and the drudges for the meanest of my people. If that be better for brave men than is swift death, then comfort your-

selves in the thought.

"As for your white brethren who await you at the mouth of the Great River, within a week my war parties shall pour in upon them. And those who die at the first attacks will be happiest. The white men shall vanish from these shores like morning mist beneath the noonday sun. I have spoken."

At thought of the Indian raid he so solemnly foretold, my heart went sick, for back there amongst those starving colonists was Dorcas Errol.

And in her moment of supreme peril I should not be beside her to comfort her, to sustain her, to lay down my life for her dear sake.

I had tried hard and vainly to put her from my thoughts, since I had learned that her father had promised her to Smith! But now I found I had made pitifully slight progress in my task of forgetfulness.

She could not be mine. She was pledged to another. To another who, like myself, could not hope to return to her. Yet, in this moment, with degrading and lifelong slavery staring me in the face, all other emotions were thrust from my heart by that one great wave of hopeless love.

A man's heart is strangely and wondrously fashioned, is it not? (So they tell me is the skeleton of the domestic rabbit.)

"There are no terms we can make with you for our release?" queried Smith, the light dying out of his face.

"Are there any terms the caught hare may make with the panther?" mocked Powhatan.

Then breaking once more into savage wrath, he snarled:

"Terms? Yes, there be terms. Give back my dead son to me, alive to me and well, and you shall not only return to your people in safety, but I will feed them and grant them protection!"

He laughed, harshly, as he spat forth the wildly impossible conditions. And, as I have said, an Indian seldom laughs save in mockery or when inflicting pain. The king's fierce laughter was not good to hear. Yet, in the midst of his ferocious, ironic mirth, the laugh on his lips turned to a gasp. From every part of the room, the stolid warriors and councilors broke into an amazed shout.

For, through the great gaping hole in the roof thatch left by the fall of the boulder, a man had just dropped. Landing lightly on his feet, he

sprang to the dais.

It was Aquia.

The sinewy giant appeared in no way excited as he faced the king and the rest of the assemblage. His high-bred, coppery face was emotionless.

"I am here!" he said.

That was all. For, with a cry more animal than human, Powhatan had thrown himself upon the newcomer.

At first I thought he was attacking him barehanded. But I was wrong. The old monarch was hugging Aquia to him, fondling his face and head, mumbling strange, crooning words that I could not catch.

And all at once I understood. But Smith still stood open-mouthed with wonder, until Aquia said:

"The terms are fulfilled. You will hold to your share of the pact, my father?"

"The pact?" stammered Powhatan, not for the moment understanding.

"As I lay hidden on the roof, seeking a chance to save my white brothers here," explained Aquia, "I heard you take the pledge to spare these men, to set them free and to succor their followers on the coast yonder, if your son were restored to you alive and well. I am here."

"These white men be manitous after all!" muttered Powhatan. "You were on the roof? On the roof of my lodge? Did their magic snatch you from the spirit land and place you there?"

In a dozen brief, guttural sentences Aquia told his story. The white men of Raleigh's ship had not slain him, as the inquiring messenger had been led to believe, when he fled from his father's people to the English.

Instead, Raleigh had persuaded him to take service with himself and to accompany him to England. And Aquia, being cast off by his own race, had accepted.

In England he had dwelt as Raleigh's servant, until Sir Walter had been cast into prison. Then, as I knew, he had taken service under Smith, and had later come with us to America.

On learning of our plan to visit his father, Aquia had consented to join us, but had planned to hide ere he should reach Powhatan's village, for he believed his father still held wrath against him, and would

order him to death.

Then, when the war party had assailed us, Aquia had dropped at once into the long grass and undergrowth of the glade, with all the secretive power of a trained Indian warrior. He knew he could better serve us by watching over us from a point of safety than by joining us in a captivity which he was sure would have a fatal termination.

While crawling to safety through the grass he had come upon one of the braves who were stealthily approaching us in like fashion. The brave had struck at him with a hatchet. Aquia had warded off the blow and had sunk his own hatchet in his assailant's brain.

Then he had sped onward toward the shelter of the higher growth. On his way thither he was seen by one of the war party who lurked in a tree. The man in the tree was raising his bow to shoot him when Aquia had caught sight of the archer. His own arrow sped first, and the tree-climber had dropped dead.

Aquia had followed close on our trail as we were conducted toward Powhatan's village by the war party. Seeking a chance to free us, he had been near the camp, that last night, when I managed to go forth by myself into the forest. And, following me, he had shot the savage who was about to kill me.

Lurking in the woods near the village when we had entered the king's house, Aquia had bided his time, and had crept unseen from hut to hut until he neared the great house itself.

Then, when all the loungers outside were peering in through the wall crevices to one side and through the doorway in the front at something of wild interest that was transpiring inside, he managed to reach the house on the opposite side and to draw himself up to the thatch.

He had looked down through the opening just as Powhatan had voiced his iron terms for our release. Not until his father had cast aside his wonted stoic reserve and ecstatically embraced him did Aquia know he was forgiven.

Up to that moment he thought his appearance among us would be the signal for his own death. But he knew Powhatan's pledged word to be inviolable, and on that he had relied to save us. He was calmly risking his life for ours, an act which, when it was explained to him, drew from old Powhatan a snort of genuine contempt. Wheeling about on

his clustered warriors who had come crowding near the dais, Powhatan singled out the sub-chief who had been the leader of our captors. Beckoning him forward, the old king angrily demanded:

"Did you see no trace of my son when you searched the trails during the march?"

"Yes," replied the scared sub-chief. "We found his trail after the two men were slain in the glade, and again where the warrior was shot last night, and each day we saw his trail where he was following us. Each morning we saw where, in the night, he had circled our camp."

"You saw this?" roared the indignant monarch. "You saw this, and yet you set none of your braves to follow up the trails and capture him?"

The sub-chief looked foolish.

"The white men," he muttered, "told us he was not mortal, but was their red manitou servant who was accompanying them unseen, and who could strike men dead at their command. He slew three of us, and—"

"And so you didn't bother to hunt him up!" guffawed Smith. "You thought a man could leave a trail and yet be invisible! And you had no wish to share the fate of your three comrades."

The sub-chief glowered, and, at a swift nod from Powhatan, fell back among his fellows.

"Princess," went on Smith, taking Pocahontas's little hand, "all America shall one day know and honor your name. You call yourself the 'Princess of America!' Posterity will know you as the 'Preserver of America.'"

CHAPTER XXII.
AFTERWARD.

THE hopeless little settlement of Jamestown had grown. The feeble roots of colonization had at length struck deep and firm into American soil.

Thanks to Pocahontas, we had weathered that first bitter starvation year. And now, other and better folk had come out from England

by the ship-load to swell the ranks of our colony and to give it a surety of success.

The tattered sail-cloth tents and rude dugout huts had given place to log houses, and a church raised its holy tower above the clustering roofs. Jamestown was a thriving colony. Captain John Smith had not lived in vain.

But neither he nor I had been able to reap the benefits of what we had sown. Scarce two consecutive weeks had I rested in the settlement, and he had enjoyed little more repose.

We had been hither and yon; toiling, surveying, exploring, making treaties with the more distant tribes. And now I was but just returned from accompanying him on his trip of exploration to New England, where he had once purposed to plant a second colony.

I had been rowed ashore from our little ship; while Smith had gone across the harbor to consult with the captain of a larger vessel which on the morrow was to weigh anchor for England.

It was early summer twilight when I landed and walked up the dusky lane toward the settlement.

Somewhere amid the trees a belated mocking-bird was singing out its heart to the rising moon. The fragrance of wild honeysuckle was heavy on the warm air. Ahead of me twinkled the lights of the village houses.

Everything seemed wondrous beautiful and peaceful; and as I looked ahead toward the distant lighted windows, I felt a sharp tug at my heart-strings.

For it all intensified my own bitter, hopeless loneliness. Ahead of me were homes. I was homeless. In those homes were women, happily waiting for their husbands to return from their day's toil. Who, on all this broad earth, watched for me or cared if ever I should come back?

These be morbid and babyish thoughts for a man who is nearing forty. And for the most part, I had drowned them in hard work and in perilous adventure. But tonight they rushed in upon me with a force I could not stem.

And I fell to thinking miserably of that day when first our ships neared Jamestown, and of the picture of home and of love that I had so eagerly, so hopefully set before Dorcas Errol. The memory well-nigh unmanned me; for strive as I would, I could not forget her, nor

abate one atom of my mighty love for her. During my few visits to Jamestown, I had avoided her.

I felt sure she would understand why. A woman, I think, always knows when a man loves her. And, when I was near Dorcas, I could not for the life of me keep the love out of my voice and my eyes.

And even such unspoken adoration was not seemly toward a betrothed woman; nor was it loyalty to my stanch comrade, Smith. Wherefore, I had kept away, not only from Dorcas, but from Jamestown as well.

Nor had I been able to talk of her with Smith. That very day, as our ship had drawn into harbor, he had clapped me on the shoulder in high glee, and had exclaimed:

"Well, lad, the New England work is done. The savages be at peace with us, and Jamestown flourishes. 'Tis time to draw breath and to enter into the benefits of our labor. My own wandering days are done. I shall settle down now upon my plantation. And next week Dorcas and I shall marry!"

His blithe words had been as gall to me. Yet I had forced myself to make fitting reply of a sort, and had soon found excuse to go to another part of the deck where I could be alone with my keen wretchedness.

To-night, as I swung up the lane toward Jamestown, my resolve was made. I would at once take up a plantation somewhere far beyond reach of the settlement, and there would eke out the rest of my miserable life alone with my bitter-sweet memories.

So deep was I in my thoughts that I did not raise my eyes until just beyond a sharp turn in the lane I came suddenly upon a white-clad figure. It was a woman. And my heart as quickly as my eyes told me it was Dorcas Errol. Also, that she was weeping.

At sight of me she furtively dried her eyes, and spoke my name in a cordial greeting that was none the less tremulous.

"My father told me the New England ship had been sighted," she said, talking hastily to hide the tremor in her voice. "And he bade me come down toward the dock to meet Captain Smith on his return. He is not with you?"

"No," I said dully. "He stopped to speak with the outward-bound ship's captain, to order from England some household goods, I believe.

He tells me your marriage is to be next week."

She did not answer, but stood, her hands clasped, looking at me as though I had struck her.

"Next week?" she murmured at last. And her sweet voice was dead.

For a minute we two stood there looking dumbly at one another, in the moonlight, while the mocking-bird in the holly-tree near by sang his heartbreak song, and the flower fragrance filled our senses.

We looked deep into each other's eyes, this maid whom I loved and I, and each read there the soul and the sorrow of the other.

Then—I know not how it chanced—of a sudden I found myself clasping Dorcas to my breast, pouring forth Heaven-knows-what mad words of love, covering her white, upturned face with a thousand kisses.

And her dear arms were about my neck, and her wondrous eyes were looking love into mine. Oh, the miracle of it all! I shall be dust when I forget one atom of it.

It may have been a minute, it may have been a century, that we stood clasped thus, in a paradise of our own. Then I grew sane. Very gently I released her and put her from me.

"I crave your forgiveness," I panted. "I did not mean to be so base. I entreat you to forget it."

"But why?" she sobbed. "Why? We love each other. I have loved you ever since that terrible night in London. Even in the shipboard days when I strove so valiantly to hate you. We love each other, and we belong to each other. Why should you call it 'base'?"

"It is not base for you," I returned, "for you do not stop to realize that you are betrothed to another man. But, for me, who am that man's sworn comrade, there is no excuse. Oh, I have betrayed the trust he places in me! I shall never dare look him in the face again. I must go. I can never see you again, dear heart. And so, good-by, and Heaven bless you!"

"No!" she wailed. "No! It is not wicked. I have never loved Captain Smith. My father ordered me to wed him. And—and I thought I could obey even though it broke my heart. But, with the memory of your kisses on my lips, I know now I *cannot*."

"Oh, it was disloyal of me!" I groaned. "It was unforgivable."

"Yes," said a heavy voice behind us. "I think you are right, Master Clyde. But when the steed is stolen, what boots it to moan because the stall door was not locked?"

We turned to confront Captain John Smith. He had come up the lane from the dock, unnoticed by us. In the moonlight his keenly expressive face was drawn and ghastly.

"You have heard?" I queried, as Dorcas shrank back.

"I have heard enough," he answered heavily.

"I have no excuses," said I, "but this lady is blameless."

"No, no!" cried Dorcas, her fear giving place to her love. "It is I—and I alone who am to blame! I—"

I stepped between her and Smith.

"Captain," I began, "I have wronged you. You will demand satisfaction, of course. I am at your service."

He made no reply for the moment, but stood tugging at his great beard and looking from one to the other of us from under his bushy brows. At last he spoke.

"Dorcas," he said very gently, "as I drew near just now, I heard you cry out that you have never loved me, and that you know now you cannot force yourself to marry me. Is that true?"

She nodded her head.

"I am sorry," she added simply.

"Clyde," asked Smith, "how long have you loved Mistress Errol?"

"From the first," I made curt answer.

"And you?" he asked her.

"Always," she replied.

He looked down, in thought, and for a time none of us spoke.

"You loved her," said Smith at last, "yet never till to-night told your love?"

I assented.

"For all these long months," he resumed, "you have been my true comrade even though you believed I had won the woman you loved. I wish I had known. And yet—I loved her, too. More perhaps than either of you could understand—or would care to understand."

To hear bluff, swaggering Captain John Smith speak thus of loving, was unbelievable. Yet we, who noted the new tone in his voice as he spoke, could not doubt his words.

"I am so sorry! So sorry!" breathed Dorcas, laying one hand impulsively on his arm.

But Smith drew back from the touch as though it burned him. He turned again to me.

"I tricked you into coming to Virginia," he said, "and I am repaid. Listen to me, both of you. In half an hour the council shall receive an order from me, as president, sanctioning and commanding your marriage to each other. Even Mark Errol dare not disobey that."

"Oh!" cried the girl in amaze.

"If I loved you less," he said simply, "I think I could not do it. You do not understand that now. But some day you will."

He stepped forward and held out his hand to me, his eyes misty with unconcealed emotion.

"Good-by, lad," he said almost affectionately. "We have been leal comrades, you and I. And now we come to the parting of the ways. To-morrow a ship sails for England, and she will carry a certain Captain John Smith—soldier of fortune and utter failure."

"You are going back to England?" I cried, incredulous. "Why, your whole life is bound up in the Americas!"

He laughed bitterly.

"I have two children," he murmured. "One is Virginia, one is New England, and I own not one foot of ground in either. I have carved this colony out of the wilderness. I have saved it from destruction. And yet its people hate me and secretly conspire for my ruin. I had a friend. I had a—sweetheart. Henceforth, I shall have neither.

"My life-work shall endure, but I shall fail. A hundred years from hence, when Virginia and New England are flourishing provinces, the name of the man who made them will be forgotten."

"It will never be forgotten," cried Dorcas eagerly, "either by this country or by us!"

He smiled sadly, then, stooping with the grace of a courtier, he kissed her white little hand.

"It is better," he said bravely, "that a man's work should endure than his happiness, or even his memory. Yet you two will think of me, sometimes—perhaps?"

Ere we could reply he had strode past us and was out of sight beyond the bend of the lane. We never saw him again.

Nor did America.

And so, our arms about each other, Dorcas Errol and I walked toward Jamestown and—happiness!

The End.

Appendix
Original source publication

This novel was published complete in the April 1912 issue of *Argosy*.

Aside from obvious punctuation and spelling errors, the following change was made in Chapter V:

Captain Smith is assumedly a braggart.
   was changed to
Captain Smith is assuredly a braggart.

The cover image on the next page, and the opening illustration used as a frontis for this book, are by Clinton Pettee, whose most famous single illustration is undoubtedly the cover of the October 1912 issue of *The All-Story Magazine,* which featured the first novel of Edgar Rice Burroughs' Tarzan of the Apes.

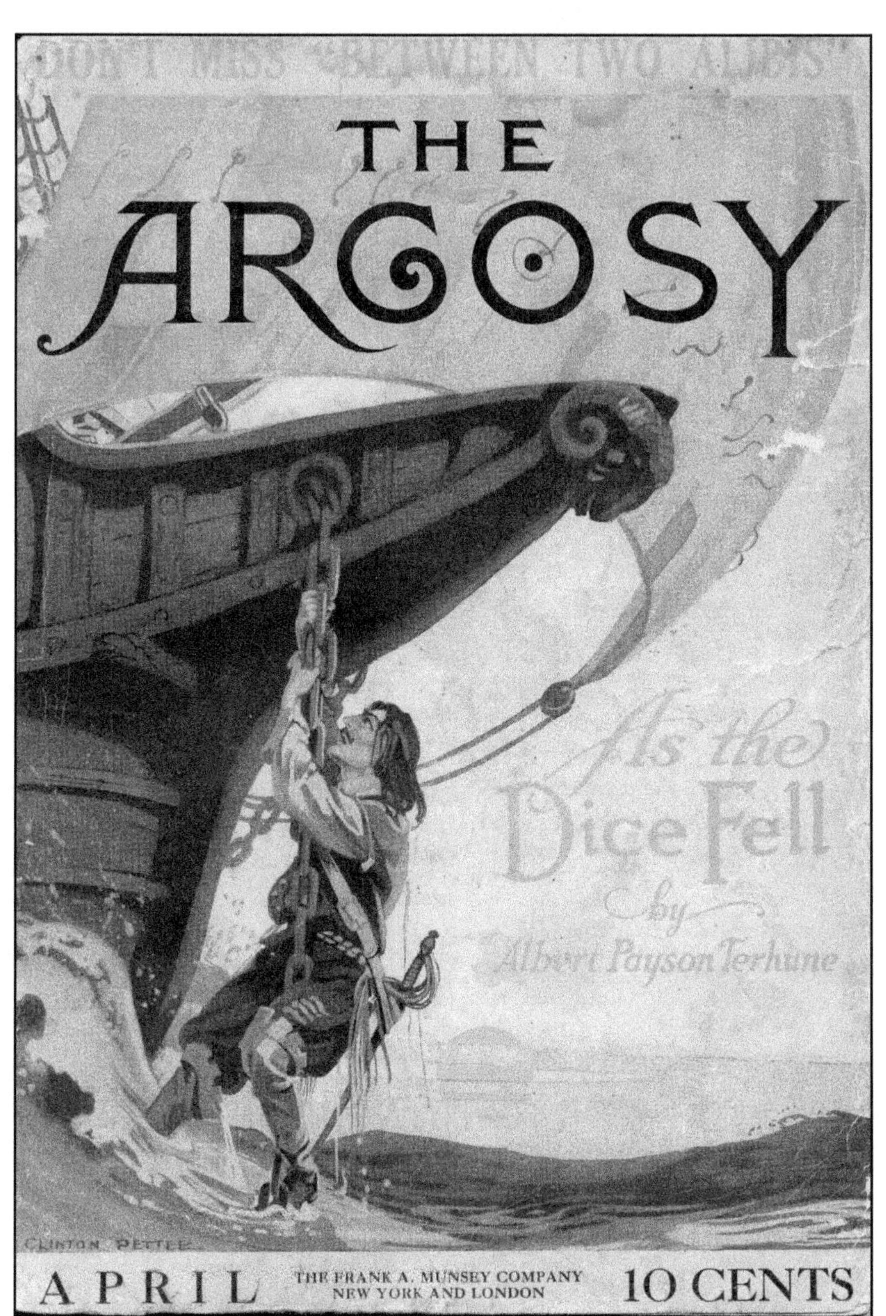

**Turn this book over for another complete novel
by Albert Payson Terhune!**

119